A Perfectly Proper Paranormal Museum Mystery

ALSO BY KIRSTEN WEISS

The Perfectly Proper Paranormal Museum

Pressed to
DEATH

A Perfectly Proper Paranormal Museum Mystery

by

KIRSTEN WEISS

MIDNIGHT INK
WOODBURY, MINNESOTA

FIRST EDITION
First Printing, 2017

Book format by Cassie Kanzenbach
Cover design by Kevin Brown
Cover illustration by Mary Ann Lasher-Dodge

Midnight Ink, an imprint of Llewellyn Worldwide Ltd.

Library of Congress Cataloging-in-Publication Data

Names: Weiss, Kirsten, author.
Title: Pressed to death / Kirsten Weiss.
Description: First edition. | Woodbury, Minnesota : Midnight Ink, [2017] |
   Series: A perfectly proper paranormal museum mystery ; #2
Identifiers: LCCN 2016049794 (print) | LCCN 2016058939 (ebook) | ISBN
   9780738750316 | ISBN 9780738750750
Subjects: LCSH: Paranormal fiction. | GSAFD: Mystery fiction.
Classification: LCC PS3623.E4555 P74 2017 (print) | LCC PS3623.E4555 (ebook)
   | DDC 813/.6—dc23
LC record available at https://lccn.loc.gov/2016049794

Midnight Ink
Llewellyn Worldwide Ltd.
2143 Wooddale Drive
Woodbury, MN 55125-2989
www.midnightinkbooks.com

Printed in the United States of America

To Karen, Raymond, and Alice

ONE

I WAS GOING TO jail.

Worse, my arch nemesis would be the one to drag me from my own paranormal museum.

"I do not traffic in stolen goods." My voice cracked on the final word. You'd think my innocence would go without saying, but Detective Laurel Hammer's loathing for me was irrational.

So I was saying it. I crossed my arms, defiant. The photos of executed murderers watched, impassive, from the museum's glossy white walls.

GD, the museum's ghost detecting cat, hopped off the haunted rocking chair in the corner. He landed, silent, on the checkerboard floor and cocked his sleek black head.

Blue eyes crackling, the detective planted her hands on the glass counter and loomed over the tip jar. Looming—of the tall and blond, beautiful and terrifying variety—was Laurel's signature move.

I edged away, dropping my arms to my sides. Unable to meet her gaze, I focused on her manicure, pale pink and elegant.

"Mr. Paganini says otherwise." She blew a wisp of short, side-swept hair out of her eyes. "He reported his antique grape press stolen from his winery, and said it was in your possession."

I shivered, tugging my black *Paranormal Museum* hoodie closer around my matching tank top. The museum was freezing, and I turned to the thermostat to escape her glower. The seven a.m. sun slanted through the blinds. I winced at the morning light as I pretended to adjust the heat. It was going to be another warm autumn day in California's Central Valley. There was no sense in turning down the AC.

"I bought the press from Herb Linden," I said. "My collector. I have a copy of the receipt."

I never should have done business with a man who lived with his mother and worked out of the trunk of a VW. But paranormal museum curators had to take what they could get. I'd taken over the museum less than a year ago. It wasn't the only paranormal museum in the country, but I was determined to make it the best. Or at least make a decent living off it. That wouldn't be possible from jail. What was the penalty for trafficking in stolen goods?

"Stolen is stolen." Laurel gazed at me coldly.

"It's not stolen! Look around you. Do you see anything in this museum worth going to jail for?" I motioned to the glass-enclosed shelves filled with haunted objects. Below the room's shiny black molding hung a rogues' gallery of haunted photos. Two doors, set in the wall to the right of the cash register, led to the Fortune Telling Room and my gallery space, which was currently packed with Halloween-themed art. A false bookcase was embedded in the opposite wall. Push the correct book and it swung open to the Fox and Fennel tea room, owned by my friend Adele (and, most importantly, to our shared bathroom).

Laurel's lip curled. "This isn't a museum, it's a con game."

"Con game?" I sputtered. I might be uncertain about the existence of the paranormal, but I believed in my museum. It was fun, spooky, and had an ounce of historical relevance. I drew a deep breath. Obviously, rational discourse wasn't working. I needed to take a different tack.

Flattery. "Actually, Laurel, if it weren't for you, the museum might not exist at all. I don't think I ever got a chance to thank you for helping me out with that fire last winter. We've completely remodeled the—"

"Stop trying to butter me up." The detective barred her teeth. "If your collector stole that grape press—"

"He didn't. Look, the receipt is right here." I drew a thick binder from beneath the cash register and flipped through the pages. Swiveling the open binder, I pushed it across the counter toward her.

Laurel glanced at it. "Doesn't mean a thing. I'll need to confiscate the grape press until this gets sorted out."

My mouth went dry. This had to be a mistake. "Laurel, please—"

"Detective Hammer!"

"I can't give it to you. It's not here."

"You sold it? Do you know what the penalty is for selling stolen goods?"

"It's not stolen! And I didn't sell it. It's part of my exhibit at the Harvest Festival." And also the only wine-themed haunted object I had.

October was high season for us in San Benedetto. Although sort of a cow town, San Benedetto was also known for its vineyards, and lately we were gaining a reputation for our zinfandels. In the fall, we not only had pumpkin patches and apple picking, but a Harvest Festival—put on by the Wine and Visitors Bureau—that brought in tourists from miles around. The highlight, naturally, was wine, with tastings promoting local vineyards. This was my first time participating, and I wanted my Paranormal Museum display to shine. After the wineries, the museum was the second-most-important tourist attraction in the area. Of course, there was also the giant straw Christmas Cow that someone torched every winter holiday. But it was fall, so the cow didn't count. My display at the Harvest Festival was small potatoes, yet I needed it to be a success if I wanted to lure tourists to the museum.

"Then I'll just go confiscate it at the festival," Laurel said.

Green eyes narrowed, GD Cat prowled behind her. The ghost detecting cat had taken a dislike to the detective ever since she'd helped save his life. Cats. Go figure.

Casually, I draped my hand over the counter and made shooing motions. "You can't. The fairgrounds aren't open yet." Ha!

"I'm sure I can get inside."

GD Cat hunched, preparing to pounce.

Sweat dotted my brow. Cosmic forces were clashing—Laurel and GD—and I was pretty certain I'd be the one blasted to smithereens. I hissed at the cat, "Go away!"

"I'm not going anywhere," Laurel snarled.

I hurried around the counter and scooped up GD, depositing him on the rocking chair.

"Herb may be odd, but I know he wouldn't do anything underhanded," I said. "Besides, the receipt is signed by Paganini's wife. Providence is important in my line of work." Providence helped me keep the paranormal stories behind the objects straight. And I liked saying "providence." It made me feel like a real museum curator.

Laurel snorted.

GD slunk from the chair, ears flat against his ebony head, and stalked toward her.

I edged between Laurel and the cat. "The festival only lasts for two days. Can I bring you the grape press on Sunday?"

"Why don't I just arrest you today?" Laurel reached behind her back and pulled out a pair of handcuffs.

"But... the festival!"

"You can't keep stolen goods until it's convenient for you to return them."

"I'm telling you, it's *not* stolen! That's the receipt."

The cat growled behind my ankles.

"Oh well, if you're *telling* me, then I guess I can just forget police procedure and let you keep the item."

"Would you?" I held my breath. Maybe Laurel had forgiven me after all.

"No."

My cell phone rang and I snatched it up. "Hello?"

"Madelyn, this is your mother."

"Yes." I eyeballed GD. The cat licked his paws, indifferent. "Your name shows up on my cell phone screen."

"Are you ready to go?"

"Um..."

"Good, because I'm here." My mother breezed through the door, setting the bell above it tinkling. Country-chic, she wore white jeans and a blue denim blouse. Her favorite turquoise earrings swung from her ears, and the matching silver squash-blossom necklace encircled her neck.

Tucking her phone into the pocket of her linen blazer, she stopped short. The overhead lights glinted off the silver threads in her pixie-cut hair. "Detective Hammer, what a lovely surprise. Will you be assisting us at the festival today?"

"No, I'm on duty," Laurel said.

"Oh? I was sure I heard that the police would be sending someone to help. After all, Ladies Aid funds the policeman's ball, and the Harvest Festival grape stomp is our most important fundraiser." My mother was heavily involved in organizing and promoting the grape stomp.

Laurel blanched.

"But since you're on duty," my mom went on, "what brings you to San Benedetto's third biggest tourist attraction?"

"Second biggest," I corrected.

"Third," she said, "after the Christmas Cow."

"The cow isn't even built yet," I retorted. "And Laurel's here because Mr. Paganini told the police that the haunted grape press I bought was stolen."

My mother blinked. "Not the grape press in your display at the festival?"

"That's the one."

"But you have a receipt, don't you?"

"It doesn't matter if she has a receipt," Laurel said. "If the guy who sold it to her stole it, it's stolen property."

"This all sounds like a simple misunderstanding." My mom turned to me. "Dear, we really must go. The festival starts in less than four hours. There's tons of work to do."

"Leo's not here yet." Leo was my new part-time employee. I had an employee! The museum was at that awkward adolescent stage— on the verge of growth. Hiring an employee, even if he was only part-time, was a big risk. If my projections were wrong and more help didn't result in more money, well, I was screwed. And I was responsible for Leo now, making sure he had his pay on time to buy food. It was mildly terrifying.

My mother frowned. "A bit late, isn't he?"

"Nope, early. He usually doesn't get here until nine. He's doing me a favor, coming in at seven to decorate." I wanted to put up Halloween decorations before the Harvest Festival crowds migrated to the museum.

"You're not going anywhere until this is resolved." Laurel banged her fist on the glass counter, rattling the tip jar.

Startled, GD Cat flattened his ears against his head.

The front bell jingled and Leo sloped into the museum. He ran a hand through his dyed-black hair, his watch catching on his silver skull earring. Wincing, he disentangled himself. "Hey. I'm here."

My mother's lips pursed, and I knew what she was thinking. Was a heavy metal T-shirt and jeans appropriate for my newest employee? But casual wear was another awesome bonus to working in a paranormal museum.

"Hi, Leo. Thanks for coming in at this hour." I pointed toward the Fortune Telling Room. "The Halloween stuff is in the spirit cabinet."

"Cool." He scooped up GD, stroking his ebony fur. To my surprise, the cat settled into his arms. "What's with Johnny Law?"

"Just a misunderstanding. She thinks I stole your father's grape press," I said.

"Why would she think that?" Leo asked.

"Because Mr. Paganini told me so," the detective said.

Leo rolled his eyes. "And you believed him? He's a congenital liar."

My mother laid a hand on his shoulder. "You shouldn't say that about your father, dear."

"Because it's true?"

"This seems like a waste of valuable police resources," my mom said, turning to Laurel. "I'll speak with Romeo and have this cleared up by the afternoon. Why don't we come by the police station then?"

"Who's we?" Laurel asked.

"Myself and Romeo Paganini, of course. I'm sure it would be easier for you if we resolved this ourselves rather than wasting your time with paperwork."

"Good luck with that." Shoulders hunched, Leo walked into the Fortune Telling Room.

"This afternoon, then?" My mother tucked her arms in mine and drew me from the museum. "By the way," she called over her shoulder to Laurel, "I love your new haircut—attractive *and* professional!"

I tensed, half expecting the detective to tackle me to the brick sidewalk. But we made it unscathed to my mother's butter-colored Lincoln, parallel parked in the shade of a plum tree. I slipped into the passenger seat beside her and we drove off.

The air conditioning blasted, teasing strands of my hair. I glanced over my shoulder. No blue lights pursued us, and I relaxed.

"Thanks, Mom. You're a lifesaver. I didn't think Laurel would let me go. She holds a grudge."

My mother gripped the wheel more tightly and shook her head. "You shouldn't have set her hair on fire, dear."

"I didn't set it on fire." It had been an accident. "And it just sort of smoldered." And it wasn't as if I'd forced Laurel to run into the burning museum. In fact, it had been kind of a heroic moment on her part, so I didn't get the hair obsession. It would grow back.

"She had such lovely long blond hair." My mother sighed. "Now, why would Romeo say you stole his vintage grape press?"

"I don't know," I said. "Herb bought the press from his wife. Maybe he's regretting the sale and is trying to get it back through the police instead of just asking me."

"Is it valuable?" my mom asked.

I pushed up the sleeves of my museum hoodie. I'd become a walking billboard, but when you own a business, that's par for the course. "I wouldn't call it valuable," I said. I'd paid a thousand bucks for it, which was a huge expenditure for the museum. But wine was a big deal in San Benedetto. A haunted grape press was perfect for the museum.

We glided through town, past its hundred-year-old brick and stucco buildings, past the park, its fountain decorated with pumpkins and cornstalks, and beneath the adobe welcome arch on Main Street. Soon we were driving past vineyards, their leaves green with tints of orange and purple.

In the distance, white tents rose above the vines, and I grinned. I'd always loved Harvest Festival. By this time of year, the sweltering Central California summer had given way to temperate, mid-80s bliss. And it was the start to the holiday season. Soon there'd be Halloween, then Thanksgiving and pumpkin pie, then the ill-fated Christmas Cow. And for the first time in years, I'd be home with my family. Or at least with my mom. My overachieving siblings would be scattered across the globe doing remarkable things. But hey, I was curator of *the* Paranormal Museum, and I could enjoy a real American holiday with all the sugary trimmings.

TWO

My mother steered the Lincoln down a wide road and into a dirt parking lot. Hastily erected metal fencing ringed the festival grounds. A female guard in a black *Security* T-shirt sat on a metal folding chair by the pedestrian gate.

Opening the glove box, my mother extracted her pass. "I presume you have yours?"

"Of course." Wait, did I? I'd been in such a hurry to get out of the museum ... Frantic, I dug in my hoodie pocket and extracted a laminated pass on a lanyard. I blew out my breath.

The guard glanced at our passes and waved us through the gate. I followed my mom past the pumpkin cannon and a row of kids' games—pumpkin ring toss, bobbing for apples, and one of those photo setups where you stick your head through a plywood painting of an overweight scarecrow.

My mom strode past a kid-sized hay maze. A bigger corn maze for adults had been set up on the far side of the fair. I couldn't wait to get lost in it with my boyfriend, Mason.

"So how is the grape press haunted?" my mom asked.

"Murder-suicide," I said.

She stared.

"Hey, happy spirits don't stick around to haunt grape presses," I pointed out.

Since I'd taken over the museum, I'd seen some odd things. My logical brain said there was a rational explanation. But a part of me wondered, and the wondering was fun. And the more I studied the paranormal, the more intrigued I became.

"I could have guessed that," she said. "But what does a murder-suicide have to do with a grape press. Unless..." Her blue eyes widened in horror. "No one was pressed to death, were they?"

"Good gad, no. It's not that big of a grape press. The killer worked in the vineyards and used the press. He was spurned by the vineyard owner's daughter, and he killed her and then himself."

"How delightfully ghastly. Did I tell you?" my mother asked. "I got an email from Melanie. She's singing at La Scala next summer!"

I hunched my shoulders. My sister, Melanie, was an opera singer, and my brother worked overseas in the State Department. I loved them to pieces, but constantly hearing about their triumphs got demoralizing.

"Oh, hey, there's Adele's spot," I said, anxious to change the subject.

I hurried down the path to a small white marquee, my mother trailing after me. My friend Adele Nakamoto paced inside it, her kelly-green heels kicking up straw. A matching bag swung over one arm. Need I say her Jackie Kennedy-style suit matched as well? She had plenty of room to maneuver, because aside from her, the tent was empty. A plastic sign above it read *Fox and Fennel Tea Room*.

"Hi, Adele!"

She whirled and grasped my shoulders. "Have you seen Steve?"

"I don't even know who he is."

"He's got all my supplies." She clawed a hand through her shiny black hair, loosing strands from her chignon.

"It's still early," I said.

"He's not," Adele said. "He was supposed to be here thirty minutes ago. I've got to set up the tables, put out my new menus... Did I tell you I have new menus? I do, and they cost me a fortune, and so did this booth, and if Steve doesn't get here in time I will die. I've been calling and calling and he hasn't been answering. What if he's dead?"

"Why would he be dead?" I asked. Adele had been accused of murder last winter, and she'd gotten a little quick to jump to the "maybe-he's-dead" conclusion whenever someone wasn't where they were supposed to be. Last week I'd been a teensy fifteen minutes late for our regular girls' night out and she'd called my mother, Leo, and my brother in Moscow. I'm more careful about checking my phone battery now.

Adele's brow crumpled. "I knew things were going too well."

"Don't panic yet," I said. "He's not that late. And he's definitely not dead."

"You don't know that," she said darkly. "And you don't understand. They're not just new menus, it's a new *menu*, with new tea blends. We're doing tastings! Iced, of course. Or they would be iced if the ice was here."

"He'll be here," I said.

"Then why isn't he answering his phone?"

"He's probably not answering because he's on his way and can't answer the phone while driving," my mom offered soothingly. "You know how sticky the police have gotten about that."

"Or he's dead," Adele said.

"Will your family also have a marquee this year?" my mom asked. Adele's family owned a winery called the Plot 42 Vineyard, and they'd introduced a new label, Haunted Vine, this year.

"With a name like Haunted Vine, Daddy couldn't resist having a tent again," Adele said. "He's with the other tasting tents in Section C."

"Look," I said, "if this Steve person doesn't show in thirty minutes, come find me. I'm sure we can scare up an extra table and tablecloth for you. Hey, who's managing your tea room while you're here?"

"Jorge." She wrung her hands. "I hope he's managing all right."

"He seems a capable young man," my mom said.

"He found the perfect printer for my menus. Which I don't have!" Adele wailed and stomped off.

I looked after her. We were best friends, but she was in full drama queen mode. Best to let her be.

"Well, shall we see your exhibit?" my mom asked.

"Yeah. It's over here." I led her through a row of booths to one of the larger canvas tents. Women in purple *Visitors Bureau* T-shirts bustled around it. Two were hanging a wooden sign over the tent's entrance: *Wine and Visitors Bureau and Haunted Museum*.

I sighed. The museum wasn't haunted, it was paranormal. Oh well. I was lucky the Visitors Bureau was letting me share tent space. Brushing beneath the flap, I held it open for my mother.

At the back of the tent, wine glasses were lined up in neat rows on long tables. The white tablecloths were tucked behind picket fences, bolted to the sides. Plastic grapevines twined through the slats. Cases of wine, I knew, hid beneath the tables. Many of the wineries would have their own booths, but the Visitors Bureau ran tastings on behalf of certain members.

In the center of the tent sat the antique grape press—a dark wooden barrel. A round metal crank at the top lowered a wooden lid to squish any hapless grapes. A placard hung from the crank, explaining its history and haunting. Beneath the text, an arrow pointed toward the Paranormal Museum display on the right side of the tent. A black cloth draped my table. On the rear corner of it sat a miniature trunk with a few of our burnt vintage dolls, who'd lived in the museum's Creepy Doll Room before it caught on fire and we turned it into a gallery. They were seriously freaky, with burnt hair and soot-covered faces, and I'd been happy to pack them away in my apartment. A haunted photograph of accused murderess Cora McBride held down the opposite side, next to other spooky photos.

"What do you need to do to finish setting up?" my mother asked.

In answer, I walked behind the table. Opening the box, I laid out a stack of brochures, a map that included the museum and key wineries, and some discount coupons. I arranged them in fan patterns. "Done."

"All right," she said. "Let's check out my grape stomp."

I grinned. "*Your* grape stomp?"

One corner of her mouth angled upward. "The Ladies Aid stomp. Did I tell you we took online sign-ups this year? We have more participants than ever. I think we may reach our goal of funding a mobile library."

"That's awesome, Mom."

We wended through the tents to a clearing with low wooden platforms covered in purple plastic. Wine barrels cut in half to make oversized buckets, with a spigot in the side, stood atop the platforms and weighted down the purple sheeting. A giant grape vat, the size of an above-ground swimming pool, stood off to one side. Backed against the massive vat sat a dump truck, its bed tilted, tailgate open.

A middle-aged woman strode across the straw-covered ground. Her loose, sleeveless tunic and pants flapped about her limbs, her silvery hair in a short ponytail. A coral prayer bead necklace with a red tassel dangled around her neck. Her nose was sharp as a blade, her face expressionless. She stopped in front of my mother. "Frances."

My mother nodded. "Cora."

I did a double take. This was the president of the Ladies Aid Society? The last time we'd met, she'd been armored in a chic suit and pearls, her hair in tight, marcelled waves. Now she was dressed like one of those freewheeling goddess types. "Hi, Mrs. Gale."

She smiled at me. "Hello, dear. I see you're exhibiting with the Visitors Bureau. What a lovely idea."

"Thanks."

She turned back to my mother and her face congealed. "And you. Nice grape stomp you've got here. It would be a shame if something happened to it."

A chill rippled the back of my neck.

My mother raised an imperial brow.

Cora looked like she might say something more, but she stalked away.

"What did she mean?" I laughed, unsettled. "That sounded like a mob threat."

"Never mind. What's that dump truck still doing here?" My mom walked to the giant vat and peered over the side, clicking her tongue.

I followed and peered over her shoulder. The grapes were piled on one side of the vat, beneath the dump truck's open gate.

My mom braced her fists on her hips. "Oh dear. I was certain I ordered more grapes, but that doesn't look like near enough grapes for the vat and the smaller barrel stomps. And I can't believe he just dumped the grapes and left. I thought our driver was more responsible." She blew out her breath. "Someone will need to distribute the grapes more evenly. Maddie, get in there and move those grapes."

"But … I'm not dressed for grapes." Seriously. I wasn't. I mean, I wasn't dressed for tea at the Savoy either, but grape guts are messy.

"Use the rake." She grabbed a rake leaning against the set of stairs leading to the vat and handed it to me. "I've got to get this truck moved." She strode into the tent area.

I looked at the rake, looked at the vat. Well, I'd promised to help. Climbing the steps, I leaned in and made a swipe at the grapes. The rake's tip clawed ineffectually at the pile.

Seeing purple stains in my future, I rolled up my jeans and clambered inside. A mountain of grapes sloped along the opposite side of the vat. Tentative, I raked at the top layer. A couple of bunches rolled down the pile. I was going to have to get more aggressive, and if grapes were damaged, so be it. They were all fated for stomping anyway.

I swung the rake with abandon, ripping at the pile. More grape clusters cascaded downward, spreading along the wooden vat floor. Sweat trickled down my spine.

The rake tines caught on a knotted pile of grapes. I tugged.

The grape mountain shifted sideways and I skittered back, stepped on a grape, and slid, grabbing the side of the vat for balance. Cursing, I examined my once-white tennis shoes. Why hadn't I just taken them off?

I scraped the bottom of my shoe on a bare spot on the floor, leaving a purple smear, and looked up.

A hairy arm was protruding from the pile of grapes.

THREE

Shocked, I stared at the arm. "Oh God." Tossing the rake aside, I waded through the fruit, praying the arm was attached to a live body. I tossed aside thick purple bunches. Yes, the masculine arm was connected to a shoulder, the shoulder was connected to a neck. It reminded me of that children's song about bones, and a hysterical giggle escaped my throat.

"Mom!" I shrieked, and then wondered why my first instinct was to shout for mommy. "Mom!"

I tossed aside another bunch of grapes. A man's face, splotched purple, stared out at me. Black hair, chiseled cheekbones, and deepset brown eyes, wide and blank.

Gulping, I touched two fingers beneath his jaw, hoping for a pulse. Not finding one, I shifted position, pressed harder. I swore. Fumbling in the pockets of my hoodie, I dug out my cell phone and called 911.

"Madelyn, what are you shouting about?" my mother asked from behind me. "And I gave you the rake. You're supposed to move the grapes, not stomp all over them."

"There's been …" My voice failed, throat thickening, and I coughed. "There's been an accident."

The dispatcher came on the line.

"I'm at the Harvest Festival, in the grape stomping section. I've found a body."

"A body?" my mother yelped.

I waded to her.

"You're at the Harvest Festival," the dispatcher said, "and you've found a body?"

"In the large grape vat."

"Are you certain he's deceased?"

"I'm not certain of anything right now, but his eyes are open and there's no pulse. Please send help."

"Help is on the way. Who am I speaking with?"

"Madelyn Kosloski."

"Okay, Madelyn. Just stay where you are and don't touch the body."

Too late for that. I hung up and hung my head. In San Benedetto, everyone comes when you called 911: police, fire, ambulance. I should have just called the police station, but I didn't have their number memorized.

My mother stared at the body and then glanced quickly away. "You're soaked in grape juice," she said.

I looked down. Calves splattered in purple. Shoes ruined.

Shaking her head, she helped me out of the vat. "Never mind the stains," she said. "It isn't important. Madelyn, do you know who that is?"

"No." Legs wobbly, I sat on the steps leading up to the vat. Since my return to my hometown, I'd gotten to know a lot of folks. But the dead man wasn't one of them.

She sighed and pulled her cell phone from her purse. "That's Romeo Paganini."

My stomach dropped to my grapey toes. "Oh … no." Romeo Paganini. The man who'd accused me of stealing his stupid grape press.

"Steve finally arrived, with Daddy." Adele minced toward us on her expensive green heels. "My booth is saved."

Her father, a silver-haired Asian man in khakis and a pressed white sports shirt, ambled beside her. "Good morning, Maddie, Fran. I hope you're both coming to my booth for a tasting."

My mother smiled, nodded, and turned away, muttering into her phone.

Adele stopped short. "Why are your legs purple?"

"I found a man in the vat, under the grapes." I jerked a shaky thumb over my shoulder. "The police are on their way."

Adele's eyes widened. "Police? Under the grapes? Is he dead?"

Mr. Nakamoto trotted past me, up the steps. Bracing his hands along the top of the vat, he looked inside and drew a sharp breath. "Romeo."

"Romeo?! Romeo Paganini?" Adele pushed past, shoving me sideways.

I stumbled off the steps, landing on my feet.

"I didn't do it!" Adele clapped her hands to her mouth.

Her father looped his arm over her shoulders. "Of course you didn't. No one will think you did." But he shot me a worried look. Though the real killer in Adele's case had been found, she flinched whenever she heard a siren. Still, this seemed like an overreaction, even for Adele. What was her connection to Romeo? It was a question I didn't want to ask in public.

My mom tucked her phone into her purse. "I suspect the police will want to fingerprint the vat. We should probably move away from it."

I nodded, relieved someone else was taking charge. Anyone else. The first murder mystery I'd been involved in had nearly gotten me killed. The police could manage this one.

Two stout, post-middle-aged women in jeans strode across the yard. Their sensible shoes crackled in the strewn hay. Over the hearts of their powder-blue tees were embroidered the words *Ladies Aid Society*.

"Tell me you're joking." The gray-haired woman raked an age-spotted hand through her hair, cut short and businesslike. Her lips pursed, reminding me of Janet Reno.

"I'm afraid not," my mother said. "The police are on their way."

"This was your responsibility, Fran."

"It wasn't as if I put the body in the vat," my mother said.

How had the body got there? I wondered. Had it been put in and then the grapes were dumped on top? Or had the body gone into the dump truck with the grapes, been driven here, and then dumped? I shook my head. That was a problem for the police. I wasn't investigating.

"You were supposed to take care of this," the gray-haired woman snapped. Her companion, a round-faced blonde with cornflower-blue eyes, stared at a nearby tent.

"I am taking care of it," my mother said. "The police are on their way. And I'm afraid I forgot my manners. Eliza, this is my daughter, Madelyn, the museum curator. Madelyn, this is Eliza Bigelow, the current president of the Ladies Aid Society."

Wait. Cora Gale wasn't the president anymore? And had I imagined it, or had my mom stressed the word *current*?

My mother's cheeks pinked. "And, of course, Betsy Kendle." She motioned toward the silent blonde. Betsy Kendle glanced at me and smiled, her pale brows drawn down.

Mrs. Bigelow took a deep breath, blew it out. "All right. I guess I can't blame you for this." She sounded disappointed. "Who's the stiff?"

"Romeo Paganini."

"Paganini..." Mrs. Bigelow's pale eyes narrowed. "Isn't his wife...?"

"Yes," my mom said.

The Ladies Aid president's nostrils flared. "You know what this means."

My mom bowed her head. "I'm afraid I do."

"What does it mean?" I asked.

"It means," my mother said, "that there's a hole in our community. A man is dead."

"And so is our grape stomp," Mrs. Bigelow said. "We can't have a stomp surrounded by police tape. We'll have to move the smaller stomping barrels to another section of the festival."

"There's space by the petting zoo," the blonde offered, timorous.

"Don't be daft," Mrs. Bigelow said. "All those smelly animals and kids? We'll need a different space. Fran, a word." She strode a few yards away and stood, waiting. My mother followed, meek, her shoulders nearly grazing her ears.

"Terrifying," Mr. Nakamoto muttered.

"I know," I said. "I can't believe I found another body. San Benedetto used to be such a nice, peaceful town."

"I wasn't talking about the body," he said, his expression grim.

"Do we have to wait for the police?" Adele asked. "After all, we didn't find the body."

"But I did touch the side of the grape vat," her father said. "You go. I'll stay."

Adele set her jaw. "No, I'll stay with you. After all, it isn't as if I had anything to do with this." She brushed back her curtain of black hair, sounding less than convincing.

Yes, we'd be having a chat later. Not that I was investigating the crime, but Adele had reacted too strongly to Romeo's death. I wanted to know why.

We waited, not saying much. My mother rejoined us.

"What was that about?" I asked. Sirens wailed in the distance.

She gave a quick shake of her head, lips pressed together.

There was definitely something going on here. I shifted my weight, not liking this at all. It was one thing for me to discover a dead body, another to suspect my mom was keeping information from me. Sure, it was probably just Ladies Aid business, but since the murder victim had accused me of a crime, I was feeling paranoid.

Detective Laurel Hammer strode through the tents, her lips curled. "I should have known it was you."

I wilted. Honestly, the hair-burning thing had not been my fault.

"Where's the body?" she asked.

I pointed at the vat. "The grapes were all piled beneath the dump truck, so I was using a rake to distribute them, and I saw an arm and thought he might be hurt, so I pulled some of the grapes away and took his pulse, and I think he's dead." I drew a breath. "That's when I called 911."

She mounted the steps to the vat and looked inside. "So you touched the body and interfered with the crime scene."

"I didn't know it was a 'body' until I touched it. He could have been hurt."

"Oh," she said, "he's hurt all right."

I touched my throat. "You mean he's alive?" Where was that ambulance? The paramedics?

"No, you idiot, he's dead."

My mother stiffened. "This is, of course, a tense situation. I'm sure if we all behave professionally, the crime scene will be processed more smoothly."

I stared at her. *The crime scene will be processed more smoothly?* Had she heard that on TV?

To my amazement, the detective flushed. She clomped down the steps in her heavy boots. "All right," she said. "You found the body. Then what?"

"I called 911."

"Whose dump truck is that?"

"I presume it's the truck rented by the Wine and Visitors Bureau," my mother said.

"Presume?"

"We hired our contractor, Mr. Finkielkraut, to bring a load of grapes to the festival for the stomp. He said he'd have to rent a truck."

"And what were *they* doing when you found the body?" The detective jerked her head toward the Nakamotos.

"Adele and her father arrived soon after my mom," I said. "I don't know where they were before that."

"I was arranging my booth for the Fox and Fennel," Adele said. "Then I met Daddy at the Haunted Vine booth, and we came over here to check out the grape stomp and see if Maddie needed help."

"So what's your beef with Paganini?" Laurel asked.

Adele squeaked. "What?"

"My daughter doesn't have any so-called beef with the man," Mr. Nakamoto said. "Just because she was suspected of one crime doesn't mean you can pin her with every murder in San Benedetto."

Eyes narrowed, Laurel studied Adele. "I heard you cursing him in the Shop and Go yesterday."

What? Adele hadn't said anything to me about that, and we saw each other nearly every day.

"I didn't … I don't …" Adele straightened. "You shouldn't eavesdrop."

"Life's full of unpleasant realities," Laurel said. "I heard you wish him dead."

"Not dead. I said I wished his stupid Death Bistro would … Oh, here." She dug into her purse and whipped out a folded sheet of paper, handing it to the detective.

Laurel unfolded it. Her blond eyebrows rose. "A Death Bistro?"

"Romeo wanted to rent out the Fox and Fennel for a private party. He didn't tell me it was for a Death Bistro, or that he was going to post flyers all over town."

"What on earth's a Death Bistro?" my mother asked.

"According to the flyer, they get together and talk about death or something. It's bad enough that my tea room is next door to a para-normal museum—"

"Hey!" I said. The museum was San Benedetto's second-biggest tourist attraction! Plus, Adele was the one who'd convinced me to take it over.

My friend placed a hand on my arm. "No offense, Maddie. But after that body was found in the museum last winter—"

"In your tea room!"

"Let's agree to disagree," she said.

I crossed my arms.

"You have no idea how I felt when I saw this flyer saying there would be a Death Bistro at my tea room," she went on. "My tea room is an elegant and restful dining experience. No one dies in my tea room!"

"Well," I said, "there was that one—"

"It's got a skull and crossbones on it! Have I mentioned they're posted all over town?"

Laurel folded the flyer and slid it into the pocket of her navy-blue blazer. "So Paganini's in some sort of death cult?" she asked.

"Whatever," Adele said. "It's in the flyer. And now I'm stuck with them at my tea room."

"Can I see the flyer?" I was a little disappointed Paganini hadn't approached me at the museum. But in fairness, we weren't set up for group dining, and the Halloween season was busy enough.

"No," Laurel said.

Adele reached into her bag and pulled out another one. "I've got lots. This one was at the Wok and Bowl."

The Wok and Bowl was popular, so no matter how quickly Adele had ripped the flyer off the wall, lots of people might have seen it. I shook myself. Didn't matter. I had bigger fish to fry, like my table at the . . . The blood drained from my face. "Leo. I've got to tell him what's happened."

"You won't say a word to anyone," Laurel said.

"But someone's got to tell Leo. Romeo Paganini is his father."

"Leo, the kid at your museum?" Laurel asked.

I nodded.

"The police will take care of it," she said. "Got it, Kosloski? You're not going to play private detective on this one."

"Of course not!" My face heated. The murders—two of them—last winter had been bad enough. Why would anyone think I'd want to get involved in this? Adele hadn't killed anyone over this Death Bistro. I bit the inside of my cheek. And just because I'd found the body, and my mom was acting weird, it didn't mean either of us were involved.

A tall, elegant black man, flanked by four uniformed officers, strode down the wide dirt walk toward us. He unbuttoned his charcoal-gray blazer and flashed his badge. I swallowed. Detective Slate.

"What's going on?" he asked Laurel.

She pointed to the grape vat. "Kosloski found a dead man in the vat. Name's Romeo Paganini. He had a run-in with both her and her friend, Nakamoto."

"It wasn't a run-in," Adele said.

"I've never met him before," I put in. "I told you, I bought the grape press from my collector, Herb."

Detective Slate rubbed his temple. "Herb Linden? The loon who hates cops? Great."

"I wouldn't say he hates cops." I wasn't going to argue about the loon part.

Slate glanced at the uniformed policemen. "You four, secure the scene."

Two EMTs jogged toward the police. Laurel pointed at the grape vat and they clambered inside. She jabbed a finger at me. "I don't want you talking to anybody about this but the cops. Clear?" She strode away to join the EMTs.

"Why don't you tell me what happened?" The detective's gold-flecked eyes seemed to look right inside me, as they always did. I took a step back.

A curse floated from the vat.

I explained about finding the body.

The EMTs clambered out, their black slacks damp around the cuffs. One caught Slate's eye and shook his head.

The detective nodded at him. "What's this about a grape press?" he asked me.

"I bought a haunted grape press from Herb. He bought it from Paganini's wife. He gave me a copy of the receipt, signed by Mrs. Paganini. But her husband apparently complained to the police that the press was stolen."

A thought occurred to me. Romeo Paganini had told Laurel I had the press, but how had he known? Laurel hadn't seemed to know about Herb—who'd bought the press and sold it to me—until I'd told her. So how had Paganini tracked the press to me? Had he seen it on display in the tent? But that would mean he'd been on the grounds before the Harvest Festival opened for business. He owned a winery... maybe he had a booth or tent at the fair?

Slate turned to Adele. "Miss Nakamoto?"

My friend examined her nails. "A... group he's in, called the Death Bistro, is renting out my tea shop for a private party. I didn't like the flyers he was posting. That was all."

"Hardly a reason for homicide," her father said. "Adele and I walked over here together, by which time Maddie had already called 911."

"No one's talking about homicide," Slate said. "We don't know yet how the man died."

"But it's unlikely he crawled beneath a pile of grapes to do it," I said.

Slate's forehead wrinkled.

"Sorry," I muttered. It was none of my business.

"Mrs. Kosloski?" The detective turned to my mother.

"The Ladies Aid Society manages the grape stomp," my mom said. "It's one of our most important fundraisers. I came here this morning with Madelyn to make sure everything was in order, and we found the dump truck parked by the vat. Everything else happened as Madelyn said."

"Any idea where the driver is?" the handsome detective asked.

"Nooooo." A crease formed between my mom's brows. An engine roared and she canted her head.

I followed her gaze. A dump truck trundled up the wide dirt road, halting outside the ring of truncated wine barrels. A head of spiky brown hair popped out the open window and I smothered a groan. Dieter Finkielkraut, my ex-contractor.

"Dudes! Where do you want these grapes?" he shouted.

Adele covered her face with her hands. "I can't believe this is happening."

Detective Slate strode to the truck and hopped onto the running board. He said something, and Dieter shook his head. Slate pointed and hopped off the truck. Dieter reversed into a spot beside a tent and parked.

"Mom, how many loads of grapes were you expecting this morning?" I asked.

She frowned at the vat, then at the first dump truck. "Only one."

"And Dieter was bringing them?"

She sighed. "He owed me a favor."

"If that's the load of grapes you ordered, then where did the grapes in the vat come from?"

"I don't know."

"Where did the other truck come from, for that matter?"

"I don't know that either."

Dieter wouldn't have just dumped a load of grapes and ditched a truck. If he'd had to make two trips, he would have made two trips with the same vehicle. Which meant the dump truck beside the vat wasn't the one my mom had arranged. Curious.

I shook my head. Wasn't my business. I wasn't investigating.

"And why put the body in the vat?" I said to no one.

"That," my mother said, "is an excellent question."

The phone rang in my pocket. Startled, I pulled it from my hoodie. Mason. We'd been dating for several months, and loving him had been the best part of coming home to San Benedetto. In spite of cops wrapping yellow police tape around a grape vat, my heart gave a little jump.

I answered the phone. "Mason. I'm glad you called."

There was a brief pause. "You sound kind of stressed. Problem at the festival?" His voice was a low rumble.

I laughed hollowly. "You can say that. I found a dead body in the big wine vat for grape stomping. The police are here now."

"You're kidding."

"I wish I were."

"Are you okay?"

"I'm fine. Just a little shaken."

Slate came back over to us. "Okay. You can go. We may have more questions for you later, but I know where to find you. And Maddie? This time, let the police handle the investigation."

I did not dignify that with a response. "Mason, I've got to go," I whispered into the phone.

"Do you need me there?"

I smiled. "Thanks, but I'll be okay."

"Let me know if that changes." Another pause. "You're not going to get involved, are you?"

"No! I mean, no, of course not." Was he joking?

"All right. Call me. Bye."

"Bye." I hung up.

My mother cleared her throat. "Detective, the festival opens in less than three short hours. I'd like to move the half barrels to another location so we can go ahead with the stomp."

Slate shook his head. "I'm sorry, Mrs. Kosloski, but we won't know if they're a part of the crime scene until we get a chance to examine them."

My mother drew breath to speak, then clamped her lips into a taut line. "Of course. Thank you, Detective." She gripped my arm. "Maddie, we need new barrels. Fast."

"I've got a few back at my winery," Mr. Nakamoto said. "I can call around and see if I can collect more."

My mother grasped his hands. "You're a lifesaver. Thank you, Roy. Madelyn? We need to talk." She strode toward the row of tents.

Sweating, I waved to Adele and her father and hurried after her.

My mother pulled me into a narrow gap between two tents, their canvas sides brushing our shoulders. "This investigation—"

"I'm not going to interfere!"

Her eyes narrowed. "Oh yes you are, Madelyn."

FOUR

I GAPED AT MY mother.

She gazed back at me, her blue eyes cool and calm, not a strand of silver-flecked hair out of place, blouse and jeans crisp. No, my mother had not been replaced by an extraterrestrial clone. Not even an alien would iron her jeans.

A gust of warm breeze ruffled the tent sides, brushing against the sleeve of my thin hoodie.

"I'm sorry." I rubbed my chin. "I must have heard you wrong. I thought you said you wanted me to investigate Mr. Paganini's death."

Looking past my shoulder, she drew me further into the cool shadow between the tents. "Madelyn, you have to," she said in a low voice. "Detective Hammer is going to fixate on you, given Romeo's accusations about his grape press." Her lips pressed together. "I wish you hadn't set her hair on fire."

"For Pete's sake, I didn't set her hair on fire! There was a fire. A spark somehow caught in her hair. I had nothing to do with it."

"That's as it may be, but in her mind, you ruined a lovely hair-style. Now, Eliza Bigelow is going to ask you to investigate, and you need to agree."

I blew out my breath. None of this tracked. Even if Laurel had it out for me, she wasn't the only cop in the precinct. And what was Ladies Aid's interest in the murder? "But Mom, why?"

"I think she's projecting some sort of frustrations—"

"I meant, why would Ladies Aid ask me to investigate?"

The canvas tents rustled, whispering, and she glanced behind her. "The grape stomp is the most important fundraiser we do, as you know. It's one of our few events that bring in money from do-nors outside San Benedetto."

"So move the stomp to another part of the festival. Problem solved."

My mother shook her head, her turquoise earrings swinging. "There's more to it than that."

"Do you think Mrs. Gale had something to do with this?" I asked. "It was almost as if she knew something was wrong with the stomp." *Nice grape stomp. A shame if something happened to it.*

"Of course not. Look, I know I'm asking a lot, but I'll make it worth your while, both for you and Adele."

"Adele? What does she have to do with this?"

"Nothing, as far as I know. But there's more going on than meets the eye."

"What aren't you telling me?"

My mother broke into a smile and waved. "Over here!"

Eliza Bigelow and Betsy Kendle stalked toward us, accompanied by three other women in similar powder-blue tees. They filtered into the narrow space, looking like a gang of determined blue fairies.

A shiver traced a line up my spine and I hunched my shoulders, trying to make myself smaller.

"What have you got for us?" In front, Mrs. Bigelow tossed her head, but her short gray hair remained frozen in place. Sweat gleamed in the creases of her neck.

"The police are treating the current area as part of a crime scene," my mother said. "So Roy Nakamoto, with the other vintners, is gathering new stomping barrels. I would guess they'll be here within two hours. We can move them to the area beside the food tables. Maddie was just on her way to inform the Visitors Bureau about changing the signage."

"It's too late to change the festival maps, though," Mrs. Bigelow said.

"That's unfortunate," my mother agreed. "But the new spot beside the dining area will attract walk-through traffic. Everyone ends up at the food tables."

Mrs. Bigelow's lips pinched. "What about the stands? We can't just put the stomping barrels on the ground."

My mother paled. She hadn't thought of that. "I'm confident our contractor will be able to build some simple stands in time for the stomp," she said, rallying. "It doesn't start until this afternoon."

"Who's your contractor?"

"Dieter Finkielkraut."

"Finkielkraut." Mrs. Bigelow's hazel eyes narrowed. "Is he the one who looks like a bum?"

"Most contractors of my acquaintance dress casually on the job," my mother said. "Their work is not conducive to business attire."

"Hmph. Well, it sounds as if you've got things under control," Mrs. Bigelow said grudgingly.

"But I'll need help to make sure this goes off without a hitch." My mother smiled, sharklike, and nodded at the other women. "If I may borrow some of the ladies?"

"They're very busy," the Ladies Aid president said.

"We're dealing with an emergency none of us could have foreseen," my mother said. She angled her chin down, looking up through her lashes. "I would hope we could all come together to ensure the success of our fundraiser. Cooperation is, after all, what Ladies Aid is about."

Was I imagining it or were there weird undercurrents in the cow-scented air?

A rotund woman in stretch pants stepped forward. "I've got time. I'd be happy to—"

Mrs. Bigelow shot her a look and she fell back, staring at the straw-strewn ground.

Another ripple of uneasiness shivered my skin. I edged closer to a tent. Would anyone notice if I slithered beneath the canvas and escaped?

"There is rather a lot to do," my mom said. "We'll need to put flyers up around the fairground about the shift in venue for the stomp. One of us must inform the other booths about the change, in case people ask them. Someone will have to manage and possibly assist Mr. Finkielkraut with the grapes..."

Several of the Ladies Aid ladies perked up, eyes gleaming. There would always be women attracted to bad boys.

"And I'm sure as the morning goes on, other issues will arise," my mother continued. "This is, after all, a sudden change. But I'm confident if we all come together, we can have a successful fundraiser in spite of this terrible tragedy."

Mrs. Bigelow looked like she'd choked on a lemon. "Fine. Take whoever volunteers."

Half the women edged toward my mom.

The president's nostrils flared and she stomped away.

My mother clapped her hands. "All right, ladies, we've got a grape stomp to save." She marched them off.

These were strange days at Ladies Aid. I rubbed the back of my neck. And then I remembered I had my own disaster to avert and hurried in the opposite direction, to the Wine and Visitors Bureau tent. Thankfully, the director of the Visitors Bureau was inside, her hair a storm cloud of gray. She stood beside the haunted grape press, frowning at an open envelope in her hand.

"Hi, Penny."

She looked up and stuffed the envelope into the pocket of her pale green slacks, adjusted the collar of her semi-sheer blouse. Its pattern of twisting grapes echoed the faux grapevines I'd wrapped around the haunted press.

Removing the glasses from her nose, she let them drop to her chest, where they dangled from a beaded chain. "Maddie? Is everything all right? I heard there was an accident on the grounds, but the police are keeping everyone away from the site. No one is telling me anything, aside from the fact that the grape stomp area will be out of bounds for at least the rest of the day."

I edged toward a table laden with rows of empty glasses. It was too early in the day for wine, but I suddenly, desperately, wanted a glass. "I'm afraid a man was found dead. Romeo Paganini."

Penny clapped her wrinkled hands to her mouth. "Romeo? But he's got a tasting tent! Are you sure? "

"I'm sure."

"Sorry." She raked a hand through her graying hair. "Obviously there's more at stake here than a tent at the festival. This is awful. Poor Jocelyn."

"Jocelyn?"

"His wife. Second wife." She frowned. "And his first wife died only a year ago. What a tragedy. And why am I babbling about this? Oh, because the festival is falling apart, and I'm on the board."

"I don't think it's falling apart. The Ladies Aid Society thinks it can move the grape stomp to that empty area beside the food tables."

"That might work," Penny said. "But we've already printed out the maps."

"My mother plans to post flyers with info about the change. It's all happening pretty fast, but you know Ladies Aid."

"The D-Day planners had nothing on your mother. Still, I'd better track down the other board members and help get this organized." Walking behind a table, Penny reached beneath the white tablecloth and grabbed her purse.

A man strode inside the tent. He stopped, bent, and knocked a bit of straw off the cuffs of his jeans, then smoothed the front of his tweed vest and tie. He looked like the quintessential California hipster—young, blond, and blue-eyed. A ginormous handlebar moustache and trimmed blond beard masked his even features. "Penny! Just the lady I wanted to see."

She jerked upright, her expression frozen. "Chuck. I told you we can't distribute maps to your winery. We can only hand out the official map sponsored by Wine and Visitors Bureau members."

He waved a hand. "That's fine. I get it. Actually, I was hoping I could get some of your maps to distribute at my tasting table."

"Why?" Penny asked.

I tilted my head. Penny was usually pretty free with the maps.

"People come to taste here because San Benedetto's got a cluster of wineries. But you already know that." He winked. "The map helps me out even if I'm not on it. Handing it out is a gesture of goodwill. Plus, I can put an X on the map where my winery is located."

Squaring her jaw, Penny scrounged beneath one of the tables for another box. "Fine."

Glancing at me, he smiled. "Sorry, I didn't introduce myself. I'm Chuck Wollmer. CW Vineyards." He held out his hand, and I gripped it.

"Maddie Kosloski. I own the Paranormal Museum."

"I love that place. What you've done with it was brilliant—the web cam, the art gallery…"

"I wanted fresh exhibits so people would return."

"Genius."

"Thanks. But it was more a desperation move."

"Necessity is the mother of invention."

Penny handed him a stack of maps. "If I find these in a dumpster—"

He pressed his palm to his chest. "Please. I don't trash paper. I recycle."

"Chuck…" Penny stared at him over her glasses.

"Kidding! Just kidding." He gazed, rueful, at the maps and turned to me. "Ever thought of working in a winery? I could use someone with guerrilla marketing chops."

"I think I've got my hands full with the museum."

"A consultancy?"

"The only time I like telling people what to do," I said, "is when I have the authority to make them do it."

"Deep waters, Kosloski. Deep waters." Grinning, he exited the tent.

Penny shook her head. "He's incorrigible. Was there anything else, Maddie?"

"Well, before you go, Mr. Paganini's son works for me at the museum."

Penny clapped her hands to her mouth. "The poor boy!"

"He was going to run the museum today while I managed my table, but under the circumstances, I'm sure he'll want to take the day off. And that leaves me a man short. Could someone from the Wine and Visitors Bureau watch my table? All they have to do is hand out discount coupons, and that can be done from the tasting table."

The corners of her mouth drifted upward, her eyes narrowing. "I'm sure we can come to some arrangement."

"Thanks." I headed toward the tent's entrance.

"But we'll need something in return."

Slowly, I turned to her. "Something?"

"As you've probably heard, this month the Ladies Aid Society is running their annual haunted house, sponsored in part by the Wine and Visitors Bureau."

"Ye-es."

"They've agreed to do a Haunted San Benedetto exhibit at the house, and I think this theme fits perfectly with your museum, don't you? If you put something together for us, you could even include some brochures and discount coupons for your business in the display."

"You want me to throw together a haunted exhibit? Sure. No problem." The Ladies Aid haunted house was three weeks away. It was one of my mother's favorite events, aside from the Christmas Cow, and I thought it might be fun to work with her. I grabbed the discount coupons off the table and thrust them at Penny. "Whoever's running the tastings can give these away."

"Excellent. I'll inform the president of Ladies Aid that you're on board for the haunted house."

"Thanks. You're a lifesaver."

Her eyes darkened. "Oh, no. Thank *you*."

Skin prickling, I paused in the entryway to the tent. Something didn't feel right, but finding Paganini's body had shaken me. Sinister threats were not seeping from beneath every wine barrel. I could throw together a Haunted San Benedetto table standing on my head. In fact, I could just take the stuff from the table I had in the wine tent right now and use it at the haunted house. It was Leo I worried about. Did he know what had happened to his father?

I hurried to the parking lot, pulling off my hoodie and wrapping it around my waist. The sun sat higher in the sky now, warming my bare shoulders.

Stopping beside a Camaro, I smacked my forehead. My mom had driven us here. I had no wheels.

On the far side of the dirt parking area, Dieter climbed into the dump truck.

I raced toward him. "Dieter! Hey!"

He paused, one muscular, denim-clad leg swinging out the door. His brown eyes crinkled, sparkling against his bronzed skin. "If it isn't the Mad Kosloski. What's up?"

"Can you give me a lift to the Paranormal Museum?" I panted, winded from my sprint. I needed to start working out.

"You need a ride? Sure, Mad Dog. Hop in."

I hated that nickname, but hitchhikers can't be choosers. Forcing a smile, I hurried around the side of the cab and clambered in, thudding the heavy door shut behind me. My jeans squeaked on the plasticy, canvas-looking seats. I took in the wide white steering wheel with its finger grips, the clock ticking away on the dashboard. "Thanks. Um, does my mom know you're leaving?"

He grimaced. "Don't worry. She's already talked to me about building new platforms and cutting barrels for grape stomping. It'll be easier for me to do the work at my workshop. My supplies are all there."

"You've got a workshop?"

"Of course. A little bird told me you found a body at the festival," he said. "Who was it?"

I hesitated. Laurel had told me to keep it quiet. She'd also threatened me with arrest over an innocent grape press transaction. "Romeo Paganini." My heart squeezed. Poor Leo. I knew too well what it meant to lose a father. At least I'd been an adult when my father had passed. Leo wasn't out of his teens, and his mother was gone too.

Dieter whistled. "A big time winery owner? That's going to be news."

"Did you recognize that other dump truck? The one parked by the wine vat?"

"Hey, I had nothing to do with that. I was supposed to bring a load of grapes from the Visitors Bureau at eight, and I followed my orders."

"From the Visitors Bureau?"

"Yeah, they collected the rejects for the grape stomp." He started the truck. "None of the juice from the stomp actually goes to making wine, you know."

I'd grown up in San Benedetto and knew the sad realities of grape stomping. Pressing grapes by foot might have been traditional, but it also violated all sorts of California health codes. "So did you recognize the truck?" I asked again.

41

"Nope. I'm guessing it's from one of the wineries—leased for the harvest is my bet."

Springs creaking, we jounced in time to the parking lot's potholes. "Why leased?" I asked.

"It would have a winery logo on the side otherwise."

That made sense. Dieter wasn't as goofy as he acted.

"Was Romeo one of your bookmaking clients?" I asked.

"Are you kidding? Running a winery is enough of a gamble."

Rows of vines flashed past. "The police are going to tell his son." I hoped Detective Slate did it and not Laurel.

"I guessed." He shook his head. "This isn't going to be easy."

No. Not easy.

Brutal.

"So," he said, "how many bodies have you found this year? Three?"

Or maybe he was that goofy. I sighed. "And what little bird told you I found the body?"

"Adele." His eyes softened, dreamy. "Are you going to investigate this death?"

"No! And I didn't ... Why would you ask that?"

"No reason."

Suspicious, I bit the inside of my lip. Dieter ran a side business taking bets on odd things, like if and when the San Benedetto Christmas Cow would get torched. The only year he'd lost big was when someone had driven into the cow with an RV. Not even Dieter had factored destruction-by-RV into his calculations.

Dieter grimaced. "Except I heard it looks like murder."

FIVE

DIETER DROPPED ME OFF in front of the Paranormal Museum. I gazed at its wide windows. My *Tackiest Museum in San Benedetto* "award" leaned in one corner. Orange and black streamers twisted along the sills. A sizable crowd milled inside, killing time until the Harvest Festival opened and the wine tasting began. Most wineries didn't start serving until noon, eleven thirty at the earliest.

Leo stood at the register, his black jeans and T-shirt now mourning garb.

Taking a deep breath, I walked inside. A pyramid of pumpkins sat wedged between the counter and the door.

Leo glanced up, his eyes pink. "Hi, Mad. Good crowd." His voice was dull, listless.

An ache speared my chest. I closed the door behind me and reached up to mute the bell.

He knew.

On the glass counter, GD lashed his tail. I edged out of the black cat's reach. GD knew enough not to claw the customers—he had an uncanny sense of who funded his eating habits. But the fact that I bought the kibble mattered not a whit.

"Thanks for keeping the museum open," I said.

Leo lifted a brow. "That's what you're paying me for."

"Yes, but ... I assume the police have spoken with you."

"Yeah. They told me you found Romeo."

"I'm so sorry."

He studied the counter. "What are you doing here? Aren't you supposed to be managing the booth at the festival?"

"The Visitors Bureau is taking it over for me."

"Out of the goodness of their hearts?"

"Not exactly, but I thought you'd want to take the rest of the day off."

"No. It doesn't matter."

"It matters to me. Whatever you need, Leo, just let me know."

"Thanks, but I don't need anything. And I haven't needed anything from my father for a long time."

"Even if you and your father weren't on the best terms, this still ... I lost my dad not that long ago. I know what it's like." At his death, the universe had shifted beneath my feet. "You can go home, take the rest of the day off."

Leo's neck corded. "I'm only surprised someone didn't kill him sooner. I've thought about doing it myself plenty of times."

I gazed into his eyes, which were puffy and bloodshot. He didn't mean it. "I hope you didn't tell that to the police."

He raised a dark brow. "I'm angry, not stupid."

"Have you spoken with anyone else in the, um, family?"

"I can't talk to Jocelyn," he said flatly. "She's a psycho." He drew a butcher knife from beneath the counter and set it beside the register. The blade glittered beneath the overhead lamps. "So about those decorations, did you want to carve some jack-o'-lanterns? We've got plenty of pumpkins."

"No, they'll rot before Halloween. We'd have to carve one every day. Where did you get that knife?"

He shrugged. "Tea room. Hey, when the cops came by, they asked about that grape press. I told them if you said your collector bought it from Jocelyn, he bought it from Jocelyn. She probably sold it to piss Romeo off. He cared more about wine-making than he did about her, or anyone else." The boy's chest hitched.

The four stages of grief theory may be debunked, but at least three tangled in Leo's eyes—denial, depression, anger. His pain weighted my shoulders. "Look, the festival's covered, and I'm here," I said. "Why don't you take the day off—"

His face reddened. "I don't need to."

I raised my hands in a defensive gesture. "Whatever you want is fine by me. But the offer stands. With pay."

He rubbed a hand through his hair, blew out his breath. "I don't know."

"Go, before I come to my senses. You know I'm a natural cheapskate."

"Are you sure?"

"I'm sure."

"All right then." He slithered from behind the counter. "See you tomorrow."

"Only if you're up to it."

He slouched out the door and I took his place.

Shooting me a look of contempt, GD sprang to the floor and stalked away, tail high.

"What? I was being nice!"

The museum and gallery were busy, too busy for me to think much about the murder. A middle-aged woman with blue streaks in her dark hair bought a cheerfully painted Ouija board from the gallery. A group of college kids relieved me of several *Paranormal Museum* T-shirts and shot glasses. And an elderly man with stooped shoulders bought an EMF detector, suitable for hunting ghosts or checking out how much energy really was coming out of your microwave. I'd tested mine. The answer was unsettling, but at least my garage apartment was specter-free.

Around one o'clock, my stomach growled, and I realized I was also food-free. I'd planned on grabbing a bite at the festival—Funnel cakes! Hot dogs! Drippy nachos!—and hadn't packed a lunch.

The door swung open and a blond Viking in jeans strode inside, his mane of blond hair wrapped in a ponytail. His black T-shirt strained across his brawny chest "Hey, Mad."

My heart skipped a beat. "Mason."

Leaning across the counter, he brushed a kiss across my cheek.

I shivered from the scratch of his five o'clock shadow across my skin. We worked next door to each other, and sometimes I worried we saw each other too much. But the sight of him never got boring, and my body reacted to his presence, my blood fizzing.

Stepping away from the counter, he gave me a look, his arctic-blue eyes serious. "You okay?"

Was I okay? Finding the body had been unnerving. My mother and Adele's behavior had been disturbing. And Leo ... My heart lurched.

On the bright side, I wasn't dead beneath a pile of grapes. "I'm fine."

"Whose body was it?" He watched a pair of tourists in matching, striped sweaters vanish into the Fortune Telling Room.

"Did you know Romeo Paganini?"

He shook his head. "Name sounds familiar."

"He owns—owned—a winery, Trivia Vineyards."

"Trivia?"

"It's not easy coming up with an original name in the world of wine."

"I'll take your word for it," he said. "And it was his body you found?"

Two middle-aged women in black tracksuits exited the gallery.

I nodded and smiled at them. "Mmm hmm."

"This isn't the best place to talk," Mason said. "And there's something I'd like to ask you. Can I take you to lunch?"

"I wish you could, but Leo is Romeo's son. I gave him the day off."

Mason's brow wrinkled. "Who's managing your display at the festival?"

"The Wine and Visitors Bureau."

"And what did you have to promise in exchange?"

"Just a display at the Ladies Aid haunted house. No biggie."

He quirked a brow. "Dinner tonight?"

Regretful, I scrubbed my hand over my face. "It's Saturday." Adele and I, along with our friend Harper, had a standing girls' night out at the local microbrewery.

"How could I forget?" He pursed his lips and I ached to kiss them. "Do you want me to bring lunch in?"

"Would you?"

The tracksuit ladies moved into the Fortune Telling Room.

"For you? Anything." His voice was a low rumble. He leaned across the counter, cupping my chin. His lips brushed mine, and my knees weakened.

"Hssst!"

I jerked away, looked around. We were still alone. Not even the cat was in sight.

"Hssst!" The fake bookshelf between the museum and the tea room stood ajar. A balding head, glasses glinting in the overhead light, nose twitching, edged out of the gap. "Is the coast clear?"

"Herb." I folded my arms over my chest.

"Your collector?" Mason asked. "I was starting to think he was an urban legend."

I growled in response.

Herb-of-the-potentially-stolen-grape-press slunk inside the museum and straightened his brown bow tie. His beigy clothing sagged on his narrow frame. "The cops came to my house. Mother was very upset."

"Did you talk to them?" I asked.

"Of course not! You know I don't talk to police."

"I'll pick up lunch and let you two talk," Mason said. "Chinese?"

"You know what I like."

He leered, and my cheeks warmed at the double meaning.

Sketching a wave, Mason left, and I forced myself not to ogle his departing backside as the door swung shut.

"Now, about Dion Fortune's scrying mirror," Herb said. "Since we're friends, I can drop the price to five thousand."

I whirled on the collector. "Romeo Paganini told the police that I stole that grape press."

"You?" Herb's eyes widened behind his thick lenses. "What do you have to do with it?"

"I bought it from you! The police think the press is stolen goods."

Herb straightened. "I do not deal in stolen goods. You know me better than that."

48

In truth, I didn't know him well at all, a situation that had suited us both until now.

"Who sold you that grape press?" I asked.

"You saw the receipt. Mrs. Paganini sold it to me."

"Are you sure it was Mrs. Paganini?"

His face pinched. "Of course I'm sure. Jocelyn Paganini, professor of viticulture at San Benedetto Community College. I looked her up on the college website before I went to her house. Everything's in order. What are you in such a stew about?"

"Did she contact you, or did you contact her about the press?"

"She contacted me. Said the thing was cursed, and she wanted to get rid of it."

"Tell me more about the history of the press."

"If you're worried about the curse, I performed a binding spell. The press is now relatively harmless, though I wouldn't let young lovers handle it."

I rolled my eyes. As if young lovers would embrace over a grape press!

"If the cops think the press is stolen," Herb continued, "all they need to do is ask Mrs. Paganini. I gave you a copy of the signed receipt. It seems like a lot of fuss over nothing."

"A lot of fuss? Romeo Paganini's dead, and I found his body, after being accused of stealing his property."

Herb's mouth opened. He closed it, Adam's apple bobbing, and swallowed. "Bye." He skittered through the bookcase. It closed behind him before I could react.

Cursing, I hurried after him, pressing the false book spine that unlatched the door. The case swung open and I ran into the tea room.

Women sat around tables covered by crisp white cloths. Customers lounged on soft white couches and lined up at the tea room counter, its frontage covered in misty, mint-green tiles. Behind it on wooden shelves stood tea blends in shiny metal canisters.

A metallic door clanged shut, fluttering the gauzy curtains at the front windows.

I hurried down the wide bamboo hall, past the bathrooms to the alleyway exit.

Thrusting the metal door open, I leaned outside. A battered yellow VW Bug revved its engine and sped off in a cloud of exhaust.

I returned to the museum, pressing my lips together. The cops would track Herb down eventually. After all, they knew where he lived (with his mother).

———

I drove up the dirt and gravel driveway to Adele's family vineyard. My window was down, the balmy air caressing my bare arm. I'd misspent my prior career in countries where pollution had burned my throat, twisted my gut, hung heavy in my clothing and hair at the end of the day. Since returning to California, I'd developed a mania for fresh air. Good thing, since my vintage pickup didn't have AC. I'd inherited the truck from my father, and I'd come to love sitting up high on the roads, the purr of its engine, its broad seats.

Above me, light from nearby Sacramento tinted the night sky purple, but there was no moon and the stars sparkled. On my left, twinkle lights twined around the barn that Adele's parents had converted into a tasting room. More lights glowed from the windows of their nearby two-story, white-painted Victorian. It was a larger version of Adele's, on the opposite side of the vineyard.

Parking my red truck beneath an oak, I walked past picnic tables and across the soft lawn to the house.

A feminine voice—Adele's—floated from her parents' Victorian. Something in the tone, a tension, stopped me on the porch steps, hand on the railing.

"But I thought you loved it!"

A lower voice, a man's, answered, too low for me to hear.

"Well," she replied, "*I* don't appreciate these high-pressure tactics."

I checked my watch beneath the porch light. Eight o'clock. Right on time. Feeling awkward, I rang the bell.

The voices stopped, and heels clicked across a wooden floor.

Adele flung open the door and pasted on a smile. "Maddie! Perfect timing." She grabbed a turquoise-colored purse and jacket off a nearby coat tree.

Behind her in the high-ceilinged foyer, her father spoke to a strange man, tall and emaciated and pale as a vampire. The man glanced toward me, his chill, dark eyes not registering a flicker of awareness at my presence. I waggled my fingers at Mr. Nakamoto, but Adele's gray-haired father didn't seem to notice me either.

Adele stepped onto the porch, closing the door behind her. Since the festival, she'd changed into a blue tulip skirt and a cream-colored, sleeveless top.

"How are you doing?" I asked.

"Fine," she said, her tone clipped.

"My truck's under the tree."

"Thanks for coming to get me," she said. "My car was supposed to be repaired by now."

"Was supposed to be?"

She minced across the thick lawn in her three-inch heels. "There was a delay in getting a replacement part. Don't worry, Daddy will drive me to the tea room tomorrow morning."

"How did your booth at the festival go?"

"It was a huge success. People snapped up my new menus. Oh, here. You haven't seen them yet, have you?" Opening her purse, she handed me a long piece of thick paper.

I squinted. "It's too dark to read here. I'll look at it once we get to the Bell and Brew." I opened the driver's door and slid the menu into my messenger bag on the seat, then got in. Adele climbed into the passenger side, adjusting her skirt.

"I'm sorry I missed your booth," I said. "Hopefully I'll be able to get to the festival tomorrow for another tasting of Haunted Vine." It was her family's new label, and I'd already tasted plenty, but bellying up to a bar and swishing wine was fun.

Her hand tensed on the handle. She slammed the door, setting my ears ringing. "That would be nice."

Adele was upset about something, but she'd let me know what was wrong when she was ready.

Silent, we drove into downtown San Benedetto, and I parked in a half-empty lot beside a brick bank. The Harvest Festival might flood us with tourists during the day, but they didn't spend the night. San Benedetto had returned to its sleepy, roll-up-the-sidewalks self.

Adele pointed at the bank. "Did you know the bank was constructed in the 1920s? It was built to last. This town has character because of institutions like that one, and especially because of the vineyards. We're one of the few places in America with grapevines over one hundred years old, zinfandels that weren't destroyed during Prohibition." Her dark eyes flashed in the light from the iron street lamps.

"I know," I said, puzzled. Everyone who grew up in San Benedetto knew its history. It shaped too much of our present. "I like San Benedetto too."

"Of course, change is inevitable," she continued, "but aren't some things worth preserving? Aren't the things that make San Benedetto special worth keeping?"

"Yes, they are." Opening the door, I hopped to the pavement, swinging my messenger bag over one shoulder.

She stepped out of the truck. "I knew you'd agree."

"Is something bothering you, Adele?"

"No!" She stalked across the parking lot, heels clicking on the pavement.

I hurried to follow.

A silver-haired man walking a terrier crossed our path. He tipped his hat and nodded, and I smiled. The dog tugged at its leash, straining to sniff a narrow tree trunk.

We walked through the swinging glass doors of the microbrewery. A wall of Joan Jett hammered us, and I took an involuntary step back.

Harper half rose from a booth near the back and waved, flipping her long, near-black hair over her shoulder. We made our way through the dim restaurant, past the giant copper vat and the bikers and cowboys bellied up to the bar.

Looking like a green-eyed Penelope Cruz, Harper scooted across the red Naugahyde booth. Her black knit top skimmed her curves, and I instinctually knew it was expensive.

I slid in beside her.

She slid her beer mug closer. "With all the Harvest Festival madness, I wasn't sure the two of you were going to make it."

"Did you get to the festival?" I asked.

"Not yet," she said. "I'm planning to head over tomorrow. How did it go?"

"Um…" I glanced at Adele, unfolding a napkin.

"Maddie found Romeo Paganini in the giant vat at the grape stomp," Adele said. "Ladies Aid had to shift the stomp to another part of the festival grounds. And I need a drink."

Harper blinked. "What?"

Adele caught a waiter's eye and he bustled over.

"Yes?" he asked, his gaze lingering on Harper. Men couldn't help themselves around her, and I'd gotten used to playing the Invisible Woman in her presence.

"A pumpkin ale," Adele said.

"Same for me," I said.

"What do you mean you found Romeo Paganini?" Harper asked.

"I didn't say anything," the waiter said.

"Sorry, not you," Harper said. "I'm fine."

He nodded, shot Harper a last doe-eyed look, and bustled away.

"What did you mean about Romeo?" Harper repeated.

"He's dead." I told her about finding him.

Paling, she slumped against the booth. "Romeo Paganini? But … I know him. He's a client of mine. He can't be dead!"

"A client?" I asked. As a successful financial planner, Harper worked with many of the local winery owners, including Adele's father.

Adele stared at the table, frowning.

"Good God." Harper raked a hand through her luxurious hair. "I'll need to call his wife tomorrow."

"You know Mrs. Paganini?"

She nodded. "Are you sure it was Romeo?"

"I'm sure."

"But how did he get inside a grape vat?"

"There was a dump truck nearby," I said. "He may have been killed elsewhere and then dumped in the festival vat."

"Killed?" Harper's eyes widened. "He was murdered?"

"I don't see how else he could have got in that vat," I said.

Adele jerked to life. "We need to figure this out."

I shook my head. "I'm sure the police will—"

Adele laughed, high and tinny. "I'm not. Not after they threw me in jail for a crime I didn't commit. We don't have time to wait for them."

"Why not?" I asked. What was going on? First my mother, now Adele, wanted us to play amateur detective. And when Adele said "we," I was pretty sure she meant me.

"Harper, Maddie needs our help. I bet she doesn't even have a process."

"A process?"

"For investigating," Adele said.

"I do too," I said. "I'll just do what I did last time."

"Which is?" Adele raised a brow.

"Talk to people."

"And?"

"And think about what they tell me."

"You see? Hopeless!" Adele pinioned Harper with a stare. "Since you were Mr. Paganini's financial advisor, you must know if there were any monetary motives for his murder."

"That information is confidential," Harper said gently.

"But he must have had life insurance," I said slowly. "I know you won't work with people who are parents unless they've got insurance, and Leo was Paganini's son." Which meant Leo would have some sort of safety net now that his father was gone.

Where kids were involved, Harper had strong feelings about life insurance. She was an orphan, and her parents hadn't had anything in place when they'd died. She'd been left in the care of her grandmother, and life hadn't been easy.

The aproned waiter speeded back to our table, placing our beer mugs on pumpkin-decorated paper coasters. "Can I get you something to eat?"

"Beer-battered artichoke hearts," I said.

"And wings," Harper added.

He nodded and left.

"Well?" Adele asked.

"I'm sure the police will investigate the financial angle," Harper said.

Adele pointed at Harper. "Ah ha! So there *is* a financial angle!"

Harper colored. "I didn't say that."

"But Romeo's first wife," Adele continued, "Leo's mother, died last year. Is his new wife the insurance beneficiary, or his son? Leo's what? Nineteen? Twenty?"

I leaned across the table and nudged Adele's hand. "Is there a reason for *you* to be accused of the murder? Why are you worried?"

Adele jerked away. "Of course not! I barely knew the man. Besides, you discovered the body, not me. I'm worried about you."

I wanted to believe it. On second thought, no, I didn't, because that would mean the police seriously suspected me.

Harper angled her head, her eyes narrowing. She wasn't buying it either. "Is Laurel Hammer involved in the investigation?" she asked.

"It looks that way." My stomach knotted. The only way Detective Hammer liked me was as a suspect, but I just couldn't believe a personal grudge would color her police work. I'd seen her in action in a crisis, and she'd been all business, impressive.

Harper glanced at Adele. "But Laurel's not the only investigating officer. She can't do anything without evidence, and there can't be anything implicating Maddie. She's innocent."

"What does that have to do with anything?" Adele asked. "I was innocent too."

Time to change the subject. Drawing the new Fox and Fennel menu from my messenger bag, I passed it to Harper. "Have you seen Adele's new menu?" I sipped my beer, bitter with a hint of pumpkin. Autumn was awesome for foodies.

Harper bent her head, reading. A line appeared between her brows and she craned closer to the paper menu.

"They were going like hotcakes at the Fox and Fennel festival booth," Adele said, preening.

Harper's lips quivered. "I can see why. These are, uh, different."

"Do you like them?" Adele asked. "I wanted to evoke the romance and mystery of tea, using lush descriptive phrases."

"Lush? These are pornographic," Harper said. "No wonder people were snatching them up."

Adele sucked in her cheeks. "What are you talking about?"

"Rooiboos Ecstasy," Harper read. "Nirvana in a cup. Sip this intense, cinnamon-infused red tea. Let it roll across your tongue and pierce the clouds that veil your core."

I coughed into my beer, splattering foam across the polished, wooden table.

"I don't see what's wrong with that," Adele said.

"Apple Ginseng," Harper quoted. "This forbidden fruit, a symbol for knowledge, temptation, and immortality, is mixed with a blend of exotic white ginseng and a hint of oolong for a tart, enticing, and nectarous mouthful." She fanned herself with the menu. "Is 'nectarous' an actual word?"

"Yes, it is," Adele snapped. "How old are you?"

"We need to find you a new boyfriend," Harper said. "Stat."

"I don't see what my current romantic drought has to do with my new tea menu."

Picking up the menu, I skimmed down the page. *Cacao Mint, an ambrosial eruption of sumptuous chocolate and exhilarating mint. The natural serotonin-boosting power of cacao will heat your spirits.* If sex really did sell, then Adele was onto a gold mine. "And here I've been wasting my time on sweet nothings. I can just read your menu to Mason to get him in the mood."

"You two are infantile." Adele snatched the menu from my hands. "Laugh all you want, but my business coach assured me this language would sell."

"Your business coach?" I asked.

Her cheeks pinked. "The business owner who thinks she knows everything is the business owner who goes bankrupt. Yes, I have a coach." Adele bent her head and studied the menu. Dropping it to the table, she cradled her head in her hands and groaned. "Oh, God. You're right. What have I done?"

"Authored the hottest tea menu in California," Harper said.

"How could I have missed this?" Adele asked. "It's, it's—"

"Spicy? Succulent? Stirring?" I waggled my brows and Adele burst into laughter.

"This is a disaster! Why am I laughing?"

"Because it's funny," Harper said, "and it's not a disaster. You did say the menus were popular."

Adele groaned. "I spent so much on these. Do you have any idea how much it will cost to print new menus?"

"Why not keep them and see how it goes?" I asked.

"My parents will read these!"

"So, dish," Harper said, angling herself toward me. "How are things going with the dreamy Mason Hjelm?"

I sighed, warming. "Great. He's thoughtful, he's funny, and he listens." I'd gotten lucky with Mason, and part of me wished I'd blown off girls' night for a whirl of passion in his apartment. But girls' night was sacred. Mason and I spent a lot of time together—which I loved—but I needed to tend to my friendships. They mattered.

Harper grinned. "So have you gone for a ride on his motorcycle yet?"

I opened my mouth to reply, then closed it, eyes narrowing. She knew darn well motorcycles scared me. "That is never going to happen."

"Take a chance," Harper said. "You might like it."

But I worried I was already taking too many.

SIX

I stepped out of my pickup and onto the hard-packed dirt of the festival parking lot. Turning, I grabbed a cardboard box off the passenger's seat and shut the door with my hip. The box pressed into my stomach, wrinkling my *Paranormal Museum* T-shirt.

The morning sun beat down on the white tents behind the high metal fence. I stared, remembering. Romeo's face, stained with grape juice. His unseeing eyes. The cold neck. And in spite of the warm morning sun, goose bumps shivered my flesh. It was hard to imagine the corpse had once been Leo's father.

Eyes swollen, Leo had arrived at the Paranormal Museum early in the morning, insisting he wanted to work. I wasn't sure it was a great idea, but it was Leo's choice.

I checked my watch. An hour to go until festival opening. A male security guard stood at the festival gates, his black *Security* T-shirt stretched across his broad chest, the sun glinting off his bald head. Expressionless, he watched me approach.

I showed him my pass.

He nodded, and I scuttled inside.

I wandered the empty paths, past vacant tents and festival games. My thoughts returned to the murdered vintner. Why would my mother insist I stick my nose into a police investigation? And what *had* Cora Gale meant when she'd kind-of-sort-of threatened the grape stomp?

Pausing in front of the giant grape vat, I shifted the box in my arms. Yellow police tape wrapped it like a Christmas bow.

Why had Romeo told the police I'd stolen the grape press when his wife's signature was on the sales receipt? Finding the answers to these questions wouldn't really be interfering in a murder investigation. After all, I'd been accused of theft—I had every right to learn why. And the police could hardly complain if I grilled my mother. She'd uncharacteristically failed to return any of my calls last night. Besides, Paganini's son worked for me. It would be unnatural for us not to discuss his father's death.

I moved on, making my way to the Wine and Visitors Bureau tent. It was empty, rows of wine glasses lined up on white tablecloths, plastic grapes twining the picket fencing.

My haunted grape press stood in the center of the tent. I trailed my hand over its round metal wheel. The wooden barrel was tall and narrow, which enabled it to fit easily in my three-room museum. It was an ideal exhibit. So ideal, I hadn't grilled Herb as much as I should have on the details of the sale—or the curse. Or maybe I hadn't pushed because the story of the long-ago murder-suicide was familiar and depressing.

Initially, Herb hadn't mentioned the curse. He'd just said the "angry ghost" of the killer had attached to the grape press. So which was it? Haunted by an angry ghost or, as Mrs. Paganini had apparently said, cursed? I wasn't sure if I believed in either one, but I needed to get the story straight for when the press was displayed in the museum.

Detective Laurel Hammer strode into the tent, her blue pinstripe suit creased to a knife's blade. Two uniformed policemen flanked her. An honor guard. She jerked her chin toward the grape press. "That's the one."

The policemen lifted it between them.

"What? Wait! What's going on?" I asked.

"It's evidence," she said, wrenching free the sign that explained the press's haunted history. She slapped it against my chest and I caught it with one hand.

"How is the grape press evidence?" I asked. "It wasn't anywhere near the scene of the crime."

She closed the distance between us, forcing me to step back. "Because the person who found the murder victim in a vat of grapes is the same person the victim accused of stealing this very grape press. Oddly enough, that makes it evidence."

"But—"

"I'll write you a receipt."

I drew a slow breath. Shouting wasn't going to win me any points, and I needed that grape press. "Can't you take it later today? It's our feature attraction."

"No. Also oddly enough, murder investigations do not await the pleasure of paranormal museum owners." Turning on her booted heel, Laurel followed the cops out of the tent.

Fuming, I stomped to the Paranormal Museum table. We were low on brochures and coupons, but whoever had watched my table yesterday had cleaned up. The remaining materials lay fanned out on the smooth black tablecloth. Movements jerky, I added more brochures and coupons from my box, then shoved the box beneath the table with my foot.

Laurel couldn't really believe I'd murder someone over a grape press, could she? Cracking my knuckles, I paced the tent. My brain ran in circles, an out-of-control hamster wheel. Stupid Laurel. Stupid grape press. I needed a way to divert myself until the festival opened, a way that did not involve fantasies about strangling police detectives.

Should I check out the new site of the grape stomp? I frowned, not liking the idea. Someone from Ladies Aid would just rope me into helping with the latest disaster.

Yesterday, Penny mentioned that Paganini had a tasting tent. I puzzled over the map of the festival grounds and located it, not far from the food area. Which was where the new grape stomp had been set up.

I jammed the map in the back pocket of my jeans. Oh well. I might as well kill two birds with one stone—check out Paganini's tent and do my daughterly duty. I had low hopes of cracking the case in the wine tent, but my mom was expecting something from me. It was time to put my investigative "process" into action.

I walked down the wide, straw-covered paths. Other sweating souls strode past, carrying boxes, plastic wine grapes, cases of wine. A bead of sweat trickled down my spine. It was just past ten o'clock and already steamy. The day would be hot. I hoped those tents had ventilation, since I'd be stuck inside one.

At the Trivia Vineyards tent, I stopped and gaped. A trompe l'oeil of an Italian-looking scene covered the entrance. Painted Italian cypresses framed rows of fallen Roman columns and grapevines. Two real cypresses in clay pots stood beside the entry, adding to the illusion.

I walked inside. Faux-Roman columns lined the tent behind the tasting tables. Miniature cypresses clustered in the corners. High, round tables covered in white cloths dotted the space.

A woman half-leaned, half-sat against a rough-edged marble slab balanced atop sawhorses and lined with empty wineglasses. The light filtering through the canvas gleamed off her mid-length blond hair, mussed as if she'd just tumbled out of bed. Her eyes were red-rimmed. Her loose black tunic skimmed over her trim figure and she wore matching, wide-legged slacks. A gold, tasseled bolero necklace hung around her fair neck. An open bottle sat on the table beside her. She gripped a glass filled with burgundy-colored liquid.

Glancing at me, she took another gulp of wine. "You need something?"

"I'm Maddie Kosloski," I said. "From the Paranormal Museum. I was just—"

"That damn grape press. Of course. I've told the police I sold it to that Herb person, the collector. As far as I'm concerned, it's all yours."

"Then you're Mrs. Paganini?"

She snorted. "My mother-in-law was Mrs. Paganini. I'm Jocelyn."

"Nice to meet you." I extended my hand and she took it, her grip cool and firm. What the hell was she doing here now, the day after her husband was killed? Leo had said his stepmom was psycho, and I'd assumed it was teenage hyperbole. But was she … off? Or was she just struggling through the best she could? "I'm sorry it's under such terrible circumstances. My condolences for your loss."

"Thanks." She swallowed, looked away. "Wine?"

It was a little early, but I wanted to talk to her and my blood was still pounding over the confiscated grape press. "Sure."

She poured, splashing droplets of red on the white tablecloth. "It's our Trivia cab. A full-bodied, fruity wine with hints of cocoa and cinnamon." She hiccupped.

"Why the name 'Trivia'?" I asked.

She sighed. "Everybody asks that. It was Romeo's idea, to name the winery after the Roman goddess Trivia." Her voice broke.

I averted my gaze, done playing detective. This wasn't a game. A man had been murdered, and lives would change. "I'm sorry. I should go."

"No, please don't." She touched my hand. "When I'm alone, I think. Today, I'd rather not."

I sipped the wine, unsure how to respond. The flavors were rich, complex—plum and cocoa and yes, a hint of cinnamon. Trivia Vineyards produced good wine. Seriously good.

"Thanks for clearing up the grape press confusion with the police," I said. "Unfortunately, they confiscated it this morning anyway."

Her delicate brows puckered. "What? Why?"

"I'm not sure. I guess they're looking at anything connected to your husband."

"That press. It's brought nothing but bad luck."

"Oh?"

She didn't respond, turning the goblet in her hand.

"I don't suppose you know any more about the history of the press?" I asked. "Herb told me it was associated with a murder-suicide." I grit my teeth, heat blooming across my cheeks. *Idiot*. Now wasn't the time for a casual chat about an old murder. Not with the widow of yesterday's victim.

"I don't know anything about the ghost story aside from that," she said. "But the press did come from the original winery. Constantino Vineyards? It was part of the estate when we bought it." She shook her head.

"It sounds like your vineyard has an interesting history."

She smiled faintly. "We have grapevines over a century old. That's the only history I care about. I never understood Romeo's fascination with the macabre, with death and curses."

"A friend of mine mentioned the Death Bistro he was involved in."

She wiped the corner of one eye with her knuckle. "I guess I never understood that either. I always thought it was healthy if couples had different interests. I'm not so sure anymore."

"If this wine is anything to go by, you both knew your viticulture. You don't make wine like this without some passion behind it."

"The vineyard is business. And business may be the one interest a couple shouldn't share." Her chin trembled.

"Are you sure you want to be here today?" I asked in a low voice.

She stared into her wine glass. "What you really mean is, why am I in the family wine tent, drinking before lunch?"

"People deal with loss in different ways." I set my glass on an empty table. "I'm not judging."

"Leo will." She banged her glass on the bar. There was a crack. The half-full goblet tilted and crashed to the marble, its stem broken. Jocelyn leapt backward, swearing.

Red wine spread across the marble. I grabbed a cloth napkin and blotted at the mess.

"Cheap glasses." She laughed, shaky. "Romeo wanted higher quality goblets, but I said …" She looked away, blinking rapidly.

I grabbed another napkin and scooped up the broken glass.

The tent flap rustled behind me and I turned. Two familiar-looking men walked inside. After a moment, I pulled up the name of one of them: Chuck Wollmer, who I'd met the day before in the Visitors Bureau tent. With his hipster, beach-blond good looks, he was a study in contrasts to his companion—who proved to be none other than the cadaverous man I'd seen at the Nakamoto house last night, when Adele had been so upset. They both wore jeans and white button-down shirts with the creases that only a professional laundry service can buy. Chuck had accessorized with a blue and tan striped tie that matched his camel-colored vest.

Squinting at me, Chuck stroked his beard.

Tall, dark, and creepy's gaze traveled, lingering, from my tennis shoes to the top of my head.

I crossed my arms over my chest.

"Hi, Chuck," Jocelyn said. "This is Maddie, from the Paranormal Museum."

"Of course," Chuck said. "We met yesterday. Lovely old grape press you've got." He grasped both the widow's hands between his. "Jocelyn. How *are* you?"

Mr. Mortuary focused on the widow. I'd been dismissed. But I continued to stare at him. I'd gone from never laying eyes on him in my life to seeing him twice in twenty-four hours. Weird. No, suspicious.

Jocelyn pulled free of Chuck's grasp. "Fine."

He shook his head. "I can't imagine what you're going through. Let me help you. If there's anything I can do to relieve your burden, I'm here."

"I may take you up on that," she said. "There's so much to do. I'm meeting with our financial advisor today."

He *tsked*. "You can't trust financial advisors. All they want is your money in a fund so they can earn their commission."

I stiffened. Harper was not like that. She cared about her clients and understood the needs of the local vintners.

Jocelyn shrugged. "Maybe. I'll hear what she has to say."

I stood there, awkward, not part of the conversation but not wanting to leave. Jocelyn was hurting, and halfway to drunk. But I wasn't sure if I should protect her or protect Leo from her.

Chuck gave me a significant look. "I got this."

Reaching into my messenger bag, I drew out my card and laid it beside the glass. "I'm working in the Wine and Visitors Bureau tent today," I told Jocelyn. "If there's anything you need, or if you just want to talk, that's where you can find me."

"People always say, 'if there's anything you need,' but they don't mean it."

"They mean it," I said. "They just don't know how to help. We used to bring each other frozen casseroles and potato salads, comfort food, but that's become passé."

She smiled, wan. "Thanks. I'll stop by your tent later, okay?"

I handed Dr. Death a card, too, hoping he'd give me one in return.

He didn't.

"I'm Maddie Kosloski."

"So your card says."

I could no longer ignore the brush-off. I was being well and truly dissed. Unable to figure out a way to gracefully stay, I nodded and left. My investigatory process had left me with more questions than answers.

I had twenty minutes until the festival opening, leaving me plenty of time to stop at the wine stomp.

Darn it.

I followed the scent of funnel cakes and pulled pork to a wide cluster of picnic tables surrounded by tents and food trucks. Mouth watering, I strode past.

A gang of blue-shirted women scuttled around halved wine barrels on low risers. The Ladies Aid president, Mrs. Bigelow, barked orders, looking more than ever like our ex-Attorney General.

Dieter, in stained painter's overalls and a tank top, hammered a riser leg into place. His bronzed muscles gleamed with sweat. He flipped the riser over and set it on the ground. Jumping on top, he shifted his lean hips as if riding a surfboard. "I think we got it, Mrs. K," he called.

My mother strode forward, her fresh jeans pressed, the collar of her white blouse standing at attention. "Thank you, Dieter. It might have made it through the day again, but I didn't like the way it was wobbling."

He puffed out his chest. "You were right to ask me to double check. It could have been dangerous."

I wended through the rows of stomping barrels. "Hi, Mom, Dieter. How's it going?"

"Pretty well," my mother said, "in spite of the last moment change of venue. Dieter came through like a champion yesterday, as did all the volunteers from Ladies Aid."

A gray-haired lady in the ubiquitous powder-blue T-shirt tottered forward and nudged my arm. "I think this is an even better location than the last one."

A woman cleared her throat behind us.

We turned.

Eliza Bigelow stood there, her eyes narrowed, her red-lipsticked mouth pinched.

The elderly woman gave a little jump. "Oh! I forgot I have to ..." She hurried away.

"Miss Kosloski," Mrs. Bigelow said, "am I to understand that we'll be working together?"

"Um ..." My mind tumbled. Working together? She didn't expect me to be her co-detective did she?

My mother nudged me. "Halloween," she muttered.

"Oh! Yes," I said. "The haunted house. Looking forward to it."

"Excellent. A delegation will stop by the tea shop tonight to coordinate."

"Tonight?" I yelped. I'd be working at the festival all day and had planned a nice quiet night with Mason and a pizza.

"Miss Nakamoto has agreed to keep the tea shop open late this evening, under the circumstances," Mrs. Bigelow said.

"She has?" What did Adele have to do with it?

"We'll see you at six." She nodded and strode off, pointing at two Ladies Aid volunteers. "You there! Do you call that a straight line? Those barrels look like they've been arranged by drunks!"

"She's very, er, decisive," I said.

My mother sighed. "She's a determined and effective manager. But enough about my problems. How are you?"

"The police confiscated my haunted grape press."

"But that's your key exhibit!"

"I know. Now all that's left is the sign. It's a haunted, invisible grape press." I straightened. Oh, hey. Idea! An invisible grape press!

"They can't believe either you or that grape press had anything to do with Romeo's death."

"Like you said, Laurel's getting back at me because of her hair."

"I hope that's all it is." My mom's chin dipped. "Have you made any progress on the investigation?"

"Not really. All I know is that Romeo had life insurance, and his widow is getting drunk in the Trivia Winery tent."

"And you left the poor woman alone? Madelyn!"

"Of course not. I left her with her friend Chuck."

"I'd better go talk to her. I remember how... well." She blinked, and I looked away, thinking of my late father.

I cleared my throat. "She says she told the police that she sold the press to Herb. And she also mentioned that Romeo was obsessed with death, which I could have figured out from that Death Bistro business."

"Oh yes, I remember Adele mentioning it."

"Adele felt she'd been tricked into hosting the event and the Death Bistro could damage her brand. Not that that's a motive for murder."

"Of course not. No one can possibly think Adele was involved."

"Mom, why did you ask me to investigate?"

Two gray-haired women in powder-blue tees walked past, carrying a crate of grapes. Dieter leapt forward and lifted it from their arms.

"Oh, thank you, young man," one said, tittering.

"This isn't a good place to talk," my mom hissed. "Later."

"But—"

"Later." She strode after Dieter.

"Wait!" I trotted after her. "I need Dieter at the Wine and Visitors Bureau tent."

He dumped the crate of grapes into a stomping barrel.

"Give me ten minutes," she said, "and I'll send him over."

"Thanks." I checked my watch and hurried to my tent. I had an invisible grape press to create.

SEVEN

"WILL YOU TAKE OUR picture?" Inside the stuffy tent, a giggling teenage girl handed me her camera. She mugged with two of her pig-tailed friends by the invisible grape press. Ahem, the *haunted* invisible grape press.

"Sure!" I forced a smile, not because I wasn't happy to snap a picture but because my smile muscles had been in overdrive all day. It might take a lot fewer muscles to smile than frown, but my cheeks were sore.

Dieter had come through, hastily painting an *Invisible Grape Press* sign and hanging it over the tent entrance. The Bureau had allowed us to scavenge two of their picket fence sections, and Dieter had built a small, square, fenced-off area. I'd hung my old haunted grape press tag from a picket and scrawled along the top, *It's Invisible!* It was attracting a surprising amount of visitors.

After shooting a few pictures, I handed the girls their camera. They ran from the tent, narrowly avoiding a collision with an elderly couple. The couple headed for the wine tasting at the rear of the tent.

Penny thrust a wine glass into my hand. Her fluffy gray hair had gone wild from the heat, her reading glasses barely keeping its strands in place. "Here. You need it." Grape-cluster earrings dangled from her ears and she wore a shimmery purple blouse and jeans.

I took a swallow. Oh, yum, ancient vine zinfandel. Many of our vineyards had vines over one hundred years old, and these created more complex flavors. "My favorite. Thanks."

"You done good, kid," Penny said. "The invisible grape press was a stroke of genius."

"Stroke of desperation."

"But you're still doing the haunted house."

"Of course!"

Mason ambled into the tent, caught my eye, and broke into a wide smile.

My pulse accelerated.

Hugging me around the waist, he picked me up and twirled me. I shrieked. "My wine!"

He set me down and pressed a chaste kiss on the cheek, his face rough against mine. The light touch inflamed me even more. I inhaled his scent: musk and motorcycle oil.

Face upturned, I pulled away, clutching the wine goblet in both hands. Miraculously, it hadn't spilled. "What are you doing here?" I asked, breathless.

"I closed early. Most folks are at the festival anyway, and I wanted to see you. How are things going?"

"Good. The police confiscated my grape press, but Dieter helped me make an invisible haunted grape press display. I think it's more popular than the original."

His blue eyes sparkled. "Very P. T. Barnum."

"I do have a few actual haunted exhibits on my table, so people won't think the museum is all smoke and mirrors." I motioned toward my table with the burnt dolls and eerie photos.

"Have you had a chance to enjoy the festival? It closes in an hour." One blond brow arched in invitation.

"Not yet, but I think I can sneak out." After all, the Visitors Bureau watched my table the first day in exchange for me taking over their display at the haunted house. I figured they still owed me. To Penny's credit, she did too.

"I'll just shift your coupons and brochures to the tasting table," she said. "Don't worry, we'll take care of everything. Have fun."

As giddy as the schoolgirls, I strolled out of the tent with Mason.

He draped his muscular arm over my shoulder. "So what do you think? Carnival games?"

I nodded, and my stomach rumbled. "And I'm dying for a funnel cake." All I needed was one funnel cake and I'd call the festival a success.

We wove through happy festival-goers to the food area, where Mason bought me a funnel cake—heaven!—and we stopped to watch the final grape stomp. Laughing stompers bent double, gripping the sides of their barrels and furiously stamping up and down. Their partners swept grape skins and gush from the spigot holes as juice drained into the glass measuring vials.

Someone blew a whistle and they stopped, grinning and sweating. My mother, wearing a judge's ribbon, walked up the aisle with a clipboard, scrutinizing the level of the grape juice in the vials.

I bit into the funnel cake. I think I'd read somewhere that it was about a million calories, but this was the Harvest Festival. I'd worry tomorrow about those extra ten pounds I'd been trying to lose. Besides, I'd been on my feet all day. That must have burned a ton of calories.

My mother stepped up to a microphone. "And the winners are Lucy Riesling and Ethel Merlot!"

Bare legs and hands stained with grape juice, two barefoot women in bandannas and 1950s-style skirts scrambled to the microphone. Cheering, they collected their blue ribbons from my mother.

We applauded.

"Your mom is good at this," Mason said.

"She's good at pretty much everything. It's a lot to live up to." But I was proud of her. She'd mourned my father's death, but she hadn't stopped living.

"Come on," he said. "I want to get to the shooting gallery."

"Really?" I said. "It's not boring for you compared to a real range?" Mason was ex-military and went to ranges for target practice at least twice a month.

"I can't win my girl a prize at a real range." He grasped my hand and tugged me forward.

Laughing, I let him pull me, leaving a trail of powdered sugar in my wake. We stopped before a shooting booth shaded by a red-and-white-striped awning. Rows of plastic animals glided on tracks in front of a yellow backdrop. Mason paid the barker and ruthlessly slaughtered an entire plastic African savanna.

He pointed.

The barker handed him a bear. "Vet?"

Mason grunted an assent.

"Afghanistan or Iraq?" the barker asked.

"Both."

"Helmand," the barker said. "Semper fi."

They nodded to each other, and I wondered what memories each were recalling. Mason didn't talk much about his time in the military. I listened hard when he did.

"For you." Mason held out the bear.

I nodded toward a wailing girl in a red dress, a dropped ice cream cone melting on the straw-covered ground beneath her feet. Her pink-faced mother rubbed her back and spoke in a low voice. "Thanks," I said, "but I think her need is greater."

Breaking into a smile, he nodded and walked to the mother. She looked up, surprised, and he handed her the bear. She gave it to her daughter and the tears evaporated.

"Nicely done," I said, taking his hand.

"It was your idea." He squeezed me close. "We make a good team."

We ambled through the carnival area.

"Mad," he said, "there's something I wanted to talk to you about."

"Oh?"

He stopped short, staring ahead, his brow furrowed.

Detective Slate ambled toward us. He'd slung his suit jacket over one shoulder, the top button of his shirt undone, blue tie loose. His dark skin gleamed like mahogany in the sun.

Catching sight of us, he slowed. His gaze dropped to our linked hands.

A tingling swept the back of my neck. "Hello, Detective."

He nodded. "Miss Kosloski."

"How are things going with the investigation?" I asked.

"You know I can't talk about that."

"You took Maddie's grape press display," Mason said. "Any idea when she's getting it back?"

"Hopefully soon," he said. "Mrs. Paganini has assured us it's not stolen property."

Mason's broad shoulders tightened. "Then why can't she have it now?"

"Because it may have some bearing on the investigation into Mr. Paganini's death. Enjoy your day." He strolled away.

Jaw clenched, Mason stared after him.

"Thanks for trying," I said.

"I wasn't much help."

"Honestly, the cops did me a favor. The invisible grape press got a lot more attention than the haunted grape press ever would have. So, what did you want to talk to me about?"

Color rose in his cheeks. "I got a call from an old girlfriend the other day."

"How old?"

He grinned. "Old enough. She's in town and wanted to meet up. I haven't seen her in years—not since I deployed."

"So will you see her?"

"It feels a little awkward."

I squeezed his hand and my insides quivered. "Because of me? Don't worry about it. I trust you." And I did trust him. Mason was solid in every way. Betrayal wasn't in his DNA.

He rubbed his jaw.

"Do you *want* to see her again?" I asked.

"I do, but not because there's anything left between us. The thing is, I was kind of wild before I joined up—selfish, arrogant. I didn't treat her well, and I owe her an apology."

"Ah." I visualized a younger Mason, with his bad-boy looks and minus the battle scars. I could imagine what a terror he might have once been, though it was a far cry from the man he'd become.

"Yeah. I'm surprised she wants to see me at all."

"Look," I said, "if you feel you need to apologize, then do what you need to do. I trust you. But thanks for letting me know."

"Are you sure?"

"I'm sure."

One corner of his mouth tilted upward. "Thanks."

"For not throwing a jealous tantrum? You're setting the bar too low."

"Trust me, Mad, I set the bar pretty high."

———

Inside the tent, I stuffed the remains of my festival exhibit into my messenger bag. The festival-goers were gone and the big take-down had begun, the sound of drills and metal-on-metal ringing through the grounds. Visitors Bureau volunteers folded up the tables, stuffing plastic grapes into cardboard boxes.

Mason carried sections of picket fence from my invisible grape press display to my pickup. At the tailgate, he gave me a bone-melting kiss goodbye and drove off on his Harley.

I reached in my bag for my keys. They weren't in their pocket. Heart seizing, I scrabbled in my bag, finally dumping the contents on the hood of my truck.

No keys.

I trotted back to the Visitors Bureau tent.

Penny grinned, dangling a set of keys from her fingers. "Looking for these?"

I slumped. "Thank God. If I'd dropped them somewhere in the fairgrounds..."

"One of us would have given you a ride." She handed them to me and clapped me on the shoulder. "Now go have fun with that handsome boyfriend!"

I hurried to the parking lot. My handsome boyfriend and I weren't seeing each other tonight after all—not with Ladies Aid on the march. The sky had darkened to a misty twilight. In the parking lot, I paused and squinted, searching for my truck key.

Something crunched, faint.

"Maddie, look out!"

Dieter grabbed my arm and yanked me sideways. A Buick hit the side of my thigh, rolled past, and crashed into the gate. The metal fence rippled, quivering, but stood.

"What?" I clutched my chest to keep my heart from bursting free. "Who? Is someone inside?"

"Wait here." He trotted to the Buick and peered through the open window. "Empty. Someone didn't set their parking brake." He frowned. "Shouldn't have needed to here. The ground is pretty flat."

"Yeah." I rubbed my thigh, breathing hard. It could have been an accident, but was it?

"Hey, did it hit you? Are you sure you're okay?"

"It just brushed me. I'm fine." The keys dug into my palms.

"I can drive you into town. Should I call Adele?"

"Adele." I pursed my lips. Dieter was so obvious. I didn't know why he didn't just ask my friend out.

"Or your mom. Or Adele."

"You're hopeless. But really, I'm okay. What are we going to do about that car?"

"I'll tell security. Don't worry about it."

"Thanks." Getting into my truck, I drove, alone, to the Paranormal Museum. The twilight softened the angles of Main Street's brick and adobe buildings. My safety-conscious mom had told me that the most common accident at fairs was vehicular. Someone had just forgotten to set their brake. Yeah.

My scalp prickled. Or not. But why would someone aim a Buick at me? No one knew my mom had ordered me to investigate Romeo's murder, except for Mrs. Bigelow, but we hadn't had a chance to discuss my so-called investigation yet. And so far, it had been pretty weak. But if someone *had* attempted murder by Buick... My jaw clenched. All bets were off.

Pulling into a spot in front of the museum, I grabbed my stuff and trudged inside.

Leo looked up from his seat behind the counter, his black hair falling into his eyes. He laid down his sci-fi novel beside GD, who was curled on the counter around a half-eaten stuffed mouse.

No customers wandered the room, admiring the haunted photos and glass display cases. The rocking chair in the corner swayed, empty.

I stopped midstride. "Tell me it hasn't been this slow all day." I leaned the fencing against the counter. "And where did the toy mouse come from?"

"I picked it up for GD this morning. He got bored with it after he chewed its head off. And the museum cleared out right before you walked in. We sold a ton of souvenirs, as well as a bunch of the Halloween stuff from the gallery."

"GD thanks you, and define 'ton.'"

"GD thanks no one. He's a cat." Leo reached beneath the counter and slid a binder across it to me.

I ran my finger down the column of tic marks in the gallery ledger and whistled. "October has gotten off to a good start." But October was only one month. We needed to do better. I'd been toying with the idea of selling things through the website. But I'd need a web designer for that sort of update, and I didn't have the money.

"What's with the picket fence?" he asked.

"Invisible haunted grape press."

A furrow appeared between his dark brows.

"Invisible and incorporeal grape press. Long story. I'll close up." I nodded to the tip jar. "It's all yours."

He reached for the cash. GD raised his head and growled, ears flat against his head.

"Don't worry." I scooped the cat off the counter and set him onto the floor before he could react. "You'll still get fed."

Taking a swipe at my shoelaces, GD streaked into the Fortune Telling Room.

Leo stuffed the bills into the pocket of his black jeans. "GD saw a bunch of ghosts today. I'll buy him some catnip as a reward."

Now there was an idea, mellowing the cat with psychotropics. "Good idea. Thanks."

Flipping the sign in the window to *Closed*, I locked the door behind Leo. Cool silence descended, and tension I hadn't realized I'd been carrying released. Alone at last.

I phoned my mom. The call went to voicemail. It was my third attempt to find out exactly why my mother wanted me to investigate Romeo's death.

Pensive, I checked out the gallery space. I'd recently had to replace its floor, so the checkerboard linoleum in here gleamed compared to the rest of the museum. The entire gallery sparkled beneath the Edison-style light bulbs hanging from the ceiling.

Square, ebony-painted bookshelves for this month's exhibit—Americana-style Halloween Art—lined the two smaller walls. Brightly painted Ouija boards decorated the long wall, facing the windows. For those who couldn't afford the original paintings, prints sat on low black pedestals. Other black pedestals of varying heights displayed the less-breakable works—carved wooden cats, ghosts, and witches.

I lusted after one of the original paintings: a Halloween scene, haunts peeking from the windows of a spooky gray Victorian in a pumpkin patch. But I also wanted one of the Ouija boards, purple and red with a staring eye in the center and dancing devils in the corners. I could afford neither, so I'd have to enjoy them while they were in my gallery.

Bouncing on my heels, I noted the empty spaces on the shelves and made notes. I'd need to collect new merchandise from my storage facility, otherwise known as Adele's office.

That duty done, I returned to the main room and opened the secret door to the tea shop. We both closed at five today, and Adele might need a lift home.

"—conflate the Fox and Fennel with your Bistro of Death! That wasn't part of the agreement." Adele braced her hands on the pale granite counter and leaned forward. An army of metal tea canisters gleamed in rows behind her.

I edged inside the tea room. The overhead lights gave the cream-colored floor tiles a warm evening glow, and dark bamboo, which was inlaid horizontally into the walls, softened the polished modern effect.

Adele wore a pink, Jackie Kennedy-style suit and a mulish look, her black hair in a tight bun. I knew there'd be a discreet hairnet over it—Adele was a stickler for rules when working in her tea shop.

A tall strawberry-blonde glared back at my friend. The woman wore button-up boots, jeans, and a gray blouse with mutton-chop sleeves and a high lace collar. Her hair was piled high on her head, loose, wanton, a modern-day Gibson Girl.

"What's the big deal?" The blonde sat on one of the metal barstools. "You share space with a paranormal museum."

"I do not share space with it. The Paranormal Museum just happens to be next door."

"There's a secret passage between them!" She motioned to me closing the bookcase.

"Only so the Paranormal Museum clients can access my bathroom."

"Look, it's called the Death Bistro, and it's always been called the Death Bistro. I can't exactly change the flyers." The woman brandished a sheet of paper decorated with a skull and crossbones.

"Why do you have to put them up at all?" Adele wailed. "Can't you find another place for your death thing?"

The blonde flushed, her voice rising. "No, I can't! The word has already gone out. The Death Bistro matters to people, especially now, when…" Her breath hitched, her face contorting.

Clearing my throat, I sidled to the counter. "Hi, Adele. I came to see if you needed a ride home."

Adele shot me a desperate look. "Maddie, I'm so glad you're here. This is Elthia Jaros from the Death Bistro."

Elthia drew a long, shuddering breath. She tossed her head. "We don't have enough time to move the Bistro, and we had a verbal agreement."

"You and Romeo didn't tell me about—"

"Romeo?" Elthia's face crumpled, her full lips trembling.

"Uh, Adele," I said, soothing. "Why don't you get us some tea? I know I could use some."

"Right." Adele scooted into the kitchen.

"You and Romeo were friends?" I asked the woman.

"Yes. For years. I just can't believe …" Elthia drew her lips into a taut, quivering line.

"I'm so sorry for your loss." I drew back a cushioned chair at one of the tables. To my relief, she followed my lead and came to sit across from me.

She sniffed. "He was a good man."

"You two were both members of the Death Bistro?" I asked.

She nodded. "Founding members. Contrary to what your friend thinks, the Bistro's not morbid. It's more of a momento mori. By remembering death, we remind ourselves how important it is to live. But we also help people deal with grieving. It can be cathartic, uplifting."

"And now with Romeo gone, the next Bistro is even more important," I said.

Tea cups clattered in the kitchen.

"Exactly."

"I didn't know Romeo," I said. "What was he like?" Would my mom expect me to report this investigatory conversation to her? Did I have to file reports?

"Warm, funny, intelligent." Elthia bit her lip, shaking her head. "I can't believe someone killed him. It's just … insulting!"

I thought I understood what she meant. Murder was the ultimate insult, a denial of the victim's right to live.

"I suppose," I said, "that when you have money you're bound to make enemies, no matter how good a person you are."

"His only real enemies were his family. Leo." She shuddered. "That boy is dark."

"Dark?"

"I suppose everyone thinks he's just a misunderstood teen. But he actually threatened his father once."

"Threatened?" I asked, disbelieving.

She shook her head.

"Leo works for me," I said mildly, "and he seems like a pretty normal teen. I have a hard time believing he could have been involved in his father's death."

"Who else could be responsible?" Her fingernails bit into her palms. "It's usually the family, isn't it?"

It was usually the spouse, but Jocelyn's grief this morning had seemed genuine. "Romeo owned a winery," I said. "Maybe a disgruntled employee?"

"Absolutely not." Elthia crossed her arms over her chest. "He was respected by the workers."

"What about other businesses?"

"Competitors? He wasn't involved in any dirty deals, if that's what you mean."

I wasn't sure what I meant, or what sorts of "dirty deals" a winery could be involved in. Watering down the wine?

"Romeo did well for himself," Elthia continued, "but I wouldn't call him rich. You know the old joke—how do you make a million dollars with a winery?"

I nodded. Start with two million dollars.

"Romeo worked hard," she said. "He bought the old Constantino vineyard when its vines were half dead. He rebuilt it from the ground up and put everything he had into it. He wasn't some rich dilettante."

That I could believe. The Trivia wine I'd sampled had been top notch. But San Benedetto was a town of farmers who'd become vintners. Too far inland to attract the upper crust, we nevertheless produced superlative reds. A few so-called dilettantes had moved in, mainly retirees looking for the glamour of owning a winery. They were amateurs but nice folks, willing to get their hands dirty and willing to learn. But Romeo's wine had not been produced by an amateur.

"I suppose it helped having a wife who's a professor of viticulture," I said.

"She only teaches at a *community* college." Elthia's lips curled.

I sat back, the chair creaking beneath me. And what was wrong with a community college?

Adele bustled into the tea room carrying a bamboo tray. "I thought an herbal blend would be appropriate. A mix of chamomile, lemon grass, lemon myrtle, and spearmint." She laid the sleek modern teapot on the table and set out three curving bone-colored cups on matching saucers. Drawing a chair, she sat beside us and folded her hands on the tablecloth. "Now about your Bistro of Death—"

"Death Bistro," Elthia said, her eyes glinting.

I grabbed the teapot and poured a cup for Elthia, then for myself.

"Whatever. Wouldn't you rather have it in the Paranormal Museum?"

My hand dipped, tea dribbling onto the white tablecloth. "What?"

"It's not a change of location," Adele said. "The museum is right next door, and people can enter through the Fox and Fennel."

"Um, I'm not set up to serve tea," I said.

"Of course not," Adele said. "I'll provide the tea. We can set a table up in your main room."

"But … I have a cat!" I could not host a tea and get ready for the haunted house and deal with the biggest sales month in the supernatural world. Ugh. And I was supposed to meet with Ladies Aid about the haunted house in less than an hour.

"You'll love GD Cat," Adele said to Elthia. "Did you know he sees dead people?"

"I've heard cats are more sensitive," Elthia murmured. "Maddie, could we hold the Bistro in your museum?"

"The space may be cramped," I warned.

"It's a small group," Elthia said. "I don't expect more than a dozen people."

I *could* fit a dozen people.

"Pleeease," Adele said. "It would be the perfect solution. It won't cause any real mix-ups. Plus, it will be a good promotion for the museum."

Well, maybe. I didn't see how I was going to make much money out of it if they were slugging down Adele's tea and crumpets. But no publicity is bad publicity, and Adele and I would work something out. "Why not?" I said. "When is it?"

"This Thursday," Elthia said.

"What?!" My head rocked backward. "That's in four days!"

"You won't have to do a thing," Adele said. "I'll take care of the table setup, food, and cleanup. Elthia will promote it with a big thank you to the Paranormal Museum."

I don't like short notice. Short notice gave me less time to plan for emergencies. But I could do this. "Fine." After all, I had a ghost hunter group that explored the museum after-hours on a monthly basis. I pasted on a smile. "The Death Bistro sounds fun."

Someone hammered on the tea room door. Frowning, Adele rose and opened it.

Three women in powder-blue T-shirts stalked in. My mother slunk in behind them. The president of Ladies Aid pointed a pudgy finger at me.

I flinched, icy tentacles rippling up my spine.

"We need to talk."

EIGHT

Two gray-haired women took up posts beside the tea room's front door. They clicked the bolt shut.

"I think we should hold this conversation in private," the Ladies Aid president said. "Don't you?" Mrs. Bigelow gazed pointedly at Elthia.

Elthia gulped down her tea and leapt from her chair. "I'm done here."

One of the blue ladies released Elthia, locking the door behind her.

Eliza Bigelow sat in Elthia's chair and shifted the tea things to the center of the table. "A new set up and Earl Grey, Miss Nakamoto."

Behind her, my mother hovered, awkward. My mother was never awkward.

"Yes, ma'am." Adele loaded the tea pot and cups onto the tray. Taking the half-full cup from my hand, she scuttled into the kitchen.

"Now." Mrs. Bigelow tilted her head down and lasered me with a steel-cutting gaze. "I understand you've taken charge of the

Haunted San Benedetto display at our haunted house. What exactly do you have in mind?"

"In mind?" My insides crumpled like an aluminum can. I glanced at my mother.

She examined her fingernails.

"Did you see our museum's display inside the Visitors Bureau tent?" I asked.

"I certainly hope you're not planning on repeating that," Mrs. Bigelow said. "Haunted houses are supposed to be frightening."

"No one told me the size of the space I'd be decorating," I said, stalling.

"You'll have the last room in the tour, the downstairs parlor," Mrs. Bigelow said. "It's approximately ten feet by twelve. Of course, you'll bring the grape press, but I do hope you can flesh out its story a bit more. Perhaps you can build a scene recreating the murder-suicide."

The idea left me cold, and I wasn't sure why. Historical murder and mayhem was a central theme in my Paranormal Museum. But this murder-suicide felt different, for some reason. "The police have the, erm, grape press."

Mrs. Bigelow's eyes glittered. "That shouldn't be a problem. We've got a cop. I'll look into it."

I blinked. Ladies Aid owned a cop? What were they? The Mafia?

"Your grape press won't take the entire space," she went on. "I'm envisioning multiple scenes for Haunted San Benedetto, which draw people through to the exit. And there had better be screaming."

"You mean ... in the exhibit?" Screaming? What was I supposed to do? Hide behind a wing chair and howl? I caught my mother's eye.

She shook her head, lips crimped tight.

Adele hustled into the room and laid out a new tea setting, cups rattling in their saucers. She backed away, flattening herself against the false bookcase.

"I mean, you need to scare the paying guests," Bigelow said. "Is anything in your museum actually frightening?"

"There's the McBride murder," I offered. "I could rig a swaying noose."

"And when lightning flashes, a shadow of the hanged man will appear on the wall." Bigelow added cream to her tea and swirled it, her spoon clinking against the cup. "Excellent idea. Ladies, write that down."

A woman beside the door whipped a notepad from the rear pocket of her jeans and a pen from behind her ear. She scribbled something on the pad.

Flashing lightning? Mysterious shadows? I didn't know how to do that!

"What about the third exhibit?" Bigelow frowned at the tea stain on the white tablecloth.

"The third exhibit." My mind had gone blank. It was worse than the fifth grade spelling bee. I'd known how to spell 'revision,' but all those staring eyes, waiting, expectant.

My mother cleared her throat. "The Paranormal Museum is, of course, known to be haunted."

"And not very frightening," Bigelow said.

"But séances are," my mother said. "Madelyn could bring in some of those items and set up a spooky Ouija board scene."

"I could arrange mannequins wearing ghost-hunting equipment around it," I said. "Maybe set up a video screen with our feed of the museum at night."

"Why would you have a feed of the museum at night?" Bigelow asked.

"So people can check in for ghostly activity. It's not that different from the Christmas Cow feed, where people watch to see if they can catch the cow going up in flames."

Her grip tightened on her teacup. "The repeated arson attacks on the San Benedetto Christmas Cow are no joking matter. Do you have any idea how many hours go into constructing that display?"

"Lots?" I asked.

"Hundreds."

"The feed is rather eerie though," my mother said. "A flickering green screen, mesmerizing, and then one of your volunteers could hide among the ghost-hunter mannequins and lunge for a guest. It could be terrifying."

Bigelow's eyes narrowed. She drummed her pink talons on the table. "Very well. Ghost hunters from the museum it is. You are aware, of course, that the haunted house is being held at CW Vineyards?"

I nodded.

"Miss Nakamoto?"

High heels dragging, Adele slunk to the table. "Yes?"

"I've decided to have a volunteer appreciation tea on Halloween for all those who contributed to the haunted house. We'll hold it at the Fox and Fennel. It will be called a Witches' Tea, in honor of the day, though of course will be scheduled for the evening."

Of course. That way they could all avoid giving out candy to trick-or-treaters.

"I presume you do not have the space reserved for another event?" Bigelow asked.

"N-no," Adele stammered.

"Excellent. Mrs. Kosloski, our volunteer coordinator, will work with you on the details. I expect something elegant, even if we are all wearing pointed hats. Do you understand?"

Adele snapped to attention. "Yes, ma'am."

"You may go."

Adele fled into the kitchen.

"Now, Miss Kosloski, what do you intend to do about Cora Gale?"

My mouth went dry. "Cora Gale?"

"Yes, Cora Gale! She clearly was the one responsible for sabotaging our grape stomp."

"You mean, you think she killed Romeo Paganini?"

"That's what I said, isn't it?"

"But why?"

"To ruin our Harvest Festival, of course. She knows that the grape stomp is our most important fundraiser of the year."

"Killing someone seems a little excessive," I said.

"Does it?" Bigelow leaned across the table, her lips pursed. "Does it, Miss Kosloski?"

Behind her, my mom shook her head frantically.

"Why would Mrs. Gale want to sabotage the Harvest Festival?" This was ridiculous. I knew Mrs. Gale. I mean, we weren't best buddies, but she was a decent enough person. She was no killer.

Bigelow sipped her tea. "There's been a schism in Ladies Aid. Cora felt that society had changed. She believed we should continue with our charitable works but that our time together should focus more on..." Her upper lip curled. "Female empowerment."

"And so she's killing people?" I asked, disbelieving.

"And so she resigned as president last month, left Ladies Aid, and took a chunk of our membership with her, including Romeo

Paganini's wife, Jocelyn. The two likely conspired, killing two birds with one stone—Romeo and our grape stomp."

"But still, why take out the grape stomp?" I asked. I should have paid more attention to my mom's moanings about Ladies Aid politics. Who knew the organization could be so high drama?

"Because there isn't enough room in San Benedetto for two charitable societies such as ours. She wants the whole pie."

I wouldn't mind a whole pie myself right now. But Mrs. Gale as murderer? "Have you told the police your theory?" I asked carefully.

"I have. That fool of a detective did not take me seriously. I will have words with his captain. We cannot allow Cora to interfere further. Since the police are useless in this matter, I expect you to prove she was the culprit."

"But—"

"You've done it before. You can do it again. Now, how are you going to tackle this problem?"

What had my mom gotten me into? "Oh," I said, "I've got a process."

"Well, what is it?"

I glanced at the locked door. "It's secret."

"Hmph. I suppose that makes sense." Bigelow rose. "You have until this Thursday to install your Haunted San Benedetto exhibit at the haunted house."

"Thursday?!" I grasped the table, dizzy. I had to host the Death Bistro. "But that's in four days! Halloween isn't for another three weeks!"

"Didn't anyone tell you? The haunted house was so successful last year, we're holding it the last three weekends in October. Our first showing will be this Thursday night." She swept out of the tea room.

I sputtered. "Thursday? This Thursday? I can't... Mom, you've got to explain—"

She grasped my arm. "I can't protect you," she whispered, then hurried after Bigelow and her lackeys. The door snicked shut behind them.

Protect me from what? What the Hades was going on? And why did I feel like I'd just survived an interview with the Godfather?

Adele slunk from the kitchen. "Are they gone?"

"A fat lot of help you were. Coward."

"Are you kidding? Ladies Aid can make or break a business. They practically run this town."

"So the Fox and Fennel is too good for the Death Bistro, but a Witches' Tea is all right with you."

"There's a skull and crossbones on the Death Bistro flyer. That's a poison warning! Besides, this is Ladies Aid. Their tea will be the height of sophistication."

"And you're too chicken to say no."

"There is that," Adele said. "But I've got to protect my business. It's still a baby. Innocent, fragile."

That I understood. What I didn't get was how my mother could have thrown in with this lunacy. And she'd been so meek! That was the unkindest cut of all.

I groaned. "How am I going to decorate an entire room in a haunted house by Thursday?" At least I wouldn't need to be there running things on Thursday night, because I definitely wanted to check out the upcoming Death Bistro.

"And you've got a murder to solve."

"You heard that, did you?"

"I eavesdropped. Only for your own protection," Adele said hastily.

"I'm not happy about my so-called investigation." I crossed my arms over my chest. "Crime-solving is what the police are for."

"The police won't stop Mrs. Bigelow from ruining Cora Gale's reputation. And didn't you hear what I said about Ladies Aid? You can't go back on your word to their president. She'll ruin you."

"Ladies Aid tried to take out the Paranormal Museum once before, and they failed."

"That was different. Mrs. Gale was in charge then. Mrs. Bigelow is a whole other kettle of piranhas."

"She's nuts." And somehow, Ladies Aid had fallen in with her delusion. There was no way someone would commit murder just to sabotage a silly grape stomp. Was there?

———

On a whim, I cut through the tea room to the back alley and jogged up the concrete staircase leading to Mason's apartment. I rapped on the fortress-like metal security door. Waited. Knocked again. Waited.

Digging my cell phone from the pocket of my jeans, I called.

He didn't pick up.

Disappointment weighted my gut, and I blew out my breath. Wait, was he meeting with his ex tonight? He hadn't mentioned a time or date. Not that it mattered. Well, I couldn't expect him to be at my beck and call. I trudged down the steps and into the tea room.

Adele had cleared the table and sat in a booth with a laptop open before her, its bluish glow lighting her face. Her pink leather purse sat beside her on the seat. "Witches, witches, witches' tea, witches and tea," she muttered.

"Found anything useful?"

She raked her fingers through her black hair. They tangled in her bun and she yanked her hair free, scattering a band, bobby pins, and a delicate hair net. "If I'm stuck doing a Witches' Tea for Ladies Aid, I'm going to have to come up with some Halloween tea blends. I may as well create them now."

"Maybe you can just take some of your existing blends and re-word the names so they sound more magical?"

She clutched her hands to her chest. "Would you?"

"Sorry, you're on your own. I've got to plan a room at a haunted house. By Thursday. And I don't even know what the room looks like yet." I'd need to make an appointment with CW Vineyards to get into the house. It had been a while since I'd done a tasting there, but I vaguely remembered a gray-painted Gothic.

And then there was my "investigation." Mrs. Gale couldn't have anything to do with the murder, but there was bad blood between her and Ladies Aid. Detective Slate was a good cop, and I trusted him. But my mother was behaving oddly and seemed somehow involved in whatever was going on. I needed to figure out what was up. And since I really didn't want to grill the grieving son and widow of the victim, talking to Mrs. Gale seemed a decent third choice.

"I need help." Adele clutched my wrist. "I'm no writer, and I don't know anything about witches. You run a paranormal museum. You must have some ideas."

"Harper."

"What about Harper?"

I bit my lower lip. Harper lived a secret life as a strega, an Italian folk witch, and I wasn't sure how much Adele knew. A reputation for witchcraft wouldn't mix with Harper's rational, financial planner persona. "I know today's Sunday, but this is an emergency," I finally said. "We need Harper."

Adele whipped her cell phone from her pink leather purse. "You're right. She's not as close to the situation. She'll have a better perspective." She dialed. "Harper? It's an emergency—" She scowled. "No, I haven't been arrested ... No, Mad hasn't been arrested either. It's Ladies Aid! Look, can you meet Mad and me at the Book Cellar in, say, thirty minutes?" She relaxed against the booth. "Great. Thanks." She dropped her phone in her purse. "She'll meet us there."

Locking our shops, we strolled down the street, passing window shoppers and diners lounging in sidewalk cafés. The temperature had dropped to a temperate seventy-something and a breeze whispered against my bare arms. People gripe that California doesn't have seasons. It's true you have to head into the mountains to see fall color, but you can't beat the weather.

We ambled inside the Book Cellar, a combination first-floor bookstore and basement wine bar. I itched to peruse its carpeted aisles for a new mystery novel, preferably something set in a charming English village. But Adele clacked down the wide stairs to the cellar, and I followed. A hostess led us past dark wood tables sunk in low shadows, faux wine barrels set into stone walls.

Harper waited in a booth, a glass of red wine on the table before her. "I hope you don't mind ..." She struggled out of her black motorcycle jacket. "I ordered a bruschetta plate." Her plain white T-shirt gleamed against her olive skin.

I didn't need more calories, but this was a crisis. "Did you order any Gorgonzola and honey bruschetta?"

"Of course. And your favorite, Adele, the Brie and green apple."

We ordered wine before the hostess could escape—we'd been here often enough that we knew what we wanted—and sank into the booth.

"I figured you and Mason would be out tonight," Harper said.

"I'm not sure where he is." Ignoring a twinge of worry, I shifted my gaze to the menu. If Mason was out with his old girlfriend, so what? He'd told me about it, and I trusted him.

"So," Harper said. "Ladies Aid."

I told her everything. "My mother seems to be in some sort of thrall to the new president."

"That doesn't sound like your mom." A furrow appeared between Harper's brows.

"I know. When I had problems with Ladies Aid earlier this year, my mom was one hundred percent Team Maddie. But she as good as told me I was on my own with this one."

"They can't honestly think someone committed murder just to mess with their grape stomp?" Harper asked.

"This is worse than just murder," Adele said. "I have to come up with a witchy tea menu for them."

Harper's expression flickered. "Oh?"

"I thought we could help her rewrite some of her erotic tea descriptions and make them sound more magical," I said.

"I brought menus." Adele dug into her pink purse and handed them out.

A waiter stopped by, deposited drinks on our table, and whizzed away.

"Well, you can change the name of your Black Rapture to Black Magic," Harper said.

"Oh! Perfect!" Adele made a note on her menu.

We drank wine and brainstormed haunted tea names, and some of my tension slipped away. By the time the bruschetta plate was reduced to crumbs, we had five haunted-sounding tea blends.

Adele leaned against the soft leather booth and took another sip of her Cabernet. "I think that does it."

"Now we need someone who understands special effects and can help Maddie with her room at the haunted house," Harper said.

"Oh, I've already got that handled," Adele said. "Dieter."

"Dieter's a contractor," I said. "I need someone who can help me make a shadow of a hanged man appear on a wall."

Adele nodded. "Dieter can do that. He spent a year with a roaming carnival. They had a haunted house and everything."

Harper wet her lips. "Dieter is a man of many parts."

Was there a way I could talk Dieter into doing it at a discounted rate? Even though this month had started off strong, over the course of the year the museum hadn't exactly made money hand over fist. "All right," I said. "I'm desperate. I'll call him."

"Why not do it now?" Adele pulled her phone from her purse and dialed. "Dieter? We've got an emergency."

I winced. Now there was no way he'd knock down the price.

"Are you working on the Ladies Aid haunted house...? You are? Maddie's got a room and she's going to need a little help... Yes... Yes..." Adele pinked. "Thanks. Maybe you should just talk to her."

Wetting my lips, I took the phone. "Hi, Dieter."

"So what's the emergency?" he asked.

"I wouldn't call it an emergency," I hedged. "It's the haunted house. I'm responsible for one of the rooms, and Ladies Aid wants a shadow of a hanged man to appear on the wall."

"Just appear? Or be there all the time?"

"I'll take whatever I can get."

"I could do something with lightning flashes. Yeah. I can do it. No problem."

"Er, how much?"

"That depends. Is Adele going to be there?"

"Probably not," I admitted, glancing at her.

"But you two are good friends."

"Ye-es."

"Did you tell her I saved you from that runaway car?"

"It was going less than five miles per hour!"

"You could have been crushed."

"Come on, Dieter." I glanced at Adele, who was studying her nails. "You don't need me for that. What's your price?"

We haggled, and I hung up. "Well, that makes my life easier."

"All set?" Adele asked.

"The lighting effects are. I need rope for a noose—my mother should have some in her garage."

"The life of a museum curator," Harper said.

"Soon I'll be traveling the world, Indiana Jonesing my way through haunted castles in search of occult relics."

They stared at me.

"Or I'll be setting up a ghost-hunter display for the haunted house. Good thing Monday and Tuesday are my days off."

"Harper, you're the only one who's not haunted," Adele said. "I've got my magic teas, Maddie's got the museum. What are you going to do for Halloween?"

"Well, I'm not taking you trick-or-treating."

"Ha." Adele threw a wadded napkin at Harper. "Ha, ha."

They bickered, good natured, and I plotted my next steps on the back of a napkin. Solve the crime? I had a host of leads—the widow, the son, and now Cora. Ghost-detecting tech for the Haunted San Benedetto display? Easy peasy. Mannequins? No idea. A cheap video screen to hook up to the Internet?

"Does CW Vineyards even have Wi-Fi?" I gnawed my pen.

"What does that have to do with a concert in Murphy's?" Adele said.

"Oh." I folded the napkin and jammed it in my pocket. "We're talking about a concert in Murphy's now? Sorry." And I still had to flesh out my haunted and/or invisible grape press story, which meant a call to the Historical Association. Finding time to look into Romeo's death for my mom wasn't going to be easy.

It was time to cowgirl up and be a detective. Now I just needed to figure out how.

NINE

THE SUN WAS ON its way to brunch when I dragged myself from bed and stumbled to my kitchen. One diet soda and two poached eggs on toast later, I stood at the sink, gripping the 1950s-era counter. Through the floral-print curtains, sunlight splintered off the unforgiving lines of my aunt's ranch house across the drive.

I gulped orange juice and mentally organized my day. First up: an appointment at CW Vineyards to view the haunted house.

My cell phone rang.

Mason! Following the ringing, I scrambled through the nautical-themed living room. The phone vibrated on a bookshelf, shimmying toward a brass telescope in a battered leather case.

My heart nosedived. Not Mason. I didn't recognize the number.

"Hello?" I plopped onto the soft gray-blue couch.

"It's Leo. Uh, I know the museum's closed today, but I heard we were doing the Ladies Aid haunted house."

"Ye-es."

"Do you need any help?"

"I'm headed over there—"

"Great! I'll come along."

I'd planned to say I was headed over soon and didn't need anything, but something in his voice stopped me.

"That would be great. What's your address?" Leo's mother had died a year ago, and while he was old enough to live on his own, he was also young enough not to be prepared for it. Was he in his mother's house? Given his strained relationship with his father, I was fairly certain he hadn't been living with Romeo and Jocelyn.

Leo gave me directions to a house in a quiet neighborhood.

"Why don't I pick you up in an hour?" I asked.

"You're the boss."

We hung up.

I dressed in jeans and a lightweight black blouse. Grabbing my messenger bag off the couch, I trotted down the steps of my garage apartment to my truck. Window down, I drove into town. The warm morning air billowed my blouse, tossed my hair, and freedom tingled through my veins.

I parallel parked in front of the tea shop, walked to the museum, and unlocked the front door. It stuck, refusing to budge. I rattled the handle and the *Closed* sign fell from the window. Putting my shoulder to the door, I jolted it open and staggered inside.

"Breakfast time," I called, swooping the *Closed* sign off the floor. I shut the door behind me and replaced the sign.

The cat glowered at me from atop a bronzed skull, high on a display case.

Not getting any love from that quarter, I replenished his bowls and left GD to his own devices.

Leo lived in a ranch-style home surrounded by tall maples, their leaves sheer and golden. I parked beside the browning lawn and walked to the door. A pile of newspapers lay beside a withered fern. The mailbox overflowed.

I knocked. Stuff had clearly been piling up for a long while. Was Leo paying all his bills? I'd been so involved in the museum, I hadn't paid much attention to Leo's personal life. Now worry niggled my chest.

Leo wrenched the front door open and pushed past me.

I caught sight of a darkened hallway, a side table piled with unopened mail, stained tiles.

He slammed the door shut, brushing his black bangs out of his eyes. "Let's go."

Biting my tongue, I followed him to the truck. How could I get him help without offending his teen-male pride? Recommending a cleaning service was out. He worked for me, so I was fairly certain he couldn't afford a maid. I unlocked his door and we got inside the truck.

I turned down a wide suburban street. "How are you doing?"

"Fine."

"When my father died, he had things well organized. But there was still tons to do. It was overwhelming," I said. And I'd had a mother and siblings to help. We'd all chipped in after his death, but each step forward had been a painful reminder of a hard ending.

Leo grunted. "Jocelyn's taking care of the funeral."

"Do you know when it will be held?"

"No. First they have to finish the autopsy."

"So you're in limbo."

He shrugged, the seat belt rustling against his black T-shirt.

"That's rough," I said.

"Romeo hasn't been a part of my life since I was little. It's no big deal."

The hell it wasn't. I couldn't imagine being rejected by a parent, though sometimes I wished my mother would be a little less involved. I frowned. She still hadn't returned my calls.

I tightened my grip on the wheel. "Thanks for working today. It looks like this month is going to be crazy."

"What are your plans for the haunted house?"

"We're only responsible for one room." I told him about the displays. "Dieter's dealing with the hanging shadow thing. All I need are mannequins to play ghost hunters and someone to set up a video screen with a link to our web feed." Pensive, I knit my bottom lip. "The only problem is, I don't have a monitor."

"I've got an extra one. I can set it up."

"Really? Thanks!"

He shrugged.

We drove into farmland, passing an apple orchard. Rows of vineyards whipped by.

"Leo, can I ask you something about your father?"

He lifted a shoulder, dropped it.

"Who do you think might have put him in the vat?"

"Aside from me, you mean?"

"I hope you didn't say that when you talked to the police."

"Didn't have to. They grilled me about where I was the night before."

"The night before? Is that when they think he was killed?"

"I guess. They asked where I was between nine and midnight. I told them I was home."

I sighed. We'd only worked together three months, and in that time I'd gotten to know a sensitive, reliable young man. I understood why Leo resented his father. But did he have to make himself a suspect? "You obviously didn't kill your father, so who did?"

"Isn't the spouse the killer nine times out of ten?" he asked.

"I talked to Jocelyn on Saturday," I said gently. "She seemed hurt and confused by his death."

Saying nothing, Leo looked out the window. Vineyards flew past.

"Is it possible your father died of natural causes and someone put him in the vat?" I didn't believe that, but heck, it might be true.

"As a sick joke? Maybe," he said slowly. "Romeo cared more about his vineyard than he did about anything or anyone. But why put him in the festival vat? There are plenty of wine vats at his own vineyard."

I slowed beside a signpost to CW Vineyards and turned right. Though it had been a while since I'd visited, I didn't need directions to find the place. It was on the way to the Harvest Festival grounds, and the town and its farms formed an easy-to-navigate grid pattern.

Making another right, I slowed at a gated entry worthy of J. R. Ewing. Five men struggled to raise a new gate into place.

I drifted past the laborers and drove the pickup onto a gravel track. We bumped past almond trees to a parking lot. I parked beside a silver Buick, and we stared.

Before us rose a two-story Gothic Revival home painted sullen gray with white trim. Pointed arch; steep gables; diamond-pane casement windows. It looked like a cross between a church and the house in *Psycho*. No wonder they'd chosen it for this year's haunted house. On the tasting room's front porch, a sandwich board proclaimed *CW Vineyards Open for Tastings, Friday through Sunday, Noon to Six*.

A barn sprawled across a wide lawn to the south. Beside it stood a cottage, a miniature of the Gothic Revival tasting room.

"Uh oh," I said, staring at the *Open* sign.

"What?"

"If they're using the tasting room for the haunted house, some-one's going to have to clear everything out at the end of each night and re-set things so people can do wine tastings during the day." Or they'd have to at least clear the parlor, location of our spooky ex-hibit. I wasn't so sure about the upstairs rooms.

Leo made a low noise in his throat. "You're right. There's no way the winery's going to shut down tastings over October weekends."

I nodded. I really hoped this didn't mean I'd have to deal with haunted house cleanup every weekend.

We walked up the tasting room's porch steps and through the open, screened front door. The room was double the size I'd ex-pected, and not because its white walls made the room look bigger. It looked like it had once been two rooms—perhaps a living area and a parlor. To the right was a long tasting counter. To the left, bar stools surrounded tall round tables on the burnished wood floor. A second-floor loft area loaded with stacked wooden wine barrels loomed over the far wall. Wide windows looked out over the rows of vines, setting the room aglow with the late-morning sun. A nar-row set of steps led up to the second floor.

"Wow." I gnawed my bottom lip. If this was the parlor, I didn't know how the hell I was going to fill it.

The round-faced blonde, deep lines around her cornflower-blue eyes, stopped and stared at us. She shifted the bucket of plastic skulls in her arms, bunching up her pale blue *Ladies Aid* T-shirt. "Maddie? You're here to see your space?"

"Yes. Betsy, right? This is my colleague, Leo."

"Hi, Leo. I'm Betsy Kendle with Ladies Aid." She handed him the bucket. "Let me give you the tour."

"Is my mother here?" I asked.

"No, I don't think so." Her chin dipped. "Shall we?" She motioned toward the stairs.

"Maybe I should just focus on my space," I said. "It's, uh, a lot bigger than I thought."

"It will make more sense in the context of the entire house," she said. "So this room is the entry." She pointed at the tasting bar. "That's where we'll take tickets and such. And then the guests will move upstairs." She led us up the narrow, switchback staircase.

I glanced at my watch. "Maybe I should just focus on the parlor?"

"That's last on the tour." She stopped at the top of the stairs, and Leo bumped into me from behind. We stood in a hallway with doors on each side, like in a hotel or asylum. A white sheet hung behind us, acting as a barrier. "Each room has both an entry from the hallway and an exit into another room, so guests won't have to backtrack."

"What's with the sheet?" Leo asked.

"That blocks off the loft." Betsy opened a door to a mid-sized room with a fireplace and sloped ceiling. "We're going to call this the Unliving Room." She took us through the house, room by room, and I checked my watch again, fidgeting. I knew my theme—Haunted San Benedetto—so seeing the rest of the house didn't help.

More blue-shirted women passed us, hanging spiderwebs, clanking chains, testing red LED lights.

"And here's the Haunted Library." Betsy ushered us into a furniture-free white room lined with empty bookshelves. Paned windows overlooked the vineyards.

"How are they going to do tastings with the haunted house running?" I stumbled on a blue rag rug.

"They don't use the upstairs for tastings. It's normally a storage area, and we've shifted most everything onto the loft. It's only the downstairs areas where we'll have to do quick takedowns each evening and setups each afternoon. That's where you'll be."

I think I whimpered.

"Oh, don't worry," she said. "Our volunteers will deal with it. All we need from you is the initial setup. I'll take photos of everything, so we know how to put it back each night."

"That's a relief. Thanks. You guys really are organized."

"Ladies, not guys," she warbled.

We emerged from the final room at the front of the hallway, where we'd started.

"Each tour will be led by a docent, so the guests don't bump into each other as they're going up and down the stairs."

"Wow." I tried to inject some enthusiasm into it. Betsy had just saved me from some major pain.

The door opposite us opened. Head lowered, Jocelyn Paganini stepped into the hall. She stopped short, her cheeks coloring at the sight of us. Wisps of her blond hair had come loose from her ponytail and stuck to her cheeks. In her black yoga jacket, she looked like she'd just come from a run. Her mouth opened and closed, an unpleasantly surprised guppy. "Leo!"

Blank-faced, my employee crossed his arms.

Chuck Wollmer emerged from behind Jocelyn. The vineyard owner laid a hand on her shoulder. "Howdy!"

Pinking, Jocelyn shrugged away from him.

Chuck's handlebar mustache twitched. He slipped his hands into the pockets of his green *CW Vineyards* hoodie, worn over a white V-necked T-shirt and jeans. He smiled. "Getting the tour? I understand you'll be in charge of the parlor room, Maddie."

Our guide smoothed the front of her powder-blue shirt, jostling me with her elbow. "I've been showing them—"

"Leo, I've been trying to call you," Jocelyn said. "Didn't you get my messages?"

"What do you want?" Leo's brows drew down in a dark slash.

"We have a lot to talk about," Jocelyn said.

"Like how you're *managing* my money?"

"Well, yes, that and other things. There are lots of decisions to be made."

"Don't pretend I have any say in the decisions," Leo said. "You've got exactly what you wanted, and I've got nothing, no say—"

"Leo, that's not true—"

Sidling past me, he rattled down the steps. I stared after him. Was Jocelyn mismanaging Leo's inheritance? How badly did she need money?

A vein throbbed in Jocelyn's jaw.

"You're doing the right thing, Jocclyn," Chuck said.

"Am I?"

Our Ladies Aid guide cleared her throat. "What are you doing here, Jocelyn?"

"I had a business meeting with Mr. Wollmer, and he offered to show me the haunted house."

"*Business?*" Betsy arched a brow. "Well, you should know we'll be ready for any sabotage here. We won't let what happened at the grape stomp happen at our haunted house.

I laughed weakly, looking to Chuck. "I doubt we have anything to worry about. It's not as if there's some sort of conspiracy at work, though I must admit there's a certain Mafia-like efficiency to Ladies Aid," I babbled.

Chuck's shoulders twitched.

"That's why we have Maddie," Betsy said. "She's not just helping us with the haunted house. She's also investigating your husband's murder, and she's running with a hot clue."

Horrified, I gaped at Betsy. Chuck and Jocelyn's eyes burnt holes in the back of my neck.

So much for a nice quiet investigation. "I'm sure the police have everything well in hand," I said weakly.

"I'm not." Jocelyn turned and walked down the stairs.

Chuck began to follow, but Betsy placed a hand on his arm. "Oh, Chuck, we're having a problem in one of the rooms. Would you mind…?"

I slipped down the steps after Jocelyn. The passage of one day likely hadn't eased the widow's grief, but I worried about Leo. I had to talk to her.

Jocelyn rummaged behind the bar in the downstairs tasting room. She pulled out a half-empty bottle and uncorked it. "Want some?"

I shook my head. "No thanks."

"Good, because someone's removed all the glasses." She took a gulp from the bottle and rolled her eyes. "Leo. He's working at the Paranormal Museum with you?"

"For the last three months."

"How's it going?"

"Good. He's dependable, serious."

She laughed hollowly. "Are we talking about the same Leo?"

"I understand he didn't get on well with his dad."

"He hated us both. I'd hoped we could at least be civil to each other now that we've got to plan a funeral. But I guess I was stupid to expect things to change."

"Why the antagonism?" I asked.

She clutched the bottle to her chest. "Romeo left Leo's mother, and she painted his father as the bad guy. Then when his mother died last year, Leo blamed Romeo." She rubbed her neck. "In fairness, the conflict wasn't all Leo's fault. Romeo could be... unyielding. It's bad enough Romeo made enemies in the business. He shouldn't have made one of his son."

"Your husband had enemies?"

"Why else would someone sabotage our vineyard? It has to be personal, and I doubt it was one of my students, upset about a grade."

How does someone sabotage a vineyard? And why?

As I opened my mouth to ask, two women in blue T-shirts clattered down the stairs, laughing. We fell silent, watching them leave through the front door. The screen banged behind them.

"Are you really investigating the murder?" Jocelyn asked.

"Ladies Aid took the placement of Romeo's body in their grape vat as a personal insult," I said, evasive.

She glanced out the window.

Outside, Leo leaned against my pickup.

"You mentioned sabotage," I said. "What exactly happened?"

Feminine voices wafted from the second floor, and Jocelyn glanced at the staircase. "We should speak in private," she said. "Why don't you come by my place tomorrow night for drinks? Around seven thirty? And I can properly apologize about the grape press imbroglio."

"Sure." I paused. "Why would Romeo tell the police a grape press Herb bought from you was stolen?"

She took another swig from the bottle. "He loved that damn press. It was from the old country, and it came with the vineyard.

The fact that it was associated with an old murder was icing on the cake. I guess he was just desperate to have it returned."

"If it meant that much to him, I would have sold it back. Having the police show up on my doorstep kind of threw me."

"That was Romeo. He didn't like to ask. You still have it, don't you? The police didn't confiscate it?"

"Yeah, they did. But if he loved the press so much, why did you sell it?"

Jocelyn flinched, her knuckles whitening around the bottle. "Romeo Paganini took everything from me." Slamming the bottle on the counter, she strode onto the porch. The front door bammed shut behind her.

Footsteps cascaded down the stairs and Betsy emerged in the tasting room, panting. "Oh! I thought you'd left, and we haven't had a chance to go over your space."

Pensive, I jerked my chin toward the open room with the tables. "Is that it?"

"Yes. We're going to hang a divider between the tasting bar and your parlor room, here." She stood between the two open spaces, her arms in a T shape. "We'll leave space on both ends of the divider for entry and exit. When people come down the stairs, they'll turn right and enter the final exhibit, the Haunted San Benedetto room. Then they'll exit from the gap on the other side of the divider."

"Makes sense." On the plus side, I was back to a ten-by-twelve-foot space. On the minus side, I only had four days to decorate. I pointed at the loft above and the stacked wine barrels, stained with damp. "Are those safe?"

"They're empty, but we'll be sure to have them properly tied down. This is earthquake country, after all. But ... Wouldn't it be fun if the barrels teetered, making it look like they might fall on the guests below? I'll ask Dieter if he can rig something."

"I don't suppose you have any extra mannequins I can use?"

"Oh, I'm sorry. The Wine and Visitors Bureau was expected to provide all their own materials for the room."

"Do you know where I can get any mannequins?"

"Your mother might have an idea. She was in charge of collecting ours."

"Thanks." I got busy drawing diagrams in my notepad, and Betsy hustled upstairs to get busy with whatever she had to do.

Leo stormed into the tasting room, his chest heaving. Wordlessly, I handed him one end of the measuring tape and we measured the space—stairs to front door, corner to stairs.

"I think we've got it all," I said.

He released his end of the tape. It retracted, rattling across the wood floor, snapping into its container and whipping my thumb.

"Ow."

"Sorry," he said, coloring. "I guess I could have walked it to you."

"I'm feeling a little tense myself. We've got a lot of space to haunt."

"We can hang the noose over the banister," he said.

"That would be authentic, assuming anyone can get past all those wine barrels to rig one." In the nineteenth-century McBride murder, the victim had indeed been hanged from a landing banister.

"I think I can do it," he said.

"Or we can just get a ladder and attach it from this side," I said. My mother would have a ladder if Dieter didn't. "The problem is, a hanging noose doesn't take up any space. I'm going to have to fill the rest of the room with a fake paranormal museum." I didn't want to take too much stuff from the actual museum. But people paid good ticket money for the haunted house, so I couldn't skimp on my exhibits.

"What about the creepy dolls you took to the Harvest Festival?" Leo asked. "What happened to the extras?"

"Good idea," I said. "They're in the back of my closet at home." I wasn't sure why I hadn't gotten rid of them yet, except I hated throwing stuff away. And I kept finding myself glad I had them. "The invisible grape press will take up another five or six square feet, but that still leaves a lot of space."

"Can we keep the tables that are already here?" he asked.

"I'll ask. We could use them to display the dolls." A bunch of scary-looking dolls plus the grape press, noose, and ghost hunter exhibit just might be enough.

"Okay." I scribbled on my yellow pad. "Here's what I think we need. Three mannequins dressed for ghost hunting—my mom might be able to help there—plus ghost-hunting equipment."

"Which we sell at the museum."

"Right. And I can get a noose from my mom. There's bound to be some good rope in her garage, no pun intended. But we'll need tablecloths—can you stop by the party supply store and buy some cheap black-plastic table coverings?" I dug my wallet out of my bag and handed him some cash.

"What about the grape press? Are you going to be able to get it back from the cops?"

I leaned against a window sill. "I'll head to the police department today and check. But let's plan on using the invisible grape press."

"I can set up the monitor so people can watch the museum's web cam, but does this place even have an Internet connection?"

"Chuck should know. I'll ask." If I was going to snoop on my mother's behalf—was I?—this would make a good excuse to talk to Chuck. He seemed to know Jocelyn well. Maybe he had some insights into who might have killed Romeo.

Explaining about how the divider would be used, I handed Leo my notebook and crooked diagram. "Can you sketch out the room with the displays? Traffic's going to flow from the stairs, around the room, and then out the front door."

"Got it."

"Thanks." I jogged upstairs to find Chuck.

Poking my head through the open doors, I finally located him, surrounded by a gaggle of elderly Ladies Aid ladies twittering about the placement of a guillotine. Looking haunted, Chuck violently smoothed his moustache, his eyes darting around the cramped room.

I knocked on the open door. "Chuck, I have a question—"

"Of course!" He sprang from the group. "Excuse me, ladies. Duty calls." Hustling me down the hallway, he half-shoved me into the haunted library. He shut the door and leaned his muscular form against it, his shoulders sagging. "Salvation."

I grinned. "A bigger job than you expected?"

"You have no idea." He wiped a hank of blond hair from his unlined brow. "But the publicity is worth it."

"That's what I keep telling myself. I'd like to set up a monitor downstairs and run our live webcam of the museum at night. Does this building have Wi-Fi or an Internet connection?"

"Sorry, no. What if you just ran a video loop? You know, a recording?"

"That's not a bad idea." Leo could manage that for sure. "And can we use some of the tables in the tasting area?"

"Sure."

"Thanks. How did you get suckered into this?"

"I volunteered when Jocelyn was still a part of the organization." Chuck frowned. "At least I think I did. It's hard to say no to Ladies Aid."

"It's a great space for a haunted house. And Jocelyn? How do you two know each other?" I wasn't investigating. Just making small talk.

"The way most vintners know each other, I suppose. It's a small town. Winery owners have to stick together."

"But you're not a member of the Wine and Visitors Bureau?"

"Not enough bang for my buck there, I'm afraid."

"Terrible about Romeo."

"Why do I feel like I'm being interrogated?"

My cheeks warmed. "The police are managing the investigation, but I'm worried about Leo. This has hit him hard."

"And the angry-young-man shtick won't win him any points with the police." Chuck smiled, wry. "He's a teenager. Bad attitude is in the DNA. The cops must know that."

"Who do you think would have wanted to kill his father?"

Chuck rubbed his knuckles against his jaw. "To tell you the truth, Romeo was a bit of a lady's man, so any number of jealous husbands would have."

"Really? Any husbands in particular?"

"I couldn't say. And as you said, the police are handling it." He walked out.

Chagrined, I wandered to the library window. Outside, Leo leaned against my truck, his arms folded over his chest. Jocelyn was speaking to him, her posture rigid. I understood the tension between Leo and his stepmom. But there seemed to have been something between Chuck and Jocelyn, and I wasn't sure if it was romance or anger. Was Romeo the only lady's man in the mix?

TEN

I sat, parked, in front of the brick police station, clutching the wide metal steering wheel. Jocelyn had told the cops the grape press hadn't been stolen. I still didn't see why they needed to keep it—the press hadn't been anywhere near the crime scene. But Detective Hammer delighted in making my life difficult.

Sliding from the truck, I put a quarter in the meter. The station's architecture was early American slaughterhouse style, squat and mournful and designed to depress. My feet dragged as I walked up its concrete steps and pushed open the front door.

The reception area was painted the same sickly green as the interior of my old high school. High school had not been good to me.

Repressing a shudder, I strode to the window and smiled at the beefy uniformed officer behind the thick glass. "Hi, I'm Maddie Kosloski. Is Detective Slate available?"

He licked powdered sugar and yellow filling off his thumb. "I'll check." Picking up the receiver, he swiveled away from me and made a call, his voice low. He nodded, hung up. "Someone will be here shortly."

"Someone?" I clutched my messenger bag. *Not Laurel. Please, not Laurel.*

He pointed to a plastic chair. "You can wait there."

"Thanks." I slithered into the chair, bag in my lap. And waited. Checked my watch. Wondered if I should run outside and put another quarter in the meter. Waited. I rose, clearing my throat, and jerked my thumb toward the door. "I'm just going to—"

Laurel strode into the waiting room and crooked a finger. "Come with me."

Swallowing, I followed her into a hallway. No jacket today, and the sleeves of her blouse were rolled past her elbow. I couldn't blame her. The station was airless.

We passed rows of cubicles. She opened the door to a windowed conference room and bowed, mocking.

"Thanks." I walked inside.

She closed the glass door behind us. The conference room windows needed a cleaning, their miniblinds bent and dusty.

"So. Laurel," I said.

"Detective Hammer."

"Sorry. Hammer. Detective Hammer."

"What do you want with Detective Slate?"

I shoved my hands in the pockets of my jeans. "I wanted to know if I could get the grape press back by Thursday for the haunted house."

A fly crawled up the pockmarked blue wall.

"You're turning the Paranormal Museum into a haunted house? Isn't that redundant?"

I hugged my messenger bag to my stomach. "No, I got roped into doing a Haunted San Benedetto room for the Ladies Aid haunted house and charity fundraiser. It's for a good cause. Have you heard about it?"

"No," she said, impassive.

"Really? They do the haunted house every year," I babbled. "This year, they're raising money to fund a mobile library for the old folks homes in the area."

"I mean, no, you can't have the press."

My stomach knotted. "Oh."

She smiled. "We found blood on it."

"Bl ... What?" Blood? But the press hadn't been at the grape vat, and Romeo couldn't have been killed by the grape press. It was too big for someone to pick up and bash into his head. "I didn't get much chance to examine the body," I said, "but I doubt someone pressed him to death."

"Stabbed. Got any haunted daggers in that museum of yours?"

My head swam. I had exactly five, arranged in a fan-shape and inside a shadowbox. "Maybe," I squeaked.

Her smile broadened, teeth gleaming. "*Maybe* we should take a look at those knives."

The door swung open behind her. Detective Slate leaned inside, his blue suit rumpled. His amber-flecked eyes caught mine and I sucked in my breath, that odd hook catching beneath my chest.

He glanced at Laurel and canted his head toward the hall. "Got a minute?"

Lips pressed tight, she followed him outside. They closed the door behind them and spoke in voices too low for me to hear. And I was trying.

Laurel's expression fossilized. She nodded.

He walked down the hall, and I sagged against the table, heaviness weighting my chest.

Laurel opened the door. "You can go."

Scurrying past her, I speed-walked out of the police station. A green envelope was wedged beneath my truck's windshield wiper. Wrenching it free, I cursed. A ticket. I knew I should have put more coins in the meter. I opened the envelope and read the fine, letting more curses fly.

I drove, fuming, to a local taqueria and parked beside a Lexus. The owner, who looked all of fifteen, sat against the bumper, gnoshing on a burrito. I forced myself to calm down, unsure what I was more upset about—the ticket or the bloodstains on the grape press. What I needed wasn't comfort food, it was someone to thrash things out with. I called Mason.

He picked up on the fourth ring. "Hey."

"Hi, Mason. I'm on a burrito quest. Want anything from the taqueria?"

"Um, no. But thanks."

I waited for him to say more.

He didn't.

"Have you got a minute? You won't believe—"

"Mad, I can't talk right now."

I stilled. "Oh. Sorry. I'll let you go."

"No, wait. I need to talk to you, but not right now."

"Is something wrong?"

"Not wrong." He blew out his breath. "Look, I'll call you soon. Okay?"

"Sure." I gnawed the inside of my cheek. I didn't believe him.

"Mad?"

"Yeah?"

"I just wanted to say ... I love you."

I leaned against the headrest. "I love you too."

It was the first time he'd said the words. For months I'd been biting my tongue, trying not to be the first to speak. I should have been elated by his confession. But the timing was off. The whole conversation was off.

"I'll call you soon." He hung up.

I stared out the windshield. A woman pushed a stroller in the park across the street.

Had reconnecting with his ex rekindled old memories? I sighed. Of course it had. But if that was the case, why would he tell me he loved me? Out of guilt? My gaze clouded. No. There was no way Mason would cheat on me. That wasn't who Mason was, and shame prickled my chest for even considering he'd cheated. I trusted him. And the past was just that, the past, a ghost, and it only existed if we wanted it to.

Appetite gone, I walked into the taqueria and stood in line at the counter. The scents of grilled pork and beef steamed the air. Women in white aprons worked behind the glass, assembling burritos. Soon I was at the register, a young man in an apron smiling, expectant.

"A grilled veggie burrito, refried beans, hot salsa, and a diet cola." The heck with those last ten pounds. It had been a stressful day. "And a nachos with everything."

I paid and the cashier handed me my soda. Turning, I stopped short before my nose smacked into a crisp white dress shirt. I craned my neck.

The vampire from Adele's house looked down at me, his cadaverous yet oddly attractive face unperturbed, his dark eyes expressionless.

"Excuse me." He edged past, to the counter.

Who *was* this guy? I lingered, standing, when there was an empty red Formica table waiting three steps away. We got plenty of tourists, so San Benedetto wasn't one of those small towns where strangers were rare enough to ogle. But this guy kept turning up in the oddest places, and in my new role as Maddie Kosloski, PI, I wanted to know why.

I sipped my soda, checking the receipt for my number though I'd already memorized it (thirty-two).

Vampire Guy turned from the counter and scanned the room, looking for a place to wait.

Stepping forward, I smiled. "Hi, aren't you a friend of Chuck's? We met at the Harvest Festival. I'm Maddie Kosloski."

He raised a fine brow. "Did we?"

"So what brings you to San Benedetto?"

"Wine."

Either this man had no social skills or he was cagey.

"Number thirty-TWO," an aproned woman bellowed from behind the counter.

"Well, you've come to the right place." I adjusted the collar of my black blouse, which had grown mysteriously tight. "We have some excellent ancient-vine zins."

"Indeed."

"THIRTY-TWO!"

"Isn't that your number?" he asked.

"Why do you say that?"

"I was right behind you, and I'm thirty-three."

Tingling swept the back of my neck. "Oh. Right." I grabbed my paper bag off the counter. "Well, it was nice seeing you again."

"Mmm."

Swallowing, I edged away, taking a free newspaper from the rack on my way out.

Vampire Guy, one, Maddie Kosloski PI, zero. I might have to rethink my investigation process. It only worked if people actually talked to me. But at least I had nachos.

Glum, I walked to the park and across its patchwork of brown and green lawn. I sat on a hay bale dusted with autumn leaves and spread my food beside me. Heard but unseen, the creek trickled, sluggish, in the hollow.

I shook out the newspaper. The body at the Harvest Festival on Saturday was front page news: *Local Vintner Found Stabbed to Death in Harvest Festival Vat*. That explained why Laurel had let me know the victim had been stabbed—it wasn't a secret. And I was willing to bet that fact didn't make Detective Slate happy.

Laying the newspaper across my lap, I dragged a nacho through some beans and sour cream and took a bite. Heaven.

Leo had been right. As the spouse, Jocelyn made the best suspect. She'd even implied she had a motive, telling me Romeo had "taken everything" from her? Did she want to get caught? Or had she snapped? And assuming Romeo had been killed elsewhere and dumped, how could she have lifted his body into the dump truck? And why use a dump truck at all if he'd been killed near my grape press in the Visitors Bureau tent?

I bit into the burrito, swiping with a napkin at the veggie juices that trickled down my chin. Why had Mason told me he loved me? The not-knowing thrummed through my veins, an uneven electric current, setting me on edge.

Seeking distraction from that line of thought, I flipped the page. Ladies Aid and the Dairy Association were looking for volunteers for this year's Christmas Cow. I shook my head. What sort of odds would Dieter be taking on the cow's survival?

I made it through half my burrito and all the nachos and waddled to my truck. Though I'd left the windows down, the truck was an oven. The steering wheel seared my fingertips. I grabbed a dishcloth from the glove compartment and covered the wheel, then drove out of the parking lot. I had a list of things to do and questions to be answered. I needed to talk to Cora Gale. I was fairly certain she hadn't killed Romeo, but she might have some good intel. But first, I had to talk to Mom.

My truck tires crunched on the loose gravel in my mother's driveway. Tall, golden, decorative grasses clumped beneath twisted oaks. A knot at the base of my neck released. I was home.

My parents had bought the sprawling ranch house when they'd married and land was cheap. Now, developments encroached, tract houses shoving against the property lines. She'd had offers to buy it, but I doubted she'd ever leave. Too many happy memories.

A blue Prius sat parked beside my mom's Lincoln. I wedged between the Prius and an oak tree and hopped out, dried leaves crackling beneath my sneakers. Slinging my messenger bag over one shoulder, I strolled up the brick path to the front door and let myself inside.

Voices drifted from the living room, to the right. "It's a big risk," a woman said.

"But worth it," my mother said. "Things can't go on like this."

"I understand what Ladies Aid means to you. I went through it too, after ..." The speaker cleared her throat. "But now, when I look

127

back, I realize I was trying to fill a hole with something that had no meaning."

Fill a hole? Were they talking about their Ladies Aid shenanigans or something more private? My cheeks burned. And was I stooping to spying on my own mother?

"Like everything else," my mother said, "it has the meaning we give it. Intellectually, I know what you're saying, but I'm just not willing to let it go. Not yet."

I shifted. Enough. I didn't need to skulk. Slamming the door, I walked into the living room and rocked back on my heels. Cora Gale was sitting on my mother's best sofa, sipping a cup of tea.

"Hi, Mom. Hi, Mrs. Gale."

Mrs. Gale tensed on the pale green couch, her shoulders rising to her ears. Then they dropped, the lines of her blue tunic flowing around her hips. She tossed her head of loose gray hair. "Maddie, dear. How nice to see you again."

My mother frowned. "What are you doing here, Madelyn?" In her faded denim top and white jeans, she almost vanished into the background of the living room. Part shabby chic, part country kitsch, the pastel furniture was so pale it looked white in certain lighting. The walls were painted a vanilla pudding color. Distressed wood beams crossed the ceiling.

"I need rope for a noose and mannequins," I said. "I was told you could set me up."

Cora laughed. "For a noose? You're not plotting a murder, are you?"

"The Visitors Bureau drafted me into working on the haunted house," I said.

A shadow crossed Cora's face. "I'm sorry to hear it, dear."

"Why? Do you expect something to go wrong, like at the grape stomp?"

"I should hope not, but with Ladies—"

"Madelyn," my mother said, shooting Cora a repressive look, "there's rope in the garage. The mannequins—how many do you need?"

"Three. Preferably female. Oh, and I need some clothing for them too."

She flipped her hand in a shooing motion. "There's a bag of clothing for the secondhand store by the garage door. Take what you need."

"Thanks." I flopped into a soft wing chair. "I don't suppose you can tell me anything about Romeo Paganini?"

My mother shook her head. "Madelyn—"

"Because I'm afraid the wrong person may be blamed for the crime," I said.

"Not you," Cora said.

"No," I said, "I don't think so. I mean, why would the police think I killed Romeo?"

"Then I don't believe the investigation is something you want to get involved in," Cora said.

"Neither do I, but I seem to be involved whether I like it or not. The police found bloodstains on the grape press that Romeo accused me of stealing from him. And since I found the body..." I trailed off.

"Bloodstains?" my mother asked. "Does that mean Romeo was killed inside the Wine and Visitors Bureau tent?"

"Possibly." I thought about it some more. He'd been stabbed. The blood could have splattered. The police believed he was killed late Friday night. What had he been doing inside the festival grounds at that hour? And if he'd been killed in the tent, why bother moving the body into the grape vat? Unless someone who was working in the Visitors Bureau tent had killed him and moved the body to divert suspicion. But the setup for the tent was finished late Friday afternoon. The festival grounds had been closed to everyone sometime after that. No one had good reason to be inside that tent.

"Romeo could have gone inside the tent to repossess the grape press," I said.

"And then someone followed him in and killed him?" my mother asked.

We sat in silence, pondering that.

"So, Mrs. Gale. What are you doing here?" I asked.

She flushed. "Oh. Just tea with an old friend."

"Not that old." My mother laughed, unconvincing.

My eyes narrowed. They were terrible liars.

The doorbell rang, and Cora's teacup rattled in its saucer. She set it on the low coffee table. "You don't think—"

"Probably someone selling magazine subscriptions," my mother said. "Wait here." She strode from the living room.

The front door snicked open. "Betsy!" my mother shrieked. "What a surprise!"

Cora bolted from the couch, looked around wildly, and dove behind it.

I gaped, marveling at her sixty-something agility. "Um…"

"Shhh," she hissed from behind the sofa.

"Do you have guests?" Betsy's voice caroled through the hallway.

"Only Madelyn."

"Oh? Your daughter's here? What luck!"

Lurching from my comfy chair, I grabbed Cora's blue purse from the coffee table and handed it to her over the sofa.

"Thank you," she mouthed.

I dropped onto the sofa and spread my arms along its pale green back.

Betsy Kendle strode into the living room. Mouth tight, my mother trailed behind her.

"There you are." Betsy's round face wreathed in a smile. Cradling a white bakery box beneath one arm, she tugged down the hem of her *Ladies Aid* T-shirt with the other. "You left the haunted house so quickly, I didn't get a chance to tell you that you're invited to our Witches' Tea for the volunteers. You may not be a member of Ladies Aid—yet—but you're still a volunteer."

"Thanks!" Were they prospecting for new members? I couldn't imagine a more horrifying fate.

Something thumped behind me.

"What was that?" Betsy asked.

"What was what?" my mother said.

"That thump."

"Probably an animal on the roof," my mother said.

"Those darn raccoons. I hope you locked your garbage cans." Betsy wagged a plump finger at me. "Come to the tea, and be sure to bring your witch's hat!"

"Oh, I will!" Because who doesn't own a witch's hat? Seriously. I've got two, one with LED lights.

She turned to my mother. "Did you get a new car?"

"New car?" My mother canted her head, lips pursed.

"The Prius out front," Betsy said.

"Oh, that! A friend is letting me test-drive it."

"Cora Gale has a car like that."

My mom cast down her gaze, demure, and toyed with her silver squash-blossom necklace. "A male friend. Shall I take those from you?" She nodded toward the box.

"Oh! Yes." Betsy's voice hardened. "Now, you understand where to make the delivery?"

My mother reached for the box. "Yes."

Betsy stepped backward, the box out of reach. "And you know what your contact looks like?"

My mom made another unsuccessful grab. "I do."

"This is an important asset," Betsy said. "He can't be compromised. If anything goes bad—"

"I know, I know! Sanitize!" My mom snatched the box from her hands and set it on an end table. "Thank you, Betsy. Madelyn and I will both be attending the Witches' Tea, and I've no doubt the haunted house will be the success it is every year."

Contacts? Assets? Had Ladies Aid gone rogue? What was my mother into?

"More so, I hope," Betsy said. "Bye!" She waggled her fingers at me, and my mother ushered her out. The front door clicked shut.

"Is she gone?" Cora whispered.

I craned my neck, looking over the sofa back. She crouched, her blue tunic puddling on the sisal carpet. I shrugged.

My mother returned to the living room. "Clear! She's gone."

Cora clambered to her feet. Sighing, she smoothed the front of her tunic. "*Deliveries*, Fran?"

"It's just this once," my mom said.

"That's how it begins," Cora said. "You need to get out now, before it's too late."

"We've already discussed this, and you know my intentions."

"I don't," I said. "What's going on?"

Cora grasped my arm, her eyes widening. "Wait a minute. Betsy said she saw you at the haunted house. You don't think she followed you here?"

"No."

"Why would she come all the way over here to make a delivery?" Cora asked. "She's supposed to be tormenting the volunteers at CW Vineyards."

"Because she's Eliza Bigelow's second in command," my mom said, "which means she does double the work."

Cora paled. "Or Eliza suspects!"

"Suspects what?" I asked.

"I need to go," Cora said. "I knew coming here was too risky." She hurried away, pivoted, trotted behind the couch, and grabbed her purse. "Bye, Maddie. So nice seeing you again, dear." She rushed out. The front door slammed.

I lifted my brows. "Mom?"

"The rope's in the garage." Turning on her heel, she whisked the white box from the end table and strode into the kitchen.

I trotted after her. "What's in the box?"

"Nothing you need to concern yourself with." My mother laid the box on the gray granite island.

"Because it sounded a lot like Betsy is your … handler. What's the big secret? Has Ladies Aid gone to the dark side? And why did Cora threaten the grape stomp at the Harvest Festival?"

"She did no such thing."

"Yes, she did. I was there."

"No, she didn't." My mom walked to the distressed cupboard, with its missing cabinet doors, and grabbed a red coffee mug from a shelf. "Oh for heaven's sake, Madelyn. You always had the most fertile imagination. I remember when you were a little girl, and—"

"You're not going to distract me with memories of childhood. What's in the box?"

"Lemon bars, if you must know."

"Oh really?" Sliding the box closer, I lifted the lid.

My breath caught. Perfect rows of sunshine-yellow squares dusted with powdered sugar glistened inside the box, their lemony scent light in the air. In spite of my full stomach, my mouth watered. "They really are lemon bars."

"Well, what did you think? That I'm dealing narcotics?"

"Then what was with all the talk about contacts and assets and sanitizing?"

She filled the mug with water and stuck it in the microwave. "If you must know, we deliver them to our elderly members who don't get out so much."

"Mmm...lemon bars." I reached for one, and she smacked my hand away. "Ow."

"And that's what she meant by sanitize! I can't deliver germy lemon bars. Go get your rope."

Shaking the pain from my hand, I stomped to the garage and rummaged for the rope. All that fuss over lemon bars? There had to be more to the situation—Cora's panicked disapproval, the general air of menace...Or my imagination really had carried me away. Maybe the Mason situation was a case of much ado about nothing too. Maybe I'd imagined the strain in his voice, the sense that something was wrong.

But I doubted it.

ELEVEN

IN THEORY, TUESDAY WAS my day off, but when you're self-employed, there's no such thing. So there I sat on Tuesday morning, parked in front of my museum. The windows of Mason's motorcycle store were dark, a *Closed* sign in the window. I checked my watch. His place should have been open by now. Tightening my lightweight, army-green safari jacket around me, I glanced up at the windows to his apartment. The blinds were drawn.

He hadn't called.

I smoothed the thighs of my jeans. In fairness, I hadn't called him either, though I'd itched to do it. But Mason had said he'd call. We were in each other's pockets so much that I wanted to honor that.

I bit the inside of my cheek. The darkened shop left me troubled. I drew out my phone, dialed.

Voicemail.

"Hi, Mason. I'm just calling to check in. It's Tuesday morning. Your shop's closed, and I hope everything's all right. Please call when you get the chance."

Dissatisfied, I hung up. He'd said he'd call. I didn't want to be clingy, but I didn't like that closed shop.

Unlocking the door to the museum, I walked inside, scooping up the mail piled behind the door. While GD munched kibble, I rifled through the envelopes. There was only one bill—from the utility company. I laid it atop the other unpaid bills on the shelf beneath the cash register. The pile of envelopes cascaded sideways.

Shrugging out of my jacket, I hung it on the hook behind the counter and checked my watch. I had two hours before my appointment with Dieter at the haunted house. Sighing, I edged a pumpkin aside and spread the checkbook binder across the counter. The cat meowed at me from the checkerboard floor, his bowl empty.

"You've already eaten, and at least one of us in this partnership is going to be fit."

Turning his back on me, GD licked his paws.

I puzzled over the code for the grape press purchase. Was the last digit a five or a six? The black cat leapt onto the glass counter and walked across the open binder, butting his head against my hand. Absently, I scratched behind his ears. He whipped his head, his teeth nipping my palm. It was only a warning shot, and I shoved him away. He yawned, turned, and sat on one of the unpaid bills.

I tugged it from beneath his furry butt. "Thanks."

Getting my calculator from under the counter, I calculated Leo's payroll, checked the tables to figure his employment tax. Someday, maybe I'd earn enough to hire an accountant.

Purring, GD stretched, crumpling the papers.

"Oh, come on!"

He bolted to his feet, back arched, hissing.

I followed his gaze to the window, and a shadow crossed in front of the closed blinds. The doorknob rattled.

GD growled low in his throat.

Sliding off the tall chair, I walked around the counter and peeked through the blinds on the door.

Detective Laurel Hammer glared through the slats, her blue eyes blazing.

My hands fell to my sides. Why hadn't I paid attention to GD? I still wasn't sure about the cat's ghost detecting abilities, but his Laurel awareness skills were dead on.

But Laurel had caught me, fair and square. I unlocked the door and let her inside my museum.

GD dropped from the counter and streaked into the gallery.

"Detective Hammer. What can I do for you?"

She shoved the sleeve of her tan linen jacket past her elbow, exposing the blue coil of a tattoo. Her mouth twisted in a bone chilling smile. "I'd like to see those knives."

"Sure," I ground out. She had to know my knives had nothing to do with the murder. Except there had been blood on the grape press, and the murdered owner of said press had accused me of stealing it, and I had found the body.

I swallowed. Maybe my true-hearted innocence wasn't so obvious.

"Over here." Leading her to the far wall, I pointed to a set of knives arranged in a fan pattern inside a wood-and-glass shadowbox.

She blinked. "Those are throwing knives."

"From a circus. The knife thrower accidentally killed his assistant during a show. At least, the jury *thought* it was an accident."

"I can't believe people pay to see this garbage."

A shadow slunk along the checkerboard floor, and I twitched. GD Cat prowled toward the detective, his belly low to the ground. He bounded atop a shelf and wound his way past haunted articles, ears flat against his head.

Wary, I tracked GD's progress. "The knives are supposed to be cursed, or at least they were before Herb bound them."

"Bound them?" Her lips curled in a sneer. "You don't actually believe this stuff."

"I suspect curses are in the eye of the beholder."

"What's that supposed to mean?"

"If you think something's cursed or bad luck, you start to attribute every bad thing that happens to the curse. You might even subconsciously start causing bad things to happen."

"So you admit it's all fake."

"I didn't say that. Lighten up. It's almost Halloween." I motioned to the black streamers draped from the corners of the room like bunting. "Haven't you ever seen something you can't explain?"

"Yeah, the way people tend to drop dead in your vicinity, and it's never your fault."

GD crept along the high shelf, his green eyes fixed on the back of Laurel's head. He hunched, ready to spring.

"GD!" I pointed at him. "Off!"

Pulling his mouth back in a snarl, he leapt to the floor, his sneak attack spoiled.

I didn't understand GD's beef with Laurel. She'd not only helped save his life once but also delighted in making mine a living hell. But there's no accounting for cats.

Glancing at GD, the detective lifted the shadowbox from the wall. "The knives are evidence."

"Seriously?"

"Do you think I'm joking?"

My shoulders slumped. Between the haunted house and Laurel's depredations, my museum exhibits were dwindling.

The cat leapt onto the haunted rocking chair and washed his paws. His green eyes glinted.

I showed Laurel out. Keeping a wary eye on GD, I finished writing Leo's paycheck and checked my watch. Only an hour had passed, but time seemed to bend when Laurel was involved.

Stretching, I walked outside, blinking in the sunshine. Mason's shop was still closed. The blinds in his upstairs apartment were open.

My hand drifted to the phone in the pocket of my jeans, but I clenched my fist and shoved it in my jacket pocket. I'd left a message. He'd call. After all, Mason had asked for space. I needed to give it to him.

Wait? Space? Had he asked for space?

Restless, I paced, my limbs tingling. I was making myself nuts thinking about Mason. What I needed was a distraction, and after Laurel's visit, playing Nancy Drew didn't seem like such a bad idea.

I drove to the Wine and Visitors Bureau and parked in the lot beside the small "educational" vineyard. Its grape leaves had faded to yellows and purples and browns. More vines twined up the Visitors Bureau itself, dried leaves rattling against the low brick walls and creeping over the peaked roof.

Inside, I walked past the wine barrel in the lobby and veered left at a placard advertising the haunted house: *Thursdays through Sundays from 7 p.m. to 11 p.m.! Sponsored by the Ladies Aid Society in cooperation with the Wine and Visitors Bureau!*

A smaller, yellow flyer advertised a yoga retreat sponsored by the San Benedetto Rebelles. San Benedetto wasn't a hotbed for

Civil War reenactors, and California had fought with the Union. Was this Mrs. Gale's splinter group? I scanned down. Yep, her name was listed as a contact at the bottom of the flyer. I tried to picture my mom at a yoga retreat, failed. No wonder she'd stuck with Ladies Aid.

The clock above the long wooden bar read ten o'clock, too early for tastings. I wound past wine barrels stacked with *Kiss My Glass* T-shirts and corkscrews and purple wine goblets. At an open office door, I rapped on the frame.

Penny looked up from her desk, her reading glasses low on her nose.

I nodded at her *Keep Calm and Drink Wine* apron. "Are you running the tastings today?"

She sighed, dropping a sheaf of papers on the desk, and tucked a lock of fuzzy gray hair behind one ear. "Our volunteer fell ill. Don't tell me there's anyone out there?"

"Nope. You're in the clear."

"Thank goodness. What can I do for you?" Her expression shifted to alarm. "You're not backing out of the haunted house? There's no way we can throw anything together in the time we've got now."

"No, I think I've got the Haunted San Benedetto exhibit under control. I just wanted to ask about our tent at the festival last weekend. Could someone have gotten into it after hours on Friday?" If Romeo's blood was on the grape press, he'd been inside that tent.

Twin lines appeared between her brows. "I don't see why anyone would. Why do you ask?"

"It seemed like someone shifted my display around after I left Friday afternoon," I lied.

"None of the volunteers would do that, I assure you! They were under strict instructions to leave your exhibits alone."

"I was thinking more of Romeo Paganini. Could he have gone inside the tent at some point?"

She shifted a stack of brochures on her desk. "He was on the festival committee, so he'd had every right to go inside any tent he wished. But I don't remember seeing him. He was busy setting up his own tent."

"He was on the committee?"

She looked down at her plump hands, folded on the desk. "Romeo was very involved in San Benedetto's wine community. He was passionate, knowledgeable, and caring. His death was a great loss."

It sounded like a prepared statement. "Could he have gotten inside the festival grounds after hours?"

She stared over her glasses at me, her lips pursed. "So it's true. You *are* investigating."

"No. No. Of course not. That would be ridiculous. But there have been some questions about my grape press, and I'm trying to figure out a timeline."

Penny canted her head and didn't say anything for a long moment. "I have the deepest respect for your mother."

"Um. So do I?" Oh, crud. There was only one reason to bring up my mother. How many people knew she and Mrs. Bigelow had asked me to investigate? Or was there another, darker reason? "Penny, about my mom—"

She rifled through the papers. "He had a key."

"Excuse me?"

"Romeo had a key to the festival grounds. As I said, he was on the committee."

So he could have gotten into the Wine and Visitors Bureau tent after hours. My stomach twisted. Had he been killed there and bled on the grape press? I tugged at the collar of my T-shirt. What were the odds the press would be attached to a murder-suicide from the 1920s and a present-day homicide? Could it really be cursed?

Coincidence. That was all. "What time on Friday night did everyone go home?"

"As you should know, we closed the festival grounds to everyone at eight o'clock sharp."

That was probably in my information packet. But since I'd finished my setup by five thirty, I hadn't paid attention to that particular deadline. "And everyone actually left? No one lingered behind?"

"Not as far as I know. We swept the area to ensure no one was accidentally locked inside like last year."

"Who was locked in last year?"

"Mrs. Featherstone. She tried to squeeze out through the fence and got stuck, and ..." She shook her head. "It was rather a disaster, though I do believe it inspired her to lose weight. Today she's in fantastic shape."

I sucked in my gut. "So someone could have hidden and stayed behind."

"I suppose so, but as I said, Romeo had a key, so he wouldn't have had any need to sneak around."

"Would he have had any reason to meet someone there after hours?"

Penny smoothed the front of her apron. "If he did, it was for personal reasons and not festival business. You see, I was on the committee as well. I'd have known."

"Did you have a key to the festival grounds?"

She colored. "I hope you don't consider me a suspect!"

"I can't imagine a reason you'd want to kill anyone."

"Romeo was the only person on the committee with a key," she said, mollified. "The head of the security team also had one, and he wore it on his person. I believe he kept it on one of those key chains that clips to your belt."

"You were on the committee with Romeo. You knew him well?"

She bobbled her head, indecisive. "Yes and no. I knew him from the committee and his work with the wine community, of course. He was a tremendous supporter of the Wine and Visitors Bureau. But aside from the occasional wine event, I didn't know him socially. He was a lovely person, you understand, but he wasn't a farmer."

And that was the divide. San Benedetto was originally populated by farmers who grew grapes and made wine. Now newcomers were trickling in—amateur vintners and wealthy retirees—a little more elegant, more refined, less earthy. But Romeo was neither amateur nor retiree. Judging by his wine, he'd been a pro.

"Why would someone have wanted to kill him?" I asked.

"I have no idea. There were rumors, of course."

I leaned my hip against the desk. "What sort of rumors?"

"That he lived up to his name. You know what men can be like."

I stiffened. Not all men were like that. Not Mason. He was a good man, and I trusted him, and I was not going to call him even if my cell phone was burning a hole in my safari jacket pocket.

"And also ..." She bit her lower lip.

"Yes?"

"I shouldn't."

"You should."

"It's all rumor."

"I live for rumors."

"Well, I've heard there's big money moving in San Benedetto."

"Big money? Like the mob?" No matter how Mafia-like Ladies Aid had become, I didn't exactly associate them with high finance.

"No, no. An international wine conglomerate, looking to invest. Our wines have always been as good as our better-known neighbors'. We've only suffered from a lack of marketing clout."

That, and the fact that San Benedetto was hot as Hades in the summer and flat as a pancake all year round. Also, when the wind blew from the south we got a heavy dose of Eau de Cow. It tended to put a damper on the bachelorette-party vineyard limo tours.

"An international corporation could put our region on the map," she continued.

"That doesn't sound like a bad thing. Why would it get Romeo killed?"

"It wouldn't, I guess. It's just ... The vintners are being very hush hush. The only reason I know anything is I overheard two of them muttering about it at a meeting."

"Who?"

"I can't remember. But I think the vintners are afraid outside investment by a conglomerate of that size will dilute the San Benedetto brand."

"Did you ask Romeo about it?"

"He would have been the last person to ask. Romeo was determined to keep the business family-owned. He'd never dilute his family's ownership with an outside investor."

"Who was the festival's head of security?"

"You know him. He's your friend's father, Roy Nakamoto."

I shuffled back a step, bumping into a stack of boxes. "Mr. Nakamoto?" Why hadn't I known that? Oh yeah, because I'd been too focused on my own booth, and Adele found security gauche.

"The festival is run by volunteers," Penny reminded me. "As the committee's head of security, Roy made sure the grounds were opened in the morning and locked up at night. He hired a professional security company to deal with safety and security issues."

"Was he the only person who had keys to the grounds?"

"I really have no idea what the arrangements were. We trusted him to manage things."

"Who else was on the festival committee?"

She rattled off a list of names, mainly vineyard owners.

I dutifully noted them down. "Well, if you think of anything—"

"I'll let you know."

I left the Visitors Bureau. In the parking lot, I stopped beside the entrance to the educational vineyard and checked my phone.

Mason hadn't called, and I checked for a signal. All five bars were glowing. My phone was working fine.

The grape leaves rustled in the still air.

Scalp prickling, I looked up. I was alone.

My phone rang and I fumbled, catching it before it could hit the pavement. Breathless, I put it to my ear. "Hello?"

"Maddie? I'm at CW Vineyards. Where are you?" Dieter's voice crackled, irate.

I checked my watch. I wasn't late. What had put him in such a mood? "I'm at the Visitors Bureau, just a few minutes away."

"Well, hurry up, will you?" His voice lowered to a whisper. "The Blue Shirts are killing my Zen."

———

I pulled up beside Dieter's rusty blue pickup. Its bed was filled with tool boxes and ladders, ropes and saw horses. For a moment I simply sat and gazed at the two-story Gothic tasting room. A tabby cat looked up from its spot on the porch and stared back. What would it would be like to live in a home with that much space? Delightful, I guessed, until it came time to clean.

Making a pack mule of myself, I slung my messenger bag over one shoulder, the rope over the other, and hauled the box of creepy dolls from the back of my truck. Across the lawn, the barn door stood open. A curtain fluttered in the Gothic cottage beside it.

I trudged up the steps of the tasting room, nudging the door open with my hip. To the left of the stairs, a new wooden divider hung from the ceiling, splitting the tasting area in two. Yellow arrows taped on the hardwood floor directed people from the stairs through the gap and into the Haunted San Benedetto room. Another arrow directed people from the room, through the gap by the front door.

Inside "my" room, black plastic tablecloths covered the high round tables. A cheap-looking TV sat on a table against one wall. Around it clustered three naked female mannequins.

Something thunked behind me. I jumped, whirling.

Grinning, Dieter brushed his hands on his paint-spattered overalls. The stains matched those on his white T-shirt. A hole near the shoulder exposed his bronzed skin. "Scare you?"

"Did you...? How did you...?" I looked around, up. The only possible place Dieter could have come from was the loft ten feet above us, stacked with wine barrels.

"I've been practicing Parkour." He flexed a bronzed arm. "Pretty cool, eh? I am one with my environment."

"You jumped off the balcony?! Are you trying to kill yourself? I've already had one dead body to deal with. If you break your neck in my haunted room, the police will arrest me for sure."

"So what's with the naked ladies?" He jerked his head of spiky brown hair at the mannequins.

"They're ghost hunters. I've got clothing for them in the back of the truck."

"Mmm. Dress-up. I'll help." He zipped out the door. Laying my things on the hardwood floor, I followed him outside. He hopped into my truck bed and grabbed a stuffed plastic garbage bag. "This it?"

"Yeah. Have you seen Leo or my mother?" I didn't trust my tech skills with the TV setup.

"I saw your mom at her house this morning. She sent me over here with the mannequins. Your Goth kid was here when I got here. He arranged them."

"He's not Goth," I said. "He just likes to wear black."

"Whatever. I haven't seen him lately. He's probably hiding from the Blue Shirts." He dropped to the ground. "I thought I was free of this nightmare, and then I was ordered back because someone"—he glared at me—"had the bright idea of rigging the wine barrels in the loft to look like they're falling."

"That wasn't my idea. The way those barrels are jammed up against the banister, I just wanted to make sure they *don't* fall. And why don't you just say no?"

"To Ladies Aid? Are you kidding? I get more than half my work from their members."

"Coward."

He flashed his teeth. "I've got to admit, the falling barrels are going to be cool. I'm rigging a cable and pulley system ... "

I stopped paying attention and reached inside the truck for a section of picket fence. Dieter's explanation would make no sense to me, and I had enough information battling for space in my brain.

Nodding and making encouraging sounds at breaks in his mono-
logue, I followed him inside.

"It's going to be awesome," he said. "Kids will leave damp spots
on the floor."

"You're amazing, Dieter. I also need to hang a noose over the
balcony. Since you're headed up there, can you find a good spot for
it?" I tossed him the rope.

"How low do you want the noose to hang?"

"Low enough for people to notice, but too high for them to get
tangled in it or swing from. Er, do you know how to make a hang-
man's noose?"

"Doesn't everybody?" He dashed up the stairs. A few moments
later he squeezed between the stacked wine barrels in the loft and
dangled one end of the rope over the banister. "This high?"

"Higher."

"This high?"

"A little lower."

"This high?"

"Perfect." We were back where we'd started, but if I didn't order
him around a bit, he'd think I didn't care.

Returning to my truck, I grabbed more picket fencing and hefted
it inside. A noose swayed eerily from the loft railing.

Dieter bounded down the stairs and admired his handiwork,
hands on his lean hips. "What do you think?"

"Very authentic." I pulled ghost hunting equipment from my
messenger bag and laid the electronics on the table beside the TV.

"What's this?" Dieter picked up a squat, cylindrical device with
colored lights and an antenna sticking from the top.

"A REM-Pod. It picks up electromagnetic signals." Which meant the nearby TV would send it into overdrive. But the flashing lights and random screeching noises it made should startle the guests.

He squinted at it. "Portable."

"That's kind of the point."

"I mean, someone might steal it."

"Oh." And it wasn't cheap, either.

"Let me think about it," Dieter said. "I might be able to rig something to clamp it to the table without damaging it."

"Thanks. Have you figured out how to make the shadow thing?"

He tossed his head. "You mean the shadow of a body swinging from your noose? That's easy. It's fixing the front gate that's making me crazy."

"What's wrong with the front gate?"

"Chuck needed to replace it at the last minute, but the new gate doesn't fit right, and the guys who installed it messed up the hinges. So how's the murder investigation going?"

"Ask the police."

"I don't care about their investigation. I want to know what Mad Dog thinks."

"I'm not..." I hated that nickname! Suspicion tickled my spine and I crossed my arms. "Wait a minute. Why do you want to know?"

"Just curious."

"Why? Have you got odds on me solving it?" I joked.

"If I did—and I'm not saying I do—you couldn't place a bet on yourself. Conflict of interest. It's why they threw Pete Rose out of baseball."

I lowered my brows, unsure if he was ribbing me or not. "You're a paragon of virtue."

"So, seriously, how's it going?"

149

"If I were investigating—and I'm not saying I am—the field of suspects is limited. You know anything I should know?"

"I couldn't interfere."

"Right. Conflict of interest." I glanced out the window.

Leo stormed out of the cottage by the barn, jaw set, dark hair mussed.

Jocelyn trotted after him, waving her arms.

He stopped, turned, and said something, his neck corded.

She stepped back, one hand to her chest.

I wavered at the window, torn between rescue and discretion.

Chuck Wollmer stepped from the cottage and shouted something.

Leo needed a rescue. "Be right back," I said to Dieter.

I walked onto the porch and waved. "Leo! Great job in here! Thanks!"

Leo swiveled. He stared, then stalked toward me.

Chuck strolled to Jocelyn and laid a hand on her shoulder.

She shook her head. "I can't! Not now!" She hurried across the lawn, plunging into rows of yellowing grapevines.

Breathing hard, Leo leapt up the porch steps. "The tablecloths are what you wanted? I kept the receipt."

"Great." I eyed Chuck.

He eyed me right back, stroked his beard, and disappeared into the barn.

"And I'll need that receipt," I said. "How's the video of the museum at night coming?"

"It's done," he said. "Want to see?"

I followed him behind the divider into the Haunted San Benedetto room. Dieter had vanished, I presumed to do more work on the not-falling wine barrels.

150

Footsteps clattered down the stairs. Chattering women passed by on the other side of the divider, and the screen door slammed. I imagined Dieter crouching behind a barrel, hiding from the Ladies Aid Blue Shirts.

Leo showed me the video setup. The darkened museum, tinted green, flickered into view on the computer screen.

"Cool," I said.

"I'm doing a five-minute video loop of those orbs from last month."

"That'll be perfect." Ghost hunters believed orbs were ghostly apparitions. Rational Maddie said they were just dust molecules catching the light. But they could move in unexpected ways that made irrational Maddie wonder. In spite of the Paranormal Museum's cheerful, haunted ice-cream parlor appearance, it had a weird aura. And there were times, alone in the museum at night, when the hair lifted on the back of my neck and I wondered if I really was alone.

Leo checked his phone. "Hey, I've got to go. Will you be okay?"

"Sure. We're nearly done." All I had to do was dress the mannequins, arrange the creepy dolls, put out the photo and sign card for the McBride exhibit, and set up the invisible, cursed, and haunted grape press. I eyed the fragments of picket fence on the hardwood floor. Dieter had put it together the first time. I had taken it apart. How hard could it be to reassemble?

Thirty minutes later, I sucked my throbbing thumb and glared at the fence's metal locking mechanisms. The pickets were not cooperating. I drew a deep breath, and some of the pain faded from my thumb. At least it wasn't bleeding. I wasn't sure when I'd gotten my last tetanus shot.

The front screen door slammed. Someone ran behind the divider and pounded up the steps.

I knelt beside the fence. Dieter had built it to snap into place. I could figure this out. Two of the sides had already locked together. Picking up a third, I inserted the metal hinge into the opposite doodad. Sides one and two separated, clattering to the floor.

"Dammit," I muttered.

Something creaked in the loft above me.

I could keep fighting the fence, or I could swallow my pride and ask Dieter for help. "Dieter?" Craning my neck, I walked closer to the loft.

Two of the wine barrels above me quivered.

One corner of my mouth quirked upward. He'd gotten his not-falling wine barrels rigged after all. The top barrel toppled toward the banister.

"Nice—" The barrel tumbled over the railing, plummeted toward me.

Time slowed. My vision telescoped, taking in the knots in the wood, the tarnished metal bands.

I dove sideways.

The barrel crashed to the floor. There was a second bang, and pain arced through my foot.

I shrieked, loosing a baker's dozen of curses. Grabbing my foot, I rolled on the floor, eyes watering, my toes a line of fire. "DIETER!"

Footsteps thundered on the front porch. The screen door banged open and Dieter raced through the entry to my horrible, haunted room.

He took in the splintered barrel and his eyes widened. "Holy crap! What happened?"

"Your barrel rigging failed. You should have warned me you were testing it."

"I never rigged it!" He knelt beside me. "Are you hurt?"

I bit back tears. "It landed on my foot."

"You're lucky it was empty. You could have been badly hurt."

"I am badly hurt." I winced. "My foot. Ow, ow, ow."

Silver- and gray-haired women in blue shirts poured down the stairs. They clustered around me, exclaiming like a flock of startled birds.

"Did any of you go into the loft?" Dieter asked.

They all denied it.

The crowd parted, falling silent, and the president of Ladies Aid stepped forward.

Mrs. Bigelow fixing me with a freezing look. "What. Did. You. Do?"

TWELVE

I SAT ON THE tailgate of my pickup, one shoe off, my feet dangling. My toes were still attached, swollen, a Pinot color.

Gently, Dieter pressed an ice pack beneath them.

I hissed, jerking my foot away.

"I think you've got some breakage, babe." Whipping a rag from his back pocket, he wrapped it around the pack and tried again.

I sighed. *Cold good.* "I'm fine. The barrel hit me on the bounce." My foot throbbed, but the ice pack eased the pain.

He shook his head, his expression doubtful.

I growled low in my throat. "Why did that barrel fall?"

"Mad, it wasn't my fault. I didn't touch the barrels when I was in the loft, and I hadn't even started putting together the rigging."

Chuck strode out of the tasting room, deep in conversation with Mrs. Bigelow.

Dieter shot me a pleading look. "Please, Maddie. It wasn't me. You know I'm safety conscious."

"Says the guy who thinks jumping off a balcony is a good idea." But my anger subsided. Even if it was his fault, it hadn't been intentional. Dieter was careful.

"Mad, there's no way that barrel could have just fallen over. I was in the loft earlier, and I checked to make sure everything up there was stable. Barring an earthquake, they shouldn't have moved."

Chuck and Mrs. Bigelow stalked toward us, her pewter hair gleaming in the sunlight.

"What are you saying?" I whispered.

"I'm saying that was no accident."

"We have insurance, of course," Bigelow bellowed. "However, I'm not sure it covers our volunteers before the haunted house opens."

"Forget the insurance," Chuck said. "If she needs to go to the hospital—"

"For a broken toe?" Bigelow snorted. "All they can do is tape it to the toe beside it."

"How are you feeling?" Chuck asked me, stroking his beard.

"I'll live."

"Maybe you should get x-rays," Dieter said.

Mrs. Bigelow glared.

Dieter looked at me and made a face, his shoulders caving inward.

"I'll give it a day," I said. Our family had always been of the only-go-to-the-doctor-if-it-might-be-fatal school of philosophy. Leaning back, I stared at a puffy, white cloud. Oh, God, that ice pack felt good.

Chuck's handlebar moustache twitched. "How do you think it happened?"

"I thought I heard someone in the loft," I said. "Maybe they accidentally bumped a barrel." I wanted to believe it—that someone made a mistake and wasn't willing to own up to it. But could it have been intentional? I had a hard time believing anyone took my inept investigation seriously enough to want to silence me.

Bigelow's eyes flashed. "None of my volunteers were in that loft. I gave them strict instructions to avoid that space. The only person with reason to be there was Mr. Finkielkraut."

Dieter yelped in protest.

"Dieter was outside when the barrel fell," I said.

A man drifted from the barn. Tall. Dark. Vampiric. Not sparkling. "What's he doing here?" I asked.

"Who?" Mrs. Bigelow turned to follow my gaze. "It's not our business to question Mr. Wollmer's guests."

Chuck straightened, frowning. "Excuse me." He walked toward the mystery man.

Seriously, who *was* that guy? Had he flown up to the loft to drop a wine barrel on me? With his vampiric super strength, it would have been easy. I knew it wasn't nice to blame a stranger for the town's problems, but it was so easy, especially if he was a supernatural ghoul in disguise.

Dieter snapped his fingers in front of my face. "Earth to Maddie. You sure you didn't get hit on the head?"

"Of course she didn't get hit on the head," Mrs. Bigelow said.

"I want to go home." I blinked. I hadn't planned on saying that aloud.

"Then go," she said. "You have until Thursday afternoon to finish your display."

Except I didn't. Today was my last day off for the week. "Maybe Leo can finish up." I looked around and realized my phone was in the Haunted San Benedetto room with my messenger bag. "Dieter, can you grab my bag for me? I need to call Leo."

"Why?" Mrs. Bigelow asked. "He's lurking about somewhere. I saw him near the barn five minutes ago."

"Are you sure?" I asked.

"Of course I'm sure."

Huh. I'd thought he left. "I still need my phone. I'm not exactly mobile."

"I'll get your bag." Handing me the ice pack, Dieter loped toward the tasting room.

Bigelow shook her head. "I hope you're more effective with your investigation than you are with your decorating. I will have words with your mother."

I thought that Haunted San Benedetto was coming along pretty well. I just needed to dress the mannequins, set out the creepy dolls, display the materials for the hanging murder … And I was sure there was something I'd forgotten. I needed my list. "Where *is* my mother? I thought she'd be here." And it shamed me to admit it, but right then I wouldn't have minded some motherly TLC.

"She's not working this event."

"What? But she's always worked the haunted house."

Mrs. Bigelow thrust her shoulders back. "It was simply too close to the Harvest Festival for her to effectively manage both." Swiveling on her sensible heel, she marched into the tasting room.

Angry heat pulsed in my toes. Bending, I touched the ice pack to the top of my foot.

Dieter ran down the porch steps and across the lawn. He handed me my messenger bag. "I'll be right back." He raced back and disappeared inside. The screen door banged behind him.

Gingerly, I slid off the tailgate and put weight on my foot. A dull throb arced up my leg, and my jaw clenched. I limped in a circle, testing my weight.

Although it would be a godsend if Leo was still around to help Dieter, I scratched my cheek with the damp ice pack, uneasy at the idea. When you find a body in a grape vat, it's hard not to be paranoid. If Leo was still on the grounds, it meant he'd had the opportunity to tip the barrel.

I frowned down at my swollen foot. No. No way. I could see him losing his temper, hurting someone in a fit of anger. But I couldn't picture him plotting a murder, sneaking up the stairway, watching and waiting until I was in the right position.

Leo hadn't done this.

I called him.

He picked up on the third ring. "What's up?"

"Is there any chance you can come back here? I've had a minor accident and need some help finishing the job."

There was a pause. "Sure. I'll be there as soon as I can."

Had I imagined that hesitation? "Where—"

He hung up.

I exhaled sharply and regarded my sock and sneaker lying on the open tailgate. The thought of jamming my foot into either did not appeal. Slinging my messenger bag over one shoulder, I hobbled across the gravel drive and up the porch steps into the tasting room.

The fallen barrel lay on its side, against the makeshift wooden divider. A table had been overturned, and I righted it, adjusting the black cloth. The picket fence pieces rested where I'd left them on the floor. I'd leave the fence to Leo and Dieter.

I pulled the creepy dolls from the cardboard box and arranged them on two round tables.

The screen door banged, and Leo strolled through the divider and into the room.

"Hey. What's going on?"

I nodded to the barrel. "It fell from the landing, hit my foot."

"For real?" His brown eyes widened, and he yanked up his sagging black jeans. "Are you okay?"

"Yeah, but I'm limping. Can you help me? I just want to finish up and go home."

"Yeah, sure."

Together, we disassembled and clothed the mannequins. I arranged the brochures, signage, and haunted photos, and Leo snapped the fence into place. I hung my *Invisible Haunted Grape Press* sign from one of the pickets.

I sat on the overturned wine barrel, my injured foot extended. "Thanks for returning, Leo. I hope I didn't mess up your plans."

"Nah." He checked his watch. "It's okay, but if we're done, I've gotta motor."

I looked around. With sunlight streaming through its wide windows, the room didn't feel spooky. I imagined it at night, lightning flashing and the greenish video flickering. It would work. "We're good. I'll see you Thursday."

He nodded and jogged out.

My stomach rumbled, and my foot throbbed in response—which was a weird response but beyond my control. Digging my cell phone out of my bag, I called Harper.

"Harper Caldarelli."

"It's me. You doing anything for lunch?"

She hesitated. "Did something happen?"

"I'm not sure." I gazed at the loft, thoughtful.

Someone rattled down the stairs and Dieter bounded into the room. "Hey, Mad—"

I pointed to the phone. He pointed to the wine barrel. I got up, leaning on my good leg, while he hefted the barrel onto his shoulder.

"Can you come by my office?" Harper asked.

"I'll be there in fifteen minutes," I said.

"See ya." She hung up.

Dieter shifted his weight. "I really don't see how that barrel came down by itself," he said in a low voice. "They're all stacked in tight rows, but the barrel beneath the one that fell is out of place."

"Maybe that's why the top barrel fell."

"Or maybe someone nudged the barrels and doesn't want to admit it."

The skin on the back of my neck crawled. "You think a volunteer went back there for some reason?"

"I don't know why they would. Like Bigelow said, they're all busy with their own rooms upstairs. The only person with any reason to go in that loft is me, and maybe Chuck since he owns the place."

"Dieter, if you were taking odds on me solving the murder—and I'm not saying you are—how many people might have already placed bets?"

"Lots." He swallowed, his Adam's apple bobbing.

My eyes narrowed. Uh oh. There really was a bet on me. "Define 'lots.'"

"The usual gamblers. You're sort of the new Christmas Cow."

"Dieter!" My fingers curled. If I was faster on my feet, I'd have lunged for his throat.

"I mean, as an interesting local bet."

"Who?"

"Some of the Ladies Aid husbands, and husbands from the splinter group as well." His chin dipped toward his broad chest. "If I've put you in the killer's crosshairs, I'll never forgive myself."

I scrubbed my face with my hands. "So basically everybody in San Benedetto but the cops and the kids know about my so-called investigation."

Dieter straightened, indignant. "Of course not the kids. You have to be twenty-one to gamble." He grimaced. "And Maddie..."

I scowled at him.

"Your mother's down for fifty."

———

Harper's office was on the first floor of a 1960s-era building. Minus a shoe, I limped into the receptionist's room. A small fountain trickled beside a bamboo plant on a high counter.

Harper's secretary, Sal, stood behind the reception desk and stared at the closed door to Harper's office. The furrows in her lined face deepened, thick makeup caking the creases.

"Hi, Sal. I'm here to see Harper."

Wrenching her gaze from the polished wood door, Sal bit her full lip. "Um. Sorry. What?"

Harper's secretary might look like a cuddly blond grandma, but she had a mind like a steel trap. It wasn't like her to space out. "I'm here to have lunch with Harper," I said. "Is everything okay?"

"I'm not sure." Bracing her elbows on the counter, Sal dropped her voice to a whisper. "The police are here."

"One of Harper's clients died recently. Maybe they're looking for his financial information."

"I know, Romeo Paganini. I can't believe someone killed him. Such a handsome man. We were getting things together for his wife, and then—"

The office door opened and Harper walked out, her expression grim, her dark hair bound up in a bun. She walked to the reception desk, her heels clacking on the hardwood floor. Her charcoal-colored shoes matched her pinstriped pantsuit. "Sal, can you pull Mr. Paganini's files, please?"

Laurel and Detective Slate followed her into the reception area. Next to Harper, they looked shabby in spite of their navy business suits. My two best friends were fashion plates, and Harper's outfit had that too-expensive-for-you vibe.

Slate nodded to me. "Miss Kosloski."

"Hi." I leaned against the counter and tucked my shoeless foot behind the other, hoping he wouldn't notice.

"What happened to your foot?" His gaze met mine.

Harper leaned across the counter and held a low conversation with her receptionist.

"I think I might have broken a toe," I said. "Once I got the shoe off, I couldn't put it back on again."

Sal hustled into a back room.

"Too bad," Laurel said, unsympathetic.

"Well, if you're up for it," Slate said, "could you come by and take that grape press off our hands?"

"Off your hands? Yes!" I straightened, bumping my toe on the floor. Pain rocketed up my leg. I gritted my teeth and swallowed hard. "Does that mean it's not evidence? I thought there were blood stains."

He snorted. "Yeah, and they're decades old. They've got nothing to do with what happened at the festival last weekend."

"That's great news. Decades old? Did you do an analysis on the blood?"

"Not personally."

"How old were the stains?"

"Too old for us to figure out much more. I can tell you that the blood was human, from both a male and a female. We weren't able to pick up a blood type or DNA. It was too contaminated after all this time. So can you get the press? People are complaining."

Male and female? That would jibe with the murder-suicide story, even if the police hadn't been able to nail down the age of the bloodstains. "I'll pick it up as soon as I can." My ribs squeezed. "Wait, what did you mean, people are complaining?"

He motioned, dismissive. "Word got out it's cursed. Now the department's imagining everything from oppressive atmospheres to evil whispers. It's ridiculous, I know. But I'd rather get it out of the station so they can focus on police work."

"Evil whispers? What sorts of evil whispers?"

"Forget it," he said. "Cops are a superstitious bunch."

"That makes sense." Harper stared at a watercolor landscape on the wall. "Cops tend to be more psychically aware."

"Excuse me?" Laurel asked.

Harper's olive skin blushed rose. "I misspoke. I just mean they have to be more aware of their surroundings."

Laurel crossed her arms over her blue blazer. "You're right, we do. And we're pretty good at sensing when someone isn't telling us the whole truth."

"I've told you everything I know," Harper said. "Mr. Paganini didn't tell me he was moving his account. I only found out about the transfer when you informed me. It must have been a recent decision, because the paperwork hasn't made its way through the system."

"He must have been dissatisfied with something you did," Laurel said. "Or didn't do."

Harper's lips thinned. "Apparently. At heart, he was a conservative investor, and we worked together to create a conservative investment plan. That plan's remained on track. Are you sure he was moving it and not just opening a second account with a different advisor? That's one way people like to diversify their risk."

"We're sure," Detective Slate said. "It may be nothing, but we had to ask."

They were playing good cop bad cop! I hoped Harper didn't fall for their ploy. She was a good advisor and she cared about her clients. She'd never act against their best interests.

Sal emerged from the back room, a thick file in hand. She moved to hand it to Harper but Laurel intercepted her, grabbing the file.

"If we have any questions," Laurel said, "we'll call."

Harper nodded, and we watched in silence as the cops made their way out the door.

"I don't think they're going to find anything in there," Sal said.

Harper bit her lower lip.

"Harper?" I asked.

"Let's get some lunch." She disappeared into her office and reemerged moments later, a shiny gray purse slung over her shoulder. "We'll be back in an hour, Sal." She strode out the door.

I hopped after her. "Uh, Harper? Can you slow up?"

She turned onto the brick sidewalk, her brow wrinkling, and looked down. "What happened to your foot?"

"You really were out of it in there. An empty wine barrel dropped on my foot, and I couldn't get my shoe back on."

"That looks bad. Have you seen a doctor?"

"Not yet. I think it's just a broken toe."

Harper pointed to a green-painted bench on a wide strip of grass. "Sit. There's a taco truck not far from here. I'll grab us some burritos so you don't have to move."

I sagged. "Would you?"

"Put your hand on my shoulder if you need to."

I didn't, walking on my heel behind her. Lowering myself to the bench, I breathed a sigh.

"Veggie burrito, refried beans, hot salsa and everything on it?" she asked.

I nodded.

She strode down the street, disappearing around a corner.

I leaned against the bench, enjoying the warmth of the sun on my face and the people-watching. A woman bumped a stroller across a crack in the sidewalk. An elderly woman walked a Scottie dog, stopping at every lamppost. A young couple ambled past, holding hands.

My heart pinched, and I checked my phone. Nothing from Mason. Should I call him? No. He said he'd call, and I didn't want to act as worried as I was starting to feel.

A shadow fell across me, and I looked up. The woman from the Death Bistro stood in front of the bench, her blue eyes crinkled in a frown. A coil of reddish-blond hair fell from her loose bun, trailing against her neck. A cameo pulled tight the high collar of her gray, puff-sleeved blouse. Her long black skirt and boots seemed to absorb the sunlight.

Augh, what was her name again? Elvira? Elmira? Elthia! "Hi, Elthia," I said, proud I'd recalled her name.

"I'm glad I caught you. I was at the museum, but it's closed," she said accusingly.

"We're closed every Monday and Tuesday."

"But our Bistro is on Thursday!"

My shoulders tightened. "I'm sure Adele has your tea well in hand."

"It's not the tea I'm worried about, it's the space. It might be a larger crowd than expected after ... after Romeo ..." Her eyes welled with tears. She pulled a delicate handkerchief from her sleeve and dabbed beneath her nose.

"I'm meeting with his wife tonight. Should I ask if she or any of their mutual friends are planning to attend?"

"Jocelyn? She won't come. She never understood the Bistro or Romeo's passion for wine making. To her, it was just a business."

Jocelyn had admitted as much to me, and I nodded. "And you? Are you a fellow wino?"

"Guilty." She smiled. "My family owns a tiny winery. Duck Ridge?"

I nodded. I'd heard of it.

"Well, I'm no vintner. I chose to be an artist instead. But I understood the mindset." She smiled, reminiscent. "My father's got the wine bug."

"Should I invite Jocelyn?"

Elthia's delicate nostrils flared. "Under the circumstances, I don't think it would be appropriate, do you? She *is* a suspect in his murder."

"Are you certain?"

"She hated him!" Elthia bit her bottom lip, her cheeks pinking, and I wondered if she and Romeo been more than friends.

Wiping the back of her crooked index finger beneath her eye, Elthia sniffed. "I shouldn't have said that. Sorry."

"But you must have some reason to think it. Why did she hate him?"

"Everyone knew she wanted children, and he didn't." Elthia's brows pulled down. "After Leo, one was enough for him."

"A divorce would have been easier than murder," I said.

Her face tightened. "And give up all that money? Besides, Jocelyn's biological clock is closing in on its sell-by date. Unless she's got someone on a string, it'll soon be too late for her."

Leo had lost his father. Jocelyn wanted a child. The answer seemed obvious to me, but from what I'd seen of those two, they wouldn't be turning to each other for comfort any time soon.

"It wouldn't surprise me if she was trying outside her marriage," Elthia said. "If you know what I mean."

"Cheating on Romeo?" I'd sensed a strange undercurrent between Jocelyn and Chuck. Had I imagined it?

Lips pursed, Elthia unclasped a pocket watch dangling from her belt. "I'm sorry. This is … Thinking about Romeo's murder is bringing out the worst in me. I've said things I shouldn't. Look, I've got some time now. We can go over the layout for my tea at the museum."

Harper strode down the sidewalk, a large white paper bag in one hand, a carrier box with two sodas in the other. I nodded toward her. "Sorry. I'm meeting a friend for lunch."

Elthia smiled and waved at Harper.

I canted my head. They knew each other?

Smiling, Harper walked across the grass. "Elthia! How are you?"

"Do you want me to be polite or tell you the truth?" Elthia barked a harsh laugh. "You know about Romeo?"

"Yes," Harper said. "I'm so sorry for your loss."

"You've heard that we've shifted the Death Bistro to the Paranormal Museum?"

"I got the email," Harper said. "I'll be there."

"Great. So when can we go over the site?" Elthia asked me.

"Anytime tomorrow," I said. "I'll be at the museum all day."

Elthia nodded. "I'll stop by in the morning. Bye Harper, Maddie." She strode down the brick sidewalk. A foil wrapper drifted across her path and she bent, picking it up. She dropped it in a nearby wastebasket.

I eyed Harper. "You're a member of the Death Bistro?"

She reached into the sack and handed me a foil-wrapped burrito. "For the last four months now."

"You do realize Adele went bonkers when she found out she was playing host to the Bistro of Death."

"Um, yeah."

"You didn't recommend them to Adele's tea room, did you?"

She winced. "I might have suggested it. I didn't think Adele was going to react that way."

"Oh, boy. She's going to find out, and when she does—"

Harper blew out a noisy breath. "It's good money. I thought I was doing her a favor! Believe it or not, the Death Bistro members are big spenders. Besides, Adele's tea room is next door to a Paranormal Museum. She needs to lighten up."

"But the skull and crossbones!"

"I know." She groaned. "I'd totally forgotten about our new logo. But I don't think anyone will see that flyer and assume Adele is serving up poisons."

"Adele's going to think you manipulated her into playing hostess."

"I didn't mean to, I swear." Harper sat down beside me, her expression shifting. "Sometimes I wish I had the skill to manipulate people. My clients can have a tough time discussing money, making financial decisions. The answers seem obvious to me, but getting them to believe they need to change is an exercise in psychology."

"Are you talking about Romeo now?"

"I didn't say that," she said quickly.

"I saw your face when Sal said the police wouldn't find anything in that file. What gives?"

"You know I can't tell you," she said. "I didn't even tell the cops. Though I admit that's because Laurel was so nasty. I'd rather they read it for themselves."

"Read what?"

She shook her head. "Sorry, Mad. Client confidentiality."

"Your client is dead."

"But his son and widow aren't, and what's in that file affects them."

"Fair enough." When it came to financial planning, Harper was a straight arrow. If she'd decided not to tell me, her lips were sealed.

Adele could be outrageous and self-centered, but I somehow felt closer to her than to the milder, more sensible Harper. Had I put this distance between us, or had Harper? I knew about Harper's secret life as an Italian-style witch, but it still felt as if she was holding back, keeping a part of herself separate. And that was her right.

She handed me the soda, put the sack on the bench, and rubbed her hands together. Her eyes glinted like emeralds. "Now let's do some Reiki on that toe." She put my foot in her lap and raised her hands above it.

"You know," I said, "if you need to talk about anything witch-related, I'm interested."

She raised a brow, skeptical.

"I do run a paranormal museum," I said. "I've even researched stregas."

She closed her eyes. "My mother was a strega. I'm not sure what I am."

"I thought you were following in her footsteps?"

"I tried, but the old ways just seem superstitious. They don't fit me. I've been figuring out my own path."

"How?"

"Dreams, intuition, experimentation."

"Why don't you tell Adele about your witchy background?"

Her eyes flew open. "No."

"She wouldn't judge you."

"Probably not, but I'm trying to keep that life separate. If my other side became public, my financial practice would be ruined."

"I understand keeping it a secret from your financial planning clients. But isn't it hard to keep it from friends?"

"Keeping this hidden is about the hardest thing I've ever done. But I don't know how I can tell Adele now. Secrets and lies are like spider webs. The more you struggle, the tighter they knot."

THIRTEEN

San Benedetto slumbered at the dark end of a dusty twilight. I drove, my truck's headlights casting long shadows, grapevines flaring into existence and vanishing behind me.

Mason hadn't called. The thought he might be avoiding me sickened my stomach. But if he was avoiding me, why had he said he loved me?

In the distance, low mountains turned to cobalt waves. They rolled toward me, a tidal wave threatening to crush the town.

I pressed the brake, slowing at an intersection, and my toe throbbed.

Either my toe wasn't broken or there was something to that Reiki business, because I was wearing both my sneakers again. For my meeting with Romeo's widow, I'd changed out of my jeans and T-shirt into a pair of nicer jeans and a silky, cream-colored blouse. But my swollen toe put heels off limits, especially for a meeting with a potential murderess. I didn't get the sense Jocelyn was a killer, but the spouse was always the prime suspect for a reason. Just in case, I wanted to be able to at least attempt to run.

My headlights swept across a sign for Trivia Vineyards. I turned down a long gravel driveway, passing too close beneath an oak. Its branches scraped the top of my truck. Wincing, I veered left and paid more attention to the bumpy road.

It sounded like Jocelyn controlled Leo's money. If she was a solid, intelligent person, putting her in charge of Leo's finances had been a smart idea. Harper had told me too many horror stories of people who'd blown through their windfalls within a year, too inexperienced to manage the sudden wealth. Leo was only nineteen. But if this was the case, it also gave her an even bigger motive for murder—she would get her own share of Romeo's estate plus a controlling interest over Leo's.

Tuscan cypresses spiked the roadside, leading to a castle worthy of the Borgias. Lit with spotlights, its crenellated battlements of honey-colored stone gleamed like teeth. I let my pickup drift to a halt beside a turret. I'd been in the winery before, but never inside the main house. I wasn't sure where on the property Jocelyn lived.

A banner fluttered above a closed drawbridge. Short of using a battering ram and/or grappling hooks, I wasn't getting in through that entrance. I edged the truck forward, searching for a secondary driveway that would lead to the house. Had I missed it in the darkness? Driving in a slow circle around the empty parking lot, I noticed a glow of light from the side of the castle and edged closer. A set of steps led up to a smaller, open door. Light flooded from within, illuminating a raised path and a mailbox was set into the wall.

Of course Jocelyn lived inside the castle. If I had a castle, I'd live in it too. In fact, I had a full-on case of castle envy.

I needed to get out of my aunt's garage apartment.

And into Mason's?

I shook my head. Where had that come from? The idea wasn't totally out there, but under the circumstances... I wasn't even sure what the circumstances were, and that was the problem. Maybe it was time I swallowed my pride and tried calling again?

I checked my watch. It was after seven-thirty, and I was late for my meeting with Jocelyn. I'd call him afterward.

Sliding from the truck, I landed on my good foot and tested the ground with my other. My foot felt tender, but I could walk on it with only a slight limp.

A gust of wind tossed my hair. I shivered, tightening my safari jacket, feeling exposed. My footsteps crunched, loud on the loose gravel, silencing the chirps of nearby crickets. I'd spent plenty of time in rural areas, so I was comfortable with dark and quiet. But my scalp prickled.

Scanning the battlements for ghouls and hidden archers, I hobbled across the drive. A walkway made of that same honey-colored stone and lined with geraniums in terra-cotta pots led to steps and an arched door. Tarnished nail heads studded its wooden beams. Suddenly I wanted to be behind its protective weight.

The door stood ajar. A stream of cool air flowed outside, lifting the hair on my neck. Through the crack, a red tile floor; high, arched ceilings; oriental rugs; a leather couch. A soft-looking throw lay draped across the couch's back. Someone had set a low coffee table with two empty wine glasses, a bottle, and a plate of something sugary piled high.

The skin between my shoulder blades heated, and I glanced behind me. Nothing moved in the darkened vineyard.

I shrugged. Letting the AC escape seemed foolish, but Jocelyn had probably left the door open so I'd find her more easily. With a home like this, I doubted she was too concerned about electric bills.

I rapped on the door, nudging it open. "Jocelyn?"

A wall of silence descended.

Edging backward, I found a doorbell, pressed it. A chime echoed, and I waited. She knew I was coming. I was even on the fashionably late side.

Something fluttered in the darkness above me. A bat.

"Gagh!" Flapping my hands above my head, I darted inside and slammed the door. Bats eat mosquitoes, so are useful flying rodents. But I didn't want one tangled in my hair. In fact, this whole setup seemed less like a charming Tuscan villa and more along the lines of Castle Dracula. Who built a castle in flat-as-a-tabletop farm country?

Swallowing, I edged farther inside. "Jocelyn? It's me, Maddie Kosloski!"

I stopped at the low table in front of the couch. Squares of lemon bars stacked, pyramid-style, on a platter. Paired with a ... I lifted the cold wine bottle, beaded with sweat: a dry, bubbly Prosecco. Good pairing.

I returned the bottle to the table and it clunked on the mahogany. "Sorry," I said to no one, wincing. She'd obviously been waiting for me and must have popped into a back room. I was creeping myself out for nothing. Just because I'd found one dead body in a grape vat, and the door was open, and the house appeared deserted, didn't mean that Jocelyn was lying in a bloody heap somewhere. Like behind the couch.

I checked behind the leather couch.

No body.

A strange, Peter Lorre giggle issued from my throat and I clapped my hands over my mouth. Now who was being outré?

The air conditioner hummed. On one wall, picture windows glinted black against the night. A bookcase filled another wall. A wide entry cut through it and led into a larger room with cream-colored couches, soft chairs, a massive stone fireplace. A fire crackled, drawing me forward. Jocelyn was burning a fire while running the AC? The rich really did live differently.

The castle's interior looked modern and luxurious, not haunted. But that unnaturally chilled air gave it an eerie atmosphere.

I dragged my palms down the legs of my jeans. Yeah. That was why my heart pounded and my palms had grown moist. The cool air. Not the fact that I was alone in a cavernous castle, my hostess nowhere in sight.

And besides, the castle was too new to be haunted. Romeo had built it when he bought the vineyard. I knew this because neighbors tend to take note when a castle rises outside of town. It had been built at the old Constantino winery and vineyards, where the murder-suicide had occurred all those years ago. I knew what the ghost hunters who regularly investigated my museum would tell me: get a plan of the original winery and overlay it on the existing one to see if the castle had been built literally atop the old murder site, or if the murder had occurred elsewhere on the vineyard grounds.

I shouldn't leave this room. Just because Jocelyn had left the door open didn't mean she expected me to go free range.

Hovering in the open doorway between the two rooms, I gazed, wistful, at the fire. Air conditioning or not, 'twas the season of crackling fires and pumpkin pies and nogs. The fireplace was castle-worthy. Another oriental carpet spread before it, a woman's shoe standing heel-to-toe upright, and ...

I blinked, looked again, and my heart lurched. The shoe stuck out from behind one of the couches. The only way it could stand at that angle would be if it was leaning against something, or if there was a foot inside it.

"Jocelyn?" I whispered.

I swayed, dread locking me in place. Then a voice in my head told me to *move*, and I hurried forward.

Jocelyn lay behind the arm of the couch. A knife protruded from her midsection. Her eyes stared, sightless, at the beveled ceiling.

I gasped, hands to my mouth. Then I ran, not stopping until I was inside my truck. Hands shaking, I smacked all the locks down and fumbled for my cell phone. I dropped it on the floor of my truck and dove for it, hitting my head on the wheel. Cursing, I retrieved the phone and called 911.

This was not good.

———

Cold seeped from the interview room's cinderblock walls, its concrete floor. I turned up the collar of my cream-colored blouse, of my safari jacket—both useless gestures. They were too light to fight this chill. A wide "mirror" in the wall reflected my pale image. Did anyone brought in here really think it was just a mirror? In this day and age, criminals couldn't be that unenlightened.

The overhead fluorescent light flickered, and I glanced at the video camera, high in one corner of the room. A fat spider crawled across its lens, spinning a web. I clenched my hands in my lap, stilling their trembling.

Detective Laurel Hammer, rumpled and irritated, sat across from me. A coffee stain marked the right breast of her navy suit jacket. "You found both murder victims, husband and wife. How do you think that looks?"

"Bad." Poor Jocelyn. The attack must have been terrifying. I couldn't imagine dying like that. There'd been so much blood. I stared hard at the spider, trying to banish the memory.

"Mrs. Paganini cleared your name in the theft of the grape press. Did you have to shut her up to make sure her story stayed pat?"

I could have smarted off but I felt hollowed-out, bone-weary. Finding Romeo's corpse had been shocking. Finding Jocelyn's had been terrifying, because now I understood that a predator stalked San Benedetto.

Oh, God. How would Leo react? My thoughts jumbled. It was my fourth interview of the night. Laurel and Detective Slate had been tag-teaming me. I checked my watch. Morning now.

"Bored, Kosloski?"

"Tired. What's happening to our town? This used to be the place where the most nefarious thing that happened was the annual Christmas Cow arson. I don't know who killed Jocelyn Paganini. I can't imagine anyone doing it."

"Why did you go to Paganini's house?"

"I told you, she invited me. She said she wanted to talk."

"About what?"

"I'm not sure. We were at the haunted house setup yesterday, and we talked about a lot of things—Romeo's death, how Leo was dealing with it, the grape press. We were interrupted—there were so many people around—and she invited me over for drinks at seven thirty."

"You called 911 at seven fifty-two."

"I was five minutes late, and I didn't find her right away. Like I said, the door was open. It didn't seem right to just wander around the house."

"But you went ahead and did it anyway."

I knotted my fingers together.

"Did she want to talk about Leo?" Laurel asked.

"I'm not sure." Uneasy, I ran my finger inside my watchband. The detective wasn't asking this out of concern for Romeo's orphaned son.

"I hear he blamed his father for his mother's death."

My brow furrowed. "His mother died of cancer." Sympathy weighted my chest. The disease had claimed my dad, too.

"And Romeo didn't lift a finger to help pay for her treatments."

"Are you saying Leo's mother didn't get the treatment she needed?" I asked.

"I'm saying Leo hasn't been shy about how much he hated his father. I know he's said things to you."

"I'm his boss, not his confidante." But Leo *had* said things, and he'd been angry at Jocelyn as well. They'd argued at the haunted house.

No, Leo couldn't have done something this brutal.

"What? You've thought of something."

"You got me thinking of the museum," I lied. "I'm trying to remember if I fed GD."

Laurel flushed. She lurched to her feet, her metal chair scraping against the concrete floor. Lips pressed in a thin line, she stalked to the metal door, slamming it on her way out. Though I'd known it was coming, my shoulders jerked at the sound.

At least I wasn't her only suspect. But Leo? He was only nine-teen. And while I knew that didn't exempt him from being a killer, I didn't want to believe it. Sure, he had motive—his inheritance from his father would no longer be controlled by Jocelyn. His Gothic, rebel-with-a-cause image wouldn't help his case. Yes, he'd been open about his turbulent relationship with his father, but at that age, feelings ran hot—an argument the cops would make for Leo being the killer.

I sighed, scrunching in my chair, and glanced at the video camera.

The spider was gone. I straightened, looking around. In theory, spiders were good guys. Like bats, they ate other bugs. In practice, I'd rather not get too close.

At least I could now get Ladies Aid off my back about solving the crime. There was no way they could think Mrs. Gale responsible for Jocelyn's death too. She might have wanted to sabotage the grape stomp, but she wouldn't have followed up by murdering Jocelyn Pa-ganini. In any case, murdering a random vintner just to sabotage a charity grape stomp was ludicrous.

The door opened, a metallic clank. Detective Slate walked in, jacketless, his sleeves rolled up and exposing corded muscles. Dark smudges marked the skin beneath his eyes. "I'm starting to think your museum really is cursed," he said.

"The exhibits, not the museum," I corrected automatically. "Why? Did something happen at the museum?"

"No, I was talking about you. Why don't you tell me why you really went to Mrs. Paganini's home last night?"

"I already told you. Because she invited me."

"Why?"

"We'd been talking about lots of things." I crept forward, feeling my way. "She seemed to be under some stress, which I chalked up to her husband's murder."

He nodded. "But now you think it was about something else?"

"No. Now I think she suspected who the killer was and wanted to talk to me about it."

"About Leo."

My heartbeat grew loud in my ears. I'd blown it. Slate had led me down the path to the solution that lay at its end. But Leo wasn't the killer! My blood warmed and I forced a smile. "Leo is not a killer."

"But he did come up in conversation before she died."

I nodded. I couldn't lie to him. "But a lot of things came up—"

"Maddie," he said gently, "you might not be seeing Leo clearly."

"What do you mean?"

"Your father died recently, and I understand your sympathy for Leo. But could you be projecting?"

"I don't... No."

"If Jocelyn suspected him in his father's death, it might explain why she invited you to her home to talk. To warn you."

"Or she wanted to talk about the grape press."

His brows rose.

"She asked me if the police had confiscated it. At first I thought she was just being nice, but now I wonder. And I couldn't figure out why Romeo had reported it stolen. He must have known his wife sold it. It would have been much easier for him to just come to me and ask to buy it back. And it seemed like Jocelyn sold it *knowing* it would make him angry. She as much as told me so."

"So you suspected that Jocelyn killed Romeo?"

"It was a possibility."

"And you decided the smart thing would be to accept her invitation to her haunted castle alone at night?"

"I think it looks haunted too!"

He shot me a look, his mouth twisting.

Right. That hadn't been his point.

"There seemed to be some tension between her and Chuck Wollmer, the vintner," I said. "I noticed it when we were setting up the haunted house. It's going to be in his tasting room. Building. It's a big place."

"I heard you had a little excitement there."

"Excitement?"

"Your toe. You didn't just break it. Someone dropped a wine barrel on you. Leo was there at the time, wasn't he?"

"No, he'd left." At least he said he had, but it hadn't taken him long to return when I'd called. "But there were plenty of other people around—from Ladies Aid, Chuck, Jocelyn."

"Who is dead."

"I don't know that anyone dropped the barrel on me. It just fell."

"I spoke with Mr. Finkielkraut," Slate said. "He's convinced someone pushed it."

That big mouth, Dieter! "Well. I can't speak to his opinion."

The detective shook his head. "You were lucky it was empty. Those barrels weigh nearly six hundred pounds when full."

"It didn't land on me. I just caught the bounce."

"According to Dieter, it wasn't your first near miss."

"The car?"

"Funny how Dieter seems to always be on the spot when these things happen."

"But he shoved me out of the way." There was no way Dieter was responsible. Not intentionally, at least.

"Hmm."

A wave of exhaustion rolled through me and I smothered a yawn.

Slate's eyes narrowed and he looked at the mirror. "You can go. We'll be in touch."

I opened my mouth to ask about the grape press but thought better of it. Forget the press. I wanted outta here.

"Thank you." Grabbing my messenger bag off the back of my chair, I speed-hobbled from the room, then slowed. My pickup was still at the castle, and San Benedetto was too small to support a cab service. I could ask one of the police officers to give me a lift back there, but the thought didn't appeal. Slate or Laurel might change their mind and have the squad car return me to sender.

I limped down the steps of the police station to the brick sidewalk. The fog was thick, haloing the iron street lamps.

Shoving my hands deeper into my jacket pockets, I turned toward the museum and walked. Pumpkins and cheerful Halloween decorations lined the darkened shop windows. The branches of a plum tree rustled above me, and I thought I could hear the trickle of the nearby creek. All else was still, silent. Peaceful.

The knot at the base of my skull loosened. Maybe I'd grown too tired to be afraid. Or maybe I knew there was nothing to be afraid of. This was my home, my town, and I belonged to it. Logical Maddie said this might no longer be true—two people had been murdered in less than a week. I'd been gone a long time before returning home last year, and life in San Benedetto had changed. But Tired Maddie enjoyed the sting of mist on her cheeks, the soft pad of her footsteps on the sidewalk.

Ten blocks later, I stood before Mason's shop. His apartment above was dark. Shaking my head, I let myself into the museum. I slipped through the bookcase door into the tea room and fell asleep in a booth.

FOURTEEN

"Oh, for heaven's sake. Did your aunt throw you out of her garage?"

I jerked awake and upright, banging my shoulder on the table. A dozen tiny knives stabbed my abdomen. GD yowled and leapt from my lap. Outside the window, morning fog hung in a sullen gray sky.

Adele loomed over me, hands on her hips. Not a strand of hair escaped her neat chignon.

I yawned. "You're very pink today." I gestured toward her slim, Parisian-style suit.

"What are you doing sleeping in the Fox and Fennel?"

"There was nowhere to lie down in the museum."

"And you let that cat inside!"

"He must have snuck past me."

"Maddie!"

I adjusted my safari jacket. "My truck is at the murder castle. It was after three a.m. and I had to walk back from the police station."

Adele paled. "Murder castle? What...? Not Trivia Vineyards? You didn't find another body!"

"Jocelyn." I rubbed my head.

She sat across from me. "Jocelyn's dead?"

I nodded.

She leaned back in the booth and was silent for a long moment. "How awful. I only knew her to say hello, but she was a lovely woman."

"Yeah."

"And you found her? You were at the police station? The police don't think you were involved?"

"I did find both the Paganinis' bodies. But the police wouldn't have let me go if they didn't have other suspects." I didn't want to tell her about Leo.

"Why didn't you just call me to pick you up?"

"At three a.m.?"

She waved that aside. "Next time you need a lift, call. You've stepped up for me in the past. Besides, isn't that what your boyf ...best friends are for?" Looking at the ceiling, she pressed her lips together. "Harper would have given you a ride too, you know."

"Well, thanks. But it seemed easier to come here. I do need to get my truck, though."

Adele checked the slim gold watch around her wrist and nodded crisply. "I got my Mercedes back this morning. Let's go."

After making sure GD was secure in the museum, I followed her to the alley and her Mercedes, parked beside a dumpster.

I tried not to look at the stairs to Mason's apartment. Why hadn't I just banged on his door last night? He would have understood. But I wasn't sure what I would have found, and the thought that there might be something to find twisted my stomach.

We drove down the long, winding drive to the Trivia Vineyards castle. Shadows streamed from the Italian cypresses, pointing like arrowheads toward our destination. Adele dropped me in the lot, and when she was sure I was in my truck, drove off. I sat for a moment, staring at the yellow flutter of police tape by the front portal of the building. In the warm morning light, the place looked more like a sandcastle, impermanent, fragile, a sepulcher.

Shaking off my fancies, I drove to my apartment. I showered, changed into jeans and a *Paranormal Museum* T-shirt, and returned to the museum, parking in the alley. My head throbbed from lack of sleep, my brain dull, sluggish.

I stumbled through the tea shop and into the museum. The checkerboard floor swam.

GD rose on the rocking chair and stretched, yawning.

"I know how you feel." Walking behind the counter, I sat and stared at the computer. There were things I should be doing. A quick whisk with the feather duster. A review of the accounts. I turned on the computer. The screen's glow lulled me.

The bookcase swiveled open and Adele walked in, carrying a tray. She laid a cup of tea on the counter. "Have you eaten?"

"No."

She shifted a plate with a scone and a tiny pot of jam onto the counter.

"Thanks," I said.

"You're welcome. I spoke with Dieter."

"Oh? Did he have any insights?"

"Not really, but he said the odds are shifting in your favor."

"The odds?"

"Good thing I got in on the action early."

I groaned and buried my head in my hands. "Not you too?" My head jerked up. "Wait. Are you betting for or against me?"

Her eyes widened. "For you, of course! Public feeling is that now that you're more of a suspect, you'll be compelled to solve the crime."

"It's not a joke, Adele."

Her expression stilled. "I know." Her voice dropped. "It's horrible. Things like this... didn't used to happen here. It doesn't feel like San Benedetto's changed, but it has, hasn't it?"

"I don't know." I rubbed my jaw, thinking of that decades-old murder-suicide. "There have always been evil, selfish people. These murders weren't random violence, I don't think. It didn't seem like Jocelyn's home had been ransacked, like in a burglary. This has to be connected to her husband's death. And that must have been personal. A mugger wouldn't have dumped Romeo's body in the grape vat, would he?"

"You're saying because these killings are personal, it's not the same as a rise in crime like gang violence or home invasions?" Adele shook her head. "I'd like to believe that, but murder is murder. And we've seen too many killings this year. The police aren't—"

"It's not fair to blame the police. They can't stop crimes before they happen, only do their best to solve them after the fact."

"Well, they thought I was a killer once. You need to figure this out yourself. You can't trust the police to do it for you." Picking up the empty tray, she clacked from the room.

The bookcase swung shut behind her.

GD meowed.

"I haven't forgotten your breakfast." And I had no illusions about the cat snuggling up to me last night. He'd been looking for body heat, pure and simple.

I fed him, flipped the sign in the window to *Open*, and returned to the counter to contemplate my computer screen and sip tea. Adele had mixed up something dark with cocoa and cinnamon. I imagined the description: *an arousing brew of serotonin-boosting cocoa to get you in the mood for…* I bit into the scone. Apricot and coconut, a pad of butter melting into the crust. My eyes rolled to the ceiling. Heaven.

I should dust. I should do accounts. I should check the inventory. Instead, I searched the Internet for news about Trivia Vineyards and the grape press. First stop, their website, where I learned that the Roman goddess Trivia was also Hecate, Greek goddess of death and magic. Romeo's interest in death hadn't begun with the Death Bistro. It seemed to be long-standing.

The Paganinis had bought the old Constantino Vineyards five years ago. According to the website, the vineyard had been abandoned for a short period during the early 1920s. Another local farmer had bought it, producing grapes for shipping during and after Prohibition.

Although the website made it sound as if Prohibition was the reason why the winery had briefly closed, local legend said that it was the murder-suicide. Which was true?

I searched the web for info on the murder-suicide and found an article typed into a genealogy website.

October 8, 1922

The remains of Miss Alcina Constantino and Luigi Rotta were discovered in a burnt cottage on the grounds of the Constantino Vineyards in an apparent murder-suicide. A vineyard worker stated the belief that Rotta had made advances to Miss Constantino. It is believed that she spurned Rotta, and he killed her, then killed himself. Miss Constantino is survived by her father, Mr. Gian Constantino.

And that was it. I searched for another thirty minutes and turned up a link to the first article on the genealogy website. If I wanted more, it was going to cost me.

Blowing out my breath, I called the Historical Association. They'd done research for me before—for a fee.

The nice lady on the phone agreed to play Girl Friday again. "Will that be all?" she asked after taking down the information.

"No. Can you also see what you can find on the father, Gian Constantino?"

"Of course," she said. "You know, there is another source."

"Oh?" I rapped my pen on the counter. I had a good idea what she was going to suggest.

"Since you're looking at the 1920s, it might be in the police archives. As you may know, crime-scene photography was coming into its own back then. You might even find some photos."

"That's a good idea," I said, wooden. "Thanks." Giving her my credit card number, I hung up. I did not want to return to the police station and risk another run-in with Laurel. But I did have to go there to get the grape press. I checked my watch. It was only ten o'clock—too early on a Wednesday to expect many visitors to the museum.

Slinging my messenger bag over one shoulder, I opened the bookcase and stuck my head inside the tea room. Adele stood behind the long counter, straightening the metal tins on the shelves. One of her minions, a slim girl with a long blond ponytail, laid out cutlery on the white-draped tabletops.

I cleared my throat. "Adele? I need to run to the police station."

She looked up, her eyes widening. "They didn't ask you in for more questioning? I'll call my lawyer." Reaching into the pocket of her white apron, she whisked out a phone.

"No. Nothing like that. They want me to collect the grape press. Things are kind of slow right now. If I leave the bookcase open, can you take tickets if any customers stop by?"

She pressed her lips together and nodded. "How long will you be?"

"I just need to get the grape press. If anything, er, happens to delay me, I'll call you."

She shook her phone at me. "And this time, no talking to the police without a lawyer!"

I nodded meekly. "And can I borrow your dolly?"

She angled her head toward the hallway that led to the alley. "You know where it is."

"Thanks." Scuttling to her storage room, I wheeled the dolly into the alley and levered it into the back of my truck. Now that I'd committed, I wanted to get this over with.

I drove down the narrow alley, careful not to look up at Mason's window. Ribbons of fog drifted across the blue sky. On the sleepy streets, café owners set sandwich boards on the brick sidewalks. Shopkeepers propped open their doors. A city worker adjusted a fallen hay bale at the harvest display in the park.

I found an open spot in front of the brick police station and put an extra quarter in the meter, then one more, just in case. One parking ticket this month was more than enough.

Heart pounding, I dragged the dolly up the steps to the front door. A uniformed officer on his way out held the door for me. Chivalry was not dead. I thanked him and wheeled the dolly through the awful, sickly green foyer and to the front desk.

The balding desk officer sucked a bit of yellow pastry off his thick thumb. Powdered sugar dusted his neat gray moustache. He smiled, adding an extra chin. "How can I help you today?"

I straightened the dolly. "My name is Maddie Kosloski. Detective Slate asked me to pick up a grape press he'd taken as evidence."

Paling, the officer tugged at the collar of his blue uniform. "The grape press? Just a moment." He picked up the phone and turned from me, muttering.

I leaned on the dolly and tried to look like I hadn't been in police custody the night before. It wasn't as if they'd arrested me. They'd only interrogated me for hours and made it clear I was a suspect.

The desk officer swiveled back to me, his chair squeaking beneath his bulk. "Someone will be here shortly. You can wait there." He motioned to the uncomfortable-looking plastic chairs.

"Thanks." I wheeled the dolly to the chairs and sat down. My toe gave a sudden throb.

A thin, uniformed officer with wisps of hair side-combed across his head emerged from a long hallway. The desk officer pointed to me, and the thin man approached.

"You're Miss Kosloski?"

Nodding, I rose.

"May I see some identification, please?"

I rummaged in my wallet handed him my driver's license.

He inspected it, holding it inches from his nose, his gaze ping-ponging between me and the ID. Finally he handed it back. "I have some paperwork for you to fill out."

He led me to another desk and sidled behind it, pulling a clipboard from a drawer. "Here. Sign at the red X's."

I filled out the forms, shifting my weight, impatient.

When I finished, he reviewed the paperwork and nodded. "This way, please."

He led me down a hallway painted ick green, stopping outside a wooden door. Shoulders drawing together, he angled his head. "In there."

I opened the door to a closet. A mop and bucket leaned against a rack of cleaning supplies, running to the ceiling. My grape press sat, centered, on the dingy linoleum floor.

"This is your evidence room?" Shouldn't it be in a basement, somewhere harder to get to? I thought there'd be gates and locks and guards, like on TV.

"Our evidence room is in the basement. Your grape press isn't evidence."

"Then what—?" I clamped my jaw shut. Don't argue. Just take the press and go. I wheeled the dolly close to the press and sat it upright. Grasping the top of it, I rocked it toward the dolly. The blasted thing was heavier than it looked. There was a way to remove the metal bands around the barrel and take it apart, but I was too stupid to figure out how to put it back together again. My chin lowered to my chest. And people expected me to figure out a murder? I couldn't even puzzle out a grape press.

"A little help?" I asked.

He shook his head, stepping into the hall. "I'm not touching that thing."

"Why not?"

His cheek twitched, a nervous tic. "That press is your problem, not mine."

Chivalry might not be dead, but it was on life support. Wrestling the press onto the dolly, I wheeled it from the closet.

The officer skipped back as if afraid I might clip him. "You know the way out." He hurried in the opposite direction. A door slammed.

Seriously?

I wheeled the press down the long hallway. A policewoman stepped into the hall. Her mouth made an O, and she darted into an office, shutting the door. Two officers pressed against the walls as I passed.

In the entry, I bumped and scraped the dolly against the front door, knocking a largish splinter of doorframe to the linoleum. Hell.

Pretending the damage to city property hadn't occurred, I wheeled the press to the top of the steps and grimaced. Stairs.

I walked down the steps backward, careful the press didn't bump off the dolly. At the sidewalk, I heaved a sigh and wheeled the grape press to the back of the truck.

And then I saw my mistake.

My truck bed was several feet off the ground. Before, it had taken Leo and I together to load the press into my truck. Today I was alone, and frustration hardened my gut.

"Damn it!"

"That's a quarter for the swear jar," a masculine voice said from behind me.

I turned.

Detective Slate stood on the sidewalk, smiling. His blue suit jacket was open, and I caught a glimpse of a shoulder holster against his white button-down shirt.

"Thanks for picking up the press," he said. "The station was getting antsy."

"I can't believe this. Everyone treated me like I was carrying a vial of Ebola virus. What exactly is everyone so freaked out about?"

"The people who handled it complained about coldness, said they got a bad feeling when they got near it. One technician said she heard a man's scream."

A *man's* scream? That was disturbing.

Slate smiled, and my heart lightened in response. "They're letting their imaginations run away with them," he said.

"Probably."

He arched a brow. "Probably? You don't really believe in that stuff, do you?"

"I'm starting to lose faith in the rational world. But who doesn't like a good ghost story? Though I've been having trouble getting the facts on this tale." I rested my hand on the handle. "I don't suppose you'd mind taking a look at the police archives about the case?"

"You mean there actually *is* a case?"

I unfolded my notes from the back pocket of my jeans and told him about the murder-suicide. "I haven't been able to find anything online aside from one short article. The Historical Association suggested there might be something in the police archives."

He took the notepaper from me. "Sure. The last goose chase you sent me on helped solve a nineteenth-century cold case. I'm game. Need some help getting that press into your truck?"

"Yes. Thank you!" I lowered the tailgate.

He bent, reaching for the grape press.

"Careful, it's—"

He lifted it, grunting.

"Heavy," I finished, scrambling to help him slide it into the truck.

His hand brushed mine, and a shiver of awareness rippled my skin.

Ignoring it, I crawled into the truck bed and tied down the press with a length of rope.

"Can you hand me the dolly?" I asked.

He didn't respond, gazing past me, his stare distant, amber eyes dull.

"Detective Slate? Are you all right?"

He shook himself. "Sorry. What?"

"The dolly. Would you mind...?"

"Sure." He handed me the dolly, and I tied that down as well so it wouldn't slide into the press.

"You come prepared," he said.

"I come with a truck. Thanks again." I hopped out, landing on my good foot, and closed the tailgate.

"Are you okay?" he asked.

"Yeah. My foot's just a little—"

"I wasn't talking about your foot. It was a rough crime scene last night."

I looked at my tennis shoes. "Yeah. I'm sorry. I wish I could have been more helpful."

"You were." He stepped onto the sidewalk. "If you think of anything else, call me."

"I will." I got into my pickup and backed into the wide street.

He stood in front of the station, watching. I turned the corner and he disappeared from view.

My shoulders relaxed. I'd managed to avoid Laurel and collect the press, and now I had new, spooky tales of terror at the police station to include with my grape press display.

A smile tugged at the corner of my mouth. I also had a good excuse to see Mason. There was no way I was getting the grape press into the museum on my own.

My throat tightened. Did I really need an excuse to see him? He was my boyfriend. We loved each other. I missed him. And if I needed a pretext to spend time with him, then we had a problem.

Pulling into an empty spot on the street, I hopped out, glancing at the museum's window. No tourists examined the display cases. No buyers wandered the gallery aisles. This state of affairs was bad for ticket sales, but no customers meant I had time to find Mason and get help unloading the grape press.

I hobbled next door to the motorcycle shop. A teal and chrome Harley gleamed in the window. I stopped short in the doorway.

Mason stood in front of the counter, his muscles straining against his black T-shirt as he cradled a sobbing young woman in his arms.

FIFTEEN

MASON PRESSED HIS LIPS to the top of the woman's head. Her long blond hair tangled across his brawny chest, her arms wrapped around his waist. The scene was straight off the cover of an '80s romance novel, and the air whooshed from my lungs.

I backed out the door of the shop and leaned, nauseated, against my truck. There could be an innocent explanation. After all, he'd kissed the top of her head, not her lips.

Unseeing, I stared at the museum window. Maybe the woman had just gotten some bad news. I should walk back inside and find out what the hell was going on. But a part of me didn't want to know.

Unlatching my tailgate, I limped into the Fox and Fennel, my movements stiff. Women gossiped at the tables, the heady scent of fruit and cinnamon scones filling the air. I waited at the counter while Adele rang up a bill and handed change to a waitress.

My friend turned to me. "How did it ...?" Her brow furrowed. "Maddie, are you all right? What happened?"

"I'm fine," I croaked.

"You're white as a sheet. The police didn't threaten you, did they? That Laurel was always a bully! I knew I should have gone with you."

"The police were fine. I'm fine. The grape press is in my truck out front. Can one of your waiters help me bring it inside?"

"I'll ask Jorge. Are you sure you're okay?"

I stretched my lips into a smile. Mason wanted space, and it had something to do with that woman, who had to be his old girlfriend. Or could I be leaping to conclusions? Maybe she was a random stranger who'd just ... lost someone in a motorcycle accident? "Great," I lied. "And guess what—the grape press may be even more haunted than we thought."

"Oh," she said. "Good." She whisked into the kitchen and emerged with a burly young man wearing an apron over his *Fox and Fennel* T-shirt.

"Hi, Jorge," I said.

He nodded. "Maddie. What have you got?"

"Out here."

He followed me outside, and together we maneuvered the grape press onto the dolly.

Back bowed, he wheeled it into the museum. "Where do you want it?" he asked, his voice dull.

GD raised his head from his spot on the haunted rocking chair. His ears swiveled toward us, curious.

I pointed at the center of the room. "There's fine." I'd keep the press as an exhibit in the museum until I had to take it to the haunted house tomorrow.

Jorge worked the dolly out from beneath it. "You want me to put the dolly back in the storeroom?"

"That would be great, thanks."

He straightened his shoulders and wheeled the empty dolly through the bookcase door. It snicked shut behind him. The black crepe-paper bunting swayed in the breeze.

GD stretched and leapt from the chair in a smooth motion, then wandered toward the grape press. Three feet away from it, he arched his back, hissing, his fur standing on end.

"So it is haunted?" I asked.

He backed away, growling.

I swallowed, my scalp prickling. I'd never seen GD retreat like that, hadn't known it was part of the cat's repertoire. Could he smell the old bloodstains?

The bell above the front door jingled and a couple, silver-haired tourists in resort wear, walked into the museum. I sold them tickets and answered their questions about nearby wineries, pointing them out on a Visitors Bureau map.

Green eyes saucer-like, GD hunched beneath the gently swaying rocking chair, staring.

The couple walked to the grape press. "What's this?" the woman asked.

"Oh!" My signage for the exhibit was at the haunted house. "An antique grape press."

Flicking anxious glances at GD, I gave them a rundown of its haunted history. When I finished, the guests moved off to examine the glass display cases. I hurried to the computer and printed up a new sign for the press on thick, off-white paper.

GD whisked into the Fortune Telling Room, and my muscles loosened. The grape press didn't bother me, but GD's behavior was starting to creep me out.

Sitting on my chair behind the counter, I stared at the computer screen, my brain a blank. I couldn't ignore the signs any longer. Something was wrong between Mason and I. My throat closed. If all it took was one old girlfriend to bust us up, then we couldn't have been on a solid foundation.

The front door opened and Elthia breezed in. The puffed sleeve of her high-collared black blouse caught on the latch. She paused to untangle herself, her pinstriped skirt swaying about her knees. She touched a finger to her red-gold hair, piled high on her head. "Is now a good time to chat about the Death Bistro?" She clacked toward me in her button-up boots, her smile taut, her blue eyes glittering.

I'm not the most sensitive person, but even I could feel the tension vibrating off her. She was the answer to my stop-thinking-about-Mason prayers.

"I can't think of a better time," I said.

"At least we don't have to worry about Jocelyn coming." Elthia gave a strangled laugh. "She's dead."

"Where did you hear that?"

"It's in the papers. The Death Bistro phone tree is buzzing. First Romeo..." Her mouth quivered, her eyes welling with tears.

I rose and came around the counter. "Why don't you sit down?" I motioned to my tall chair behind the register. "I'll get us some tea." I hustled to the bookcase, opened it, and flagged down a young, dark-haired waiter. "Two cups of tea."

"What kind?" he asked. "Would you like to see our menu?"

"Just ... Whatever's at the top of it. Can you bring it to the museum?"

"Sure."

"Thanks." I shut the bookcase and returned to Elthia.

GD sat in her lap, his paws on her chest. She ruffled his fur, drawing deep, shuddering breaths.

"I see you've met GD," I said.

"Your ghost detector."

I rested my hand on the glass counter. "You and Romeo were more than just partners in the Death Bistro, weren't you?"

She burst into sobs. Digging a lace handkerchief from her sleeve, she blotted her eyes. "Is it that obvious?"

"It's obvious you're hurting."

"I know it was wrong and stupid. God, I hate myself. But he was so ... Romeo."

"Everyone says he was a charmer."

"It was more than that." She clutched my wrist, dislodging GD. "Do you think Jocelyn knew?"

The cat leapt to the floor and took a swipe at my shoelaces before darting into the Fortune Telling Room.

"I told myself it was okay," Elthia went on, "because Jocelyn was having an affair too. But that's crap, isn't it?"

I hesitated. "You mean you no longer think she was having an affair?"

"No. Maybe. It's just that Romeo despised Chuck Wollmer so much, and he never would tell me why. But Chuck and Jocelyn were friends, and I thought ..." She hiccupped. "Can you believe I was jealous that he might be jealous? Of his wife?"

I smiled, bitter. "I might know a thing or two about unreasonable emotions."

"Oh, God. Do you think the police will suspect me?"

"Have they spoken to you?"

"No. I'm being irrational. Sorry." She drew a ragged breath. "I came here to talk about the Death Bistro, not cry on your shoulder. And we barely know each other. This is so embarrassing."

I shook my head. "The Death Bistro is tomorrow night. How many people are you expecting?"

The tourist couple ambled out of the Fortune Telling Room and into the gallery.

She sniffed. "Eighteen now."

"Eighteen!" I eyed the room with its display cases and grape press and rocking chair in the corner. Even with the grape press moved to the haunted house, I couldn't imagine eighteen people around tables in the main room. "That will be … cozy."

The bookcase creaked open and the waiter walked in, balancing a bamboo tray. "Where do you want me to put your tea?"

"Here on the counter." I took the tray from him. "Can you get Adele? Tell her it's Death Bistro business."

He nodded and bustled out.

"I'm sure she'll have some ideas for table arrangements," I said.

"Dieter told me you were investigating the murders," Elthia said.

"He did?" Dieter!!! Even though I knew the contractor wouldn't blab to the cops, one of his clients might.

"I didn't kill anyone," she said.

"Okay." Was that the real reason she'd come here, playing true confessions?

"But Romeo was tense about something for the last six weeks or so. At the time, I thought he was keeping quiet about the problem—whatever it was—because it had to do with his wife. He knew I didn't like hearing about her." Pink stained Elthia's cheeks.

"Maybe you should tell this to Detective Slate."

"But now I wonder if it wasn't something else. I mean, someone killed Jocelyn, and it obviously wasn't Romeo."

I tried to look wise. "And you don't have any idea what he was stressed about?"

Her lips turned down. "No. If we were as close as I'd thought, he would have told me, wouldn't he? How could I have deluded myself so badly? Me! The other woman. It's such a cliché."

"Maybe he thought it would upset you?"

"Maybe." She cradled her teacup between both hands, staring into its depths. "He knew I'm a sensitive."

The bookcase opened and Adele strode in, a clipboard beneath her arm. She stopped in front of the counter and smoothed the front of her apron. "Right. How many people?"

"Eighteen," Elthia said.

Adele flipped past two pages and stopped at a sketch involving circles inside a square. She folded the extra pages under the top of the clipboard and laid it on the counter, pushing it toward Elthia. "Here's how we'll organize the tables. Would you prefer black or white tablecloths?"

"Black."

"The museum is overstuffed with death-themed decor," Adele said. "I thought something simple for the tables—just flameless candles and the table settings, which as you know are white. The stark black and white will provide an elegant and calming effect in the midst of all..." She motioned at the display cases, the empty rocking chair, the black streamers. "This."

"We'll have printed materials," Elthia said. "I was thinking—"

"They'll go on the counter so people can pick them up as they enter and exit. Given the size of the room, we simply can't expand the size of the tables, and extraneous items will make them too cluttered."

Elthia blinked. "Okay."

"Excellent." Adele picked up the clipboard. Removing two sheets of paper from the back, she handed them to Elthia. "Given the price point we agreed on earlier, I've developed two menu options. Which do you prefer?"

Elthia studied them, her brow wrinkling. "Could we combine some items from Menu A with Menu B?"

"No."

Elthia heaved a sigh. "Menu B then."

"Excellent choice. Sign here." Adele pointed and handed her a pen. Elthia signed, and Adele turned to me. "The Death Bistro starts at seven. The museum closes at five. My staff will be here at five fifteen to begin the setup. Is there anything else?"

Elthia and I looked at each other, uncertain.

"No?" I asked.

"Good." Adele turned on her heel and clacked out of the room. The bookcase closed behind her.

"That was efficient," Elthia said.

"Adele's kind of amazing that way. Um, about GD Cat—"

"He can stay."

I blew out my breath, relieved. The last time I'd tried to dislodge GD from the museum, he'd marked a trail of bloody scratches up my arms. I still had the scars.

Elthia looked around. "I'm glad we moved the Death Bistro here. The museum is much more deathy than the tea shop." Her gaze landed on the grape press and she sucked in her breath. "Is that Romeo's?"

"It's from his vineyard, yes. Jocelyn sold it to me."

Sliding from the chair, Elthia walked to the press, her palms extended. She halted a foot away and closed her eyes.

The tourist couple emerged from the gallery, the silver-haired woman clutching a black cat teapot to her chest. They halted in the entryway, watching Elthia.

"Death." Elthia moaned. "Pain, so much pain. And regret." Opening her eyes, she shuddered. "I'll tell you what I told Romeo. Get rid of this grape press. It's got something awful attached to it."

"My collector, er, bound it," I said.

"Well, he didn't do a very good job. Get rid of this press."

I wasn't selling my press. Not after everything I'd gone through.

"Can I buy this teapot?" the female tourist asked.

"Yes, of course!" I hurried to her and took the pot. "Right over here." Guiding them to the cash register, I wrapped the teapot in tissue and rang it up, keeping an eye on Elthia. She edged around the grape press, waving her hands in the air and muttering beneath her breath.

The woman leaned across the counter toward me. "Is she a witch?" she whispered.

"She told me she was a sensitive."

The woman clapped her hands together. "Oh, how interesting!"

That was one word for it. I put the teapot in a box and bagged it, handing it to the woman.

"Do you do Tarot readings?" the woman asked.

I blinked. I had once, at a party, just for fun. My readings had turned out to be weirdly accurate. I'd chalked it up to the universe playing a colossal joke, since I'm basically the anti-psychic. "Um, no, we don't."

"You should. This is the perfect place for it!" She waved, and she and her husband left.

Elthia shook her head. "We can't have this grape press here tomorrow night."

"I'll remove it." And take it directly to the haunted house.

Elthia and I went over more details, and then she left me to my thoughts. Quick as desire, they turned to Mason. That woman he'd been holding had to be his ex, and he'd been avoiding me. I couldn't deny it any longer. There was more between them than time. But Mason wasn't the sort of guy to get entangled with one woman while he was with another.

"This is ridiculous." I picked up my cell phone and called … Leo.

"Do you want me to come in today?" he asked, breathless.

"Are you sure you don't mind?" I asked. "It's kind of last minute."

"Is it busy in there?"

GD hopped onto the counter.

"Not really."

"I could do more decorating," he offered.

"And you could research the murder-suicide associated with the grape press. I searched online but couldn't find anything. The Historical Association is on the case, but maybe you can turn something up."

"I'll be there in twenty."

Twenty-five minutes later, Leo strode through the door, his expression slack and brandishing a newspaper. "Did you hear about Jocelyn?"

"I did. I'm sorry."

He stared at the checkerboard floor and clutched his black T-shirt, bunching it at his stomach. "I'm not. I wish I could be sorry, but I can't feel anything." His voice was strained.

That I did not believe. He was feeling too much and didn't know how to handle it. "Leo, you've got to stop saying things like this. Even if they're true—and I don't think they are—it makes you sound awful."

"I don't care what people think. At least I'm not a hypocrite."

Once, not so long ago, I'd been an angsty teenager. I tried to remember what it was like, and failed. "Do you care what the police think?"

"I didn't do this."

"I know. But neither did Adele, and she was once arrested for murder."

"And released. I don't know," he muttered. "Maybe spending some time in jail would be interesting."

"No," I said sharply, "it wouldn't. Look, I can only imagine how overwhelming this must be. What can I do?"

"Nothing."

This conversation was getting me nowhere. "All right. But for now, can I take your lunch order?"

"Carnitas burrito, black beans, hot salsa, everything on it."

"Great. I'll be back at..." I checked my watch. Wow, it was nearly noon. "Back in thirty minutes."

I hobbled to the local taqueria, collected our food, and returned to the museum.

We noshed at the counter, GD weaving around my ankles and hoping I'd drop something.

I tried to pick Leo's brain about the murders, anything his father might have mentioned about the grape press.

He answered in unhelpful monosyllables. Honestly, I wouldn't go back to my teen years for anything.

Chucking my trash in the bin, I hurried outside to my pickup.

Mason stood on the sidewalk watching a battered van drive away. Raking a hand through his shaggy blond hair, he turned to me. His arctic eyes warmed. "Maddie!"

My heart pounded, blood rushing to my head. How could he act like nothing was wrong? My lungs constricted. I couldn't do this. "Sorry, gotta go. I'll talk to you later!" Smiling, I waved, jumped in my truck, and drove down the street.

I winced, gripping the wheel, and glided to a stop behind a blue Passat. I'd chickened out. I should turn around, go talk to him. But when the Passat pulled forward, I kept driving, out of town and into the vineyards. Maybe I was the one who needed space? I needed to calm down, get my head clear, and then listen to whatever it was Mason had to say.

I cranked my window down and inhaled the warm autumnal air. This was my favorite season in San Benedetto—stunning weather, the excitement of harvest, pumpkin pies. But today the world seemed flat, joyless.

Turning right at the sign for Plot 42 Vineyards, I piloted my truck down the gravel road to Adele's family winery. Mr. Nakamoto had been involved in security for the festival, so he might have an idea about how someone had driven a dump truck full of grapes and a body into the grounds. Unless Romeo had already been inside, waiting for someone? But why mess with hiding his body beneath all those grapes? Dump trucks are noisy, and the killer risked attracting attention. If I was the killer, I'd just drag the body between some tents and be done with it.

A silver Lexus approached me from the other direction. It came zipping down the narrow track too fast, its rear antenna a shark fin cutting the billows of dust. I edged further to the right, slowing. The

Lexus blasted past, showering my truck with gravel. The driver, impassive behind dark sunglasses, glanced my way. The vampire!

Too late, I cranked up my window to shield myself from the dust and only trapped it in the cab.

I coughed, choking. Stupid vampire.

I parked beneath a weeping willow, beside a picnic table on a lush green lawn. The door to the tasting room, set inside an old barn twined with grapevines, stood open. In purple chalk, a sandwich board proclaimed *Yes, We're Open!* Orange and yellow chrysanthemums lined the walk.

I limped up the winding brick path. Plucking a purple grape from the vines clutching the barn, I popped it in my mouth. It burst on my tongue, heady with sweetness. Inside the barn, I shivered, wishing I'd brought my museum hoodie for the cool interior.

Wearing his black *Haunted Vine* apron, Mr. Nakamoto stood behind the long tasting bar. His diminutive wife was facing him, wrenching a cork from a bottle. She looked like an older, furious version of Adele, her dark brows drawn in a scowl.

"It's more than a business," she said, her voice sharp. "It's our life!"

He smoothed a hand over his gray hair, which was thinning at the top. "You can't deny the numbers—"

"Oh, numbers! What about our family? Your daughter?"

Cheeks warming, I backed away. They hadn't seen me, and this was a private family argument. A stone turned beneath my heel and I stumbled sideways. The pebble skittered, loud, across the brick. They looked toward the open barn doors.

"Hi," I said. "I was just looking for Mr. Nakamoto."

"You've found him," Mrs. Nakamoto snarled. Slamming the black bottle on the counter, she stalked from the barn, rubbing her hands on her *Haunted Vine* apron.

I pointed over my shoulder at my truck. "I can come back later."

"Nonsense." Mr. Nakamoto smiled thinly, looking past me. "What can I do for you?"

I'd known Adele's father since I was a kid and there was no use going at this sideways, especially when he clearly wanted to run after his wife. "It's about the security for the festival grounds. How could someone have gotten a dump truck full of grapes in there before it opened?"

"We checked the locks," he replied. "None had been damaged. Which means either the person who drove that truck was a skilled lockpick, or they had a key."

A bird buzzed me, settling on a beam over the door. I edged back into the barn, out of range. Rows of barrels stacked on their sides lay along one wall. Racks of Haunted Vine-themed souvenirs and a table piled with *Haunted Vine* and *Plot 42* T-shirts stood in the center of the barn.

"And who had keys?" I asked.

Untying his apron, he tugged it over his head. "Just myself and Romeo. Is that all?"

Footsteps padded on the path behind me.

"Yeah. Thanks."

"Any time." He hurried past me, bumping shoulders with his fellow vintner, Chuck Wollmer.

"Sorry," Mr. Nakamoto panted.

"Whoa there," Chuck said, laughing. "You got a minute, Roy?"

"Not now. Sorry." Mr. Nakamoto sped off in the direction his wife had taken, into the vineyard.

Chuck tugged on his beard, his handlebar moustache twitching. Buried in a wreath of blond facial hair, his lips looked soft and pink. "What was that about?"

It was none of his business, or mine for that matter. "We're all upset about Jocelyn's death."

"I read about it in the paper this morning," he said. "It's hard to believe. Was it suicide, do you think?"

"Why do you think it was suicide?"

"She was devastated by Romeo's death."

Devastated enough to kill herself? "I, uh, found the body."

"So the rumors are true. You're investigating the crime."

"Just because Dieter says I'm investigating," I said hotly, "doesn't mean I'm investigating."

"Actually, it was that obnoxious woman from Ladies Aid."

"Which one?"

Chuck smiled. "They can be a handful, can't they? I almost regret having agreed to host their haunted house."

"Why did you?"

He shrugged. "I needed the publicity. Running a vineyard is easy. Selling the wine is another story."

I eyed him. If he'd been having an affair with Jocelyn, he sure didn't seem broken up by her death. "Assuming it was murder," I said, "who do you think could have killed her?"

"Why ask me?"

"Sorry, I thought you were friends. You seemed close."

He shook his head. "Romeo and I were … Well, I won't say we were friends, but we were comrades in arms. He was a tremendous help when I started CW Vineyards, giving me all sorts of time and advice. After he died, well, I figured I owed him. The least I could do was help Jocelyn."

"Oh?"

"You know what it's like after someone in the family dies. There's all sorts of things to deal with. And she had the vineyard to manage as well." Chuck colored. "And, well, she does know her viticulture."

"So she was giving you growing advice on the side."

"Here and there." He gazed at the stacked barrels. "It's hard to believe—back-to-back murders in a place like this. I moved to the countryside to get away from big city crime and hassles."

"In fairness, San Benedetto is still a safe town. I walk alone at night and no one's ever bothered me."

"Maybe you should rethink that. I admit, I'm having second thoughts about my move." He shook his head. "San Benedetto has its charms, but I'm not sure it's worth it."

"Because of the murders?"

His lips thinned. "They've changed things. For everyone."

I exhaled slowly. The murders had left a taint, and there was only one way to free ourselves from its weight. Find the killer, bring him to justice.

SIXTEEN

I SAT IN MY truck beneath the weeping willow and regarded the Nakamoto barn. Fluffy white clouds scudded across the blue sky.

A bead of sweat trickled down my back and I leaned closer to the open window, unsure where to go next. If I was a real detective—or at least one of the detectives on TV—I'd return to the scene of the crime. Jocelyn had said there'd been sabotage at the winery, and I should explore that. But if I was the killer, common wisdom held, I might return to the scene of the crime too. I'd already given the police enough reason to suspect my motives.

Besides, I wasn't a real detective. I didn't even play one on TV.

My cell phone buzzed in my messenger bag. I extracted it from its pocket. A message from my mother glowed on the screen. She'd recently discovered texting, and she used whole words and grammatically correct sentences like an irate schoolteacher:

Madelyn, I took some pictures at the crime scene and thought they might be of help. I'm sorry I forgot to give them to you earlier. Your mother.

I checked the attachments. Somehow, my mom had found time to shoot these photos. A picture of the grape vat, its sides shining in the sun. Romeo's body glimpsed beneath the grapes. The dump truck, tailgate down. Some shots of the ground—had she been trying to document footprints? Sheesh.

What was my mother's angle in this mess? The excuses she'd given me hadn't rung true, and this sure wasn't about winning her bet with Dieter.

I gritted my teeth. Time to cowgirl up. I revved the engine and drove. Ignoring the *Closed* sign on the sandwich board by the entrance, I turned down the gravel drive to Trivia Vineyards. The Italian cypresses made pointed shadows on the ground. Rows of vines the color of Mardi Gras fanned from the road, rippling away from me. I glanced at the trail of dust in my rear view mirror.

The winery's sandcastle doors stood shut, its narrow windows casting a dead stare over the empty parking lot. Trivia might be closed for tastings, but it was a working vineyard. And you don't just walk away from a farm, not during harvest season. The grapes would need to be crushed, the stems removed, the grapes macerated to add color, flavor, and tannin to the wine. There should be workers here. This was farm country, and the harvest stopped for no one, not even the police.

Stepping from my truck, I limped toward a Tuscan-looking barn, a two-story stone building with a sloping roofline and tiles the color of dried blood. Behind it, a narrow road led to a dirt parking area littered with pickups and battered cars.

I found an unlocked wooden door and walked inside a wide room. It was cool, dimly lit, and smelled of red wine vinegar on an old sponge. Steel fermentation vats scraped the peaked ceiling. A commercial fan rattled above me.

Something metallic clanked.

Uneasy, I licked my lips. "Hello?"

A bulky man in jeans and a plaid shirt emerged from between two of the vats, grease smudging his pockmarked cheek. He wiped his broad hands on an oily cloth. "Winery's closed."

"I know," I said. He had no reason to talk to me. Being upfront was my best chance at getting information. "I'm Maddie Kosloski. I found Jocelyn last night. She'd invited me here to tell me about the sabotage and some other things that were bothering her at the winery. She never got the chance. I thought you might know something about the problems."

A pulse beat in his jaw. "Even if I did, why would I tell you?"

That was a stumper. "Because I want to help?"

"We've got cops for that, honey."

"Riiight."

"This part of the winery is off limits. You need to go."

Another man emerged from the vats. Dieter. He tucked a greasy rag into the pocket of his paint-spattered overalls, looked up, and grinned. "Mad Kosloski! You here to update us on your investigation?"

I crossed my arms over my chest. "Wouldn't that be cheating?"

His eyes widened in faux-sincerity. "The more accurate the odds, the more fair it is to all involved."

"What are you doing here?" I asked.

Dieter jerked his head at the vats. "Problem with one of the valves. What are you doing here?"

"I came to ask about sabotage that apparently occurred at Trivia," I said. "Jocelyn invited me over last night to discuss it."

Dieter whistled, his expression shifting to sympathy. "You found her body, too? That's rough."

215

I nodded.

He turned to the other man. "The papers didn't say anything about sabotage. What happened?"

The man cut a glance to me and Dieter shrugged. "She's cool, Jake. You can tell her."

The workman frowned. "Someone turned the taps on the cellar casks. By the time we discovered it, half a million dollars of wine had drained onto the floor."

My jaw dropped. Half a million dollars? That would have been devastating. "When did this happen?"

"We discovered the loss on Friday night. Romeo was so angry he lost all his English. He took off in the truck we'd leased for the harvest."

"Did he suspect who was responsible?"

"I guess so. We figured it was that punk kid of his, Leo. He'd been here earlier that day."

Leo had been working at the museum on Friday, from after lunch until he left around six. "Do you know what time it happened?"

"Late afternoon, early evening, your guess is as good as mine."

"I have a hard time believing Leo would have done something like that," I said.

"He might not have realized how bad the damage would be. And it's the easiest kind of sabotage. Just turn a tap and let the wine flow." Jake's skin darkened. "All that work, all that grape, gone."

Scrounging in my messenger bag, I pulled out my cell phone and brought up one of my mother's pictures of the crime scene. "The truck that Romeo took on Friday night—was this it?" I showed him the photo of the dump truck.

He nodded. "Looks like it."

"Thanks." So Romeo had torn off in the truck, furious about the loss, and wound up dead. If he'd gone looking for the saboteur, could his murder have been self-defense? Even if Leo hadn't drained all the wine onto the floor, if his father had thought he'd done it, and gone after him at his home … it was possible. And then Leo had taken his father's dump truck and his key to the festival grounds and dumped the body in the vat?

But Jocelyn's death couldn't have been self-defense. That was murder, plain and simple. Had she confronted Leo and he'd silenced her?

No. I couldn't believe it. Maybe Detective Slate was right and I was refusing to see the obvious with Leo. But my instincts hadn't led me astray yet. I didn't think they were wrong about Mason either. I needed to stop avoiding him and deal.

"Who else was at the winery around that time?" I asked.

"Don't ask me. It wasn't my job to count heads. I was busy talking to the guy from Duck Ridge. We're—we were—talking about collaborating on a limited edition red blend."

"A blend?" I assessed the man, his grizzled cheeks, casual jeans. "Wait, what do you—?"

"I'm the vineyard manager." He smiled, wry. "It's not as glamorous a job as it sounds."

"Was that the only sabotage you experienced?" I asked.

The manager laughed, mirthless. "Isn't it enough?"

"Did Jocelyn and Leo have any enemies?"

He shook his head. "Don't know. We didn't have that kind of relationship. I just work here. For now, at least."

The air conditioner rattled.

I gazed at the metal vats. All that work. All that wine. "What happens to Trivia now?" I asked.

"Hell if I know. I guess the kid gets it. If he's got any brains, he'll sell."

"Why?" I asked.

Jake cocked a brow. "You think Leo knows how to manage a winery?"

My cheeks warmed. No, I didn't.

A door closed somewhere.

"Well, thanks," I said.

"Thanks for what?" Laurel asked from behind me.

I gasped, pivoting.

Planting her hands on her hips, she nudged open her black blazer, exposing the gun holstered at her hip. A badge glinted on one side of her belt.

Detective Slate stood next to her. "I'd be interested to know that as well," he said.

"I thought I'd dropped my ... pepper spray in the parking lot last night," I lied. "I just returned to see if anyone had found it." Behind my back, I crossed my fingers. As lies went, this one was on shaky ground.

"Pepper spray?" Laurel's voice whip-cracked. "Or mace?"

"Mad definitely said pepper spray," Dieter said, giving me a warning look. "But I didn't notice any. Did you, Jake?"

The other man shrugged. "Nope."

"You should have asked us," Detective Slate said. "We searched the lot."

"I don't suppose you found it," I said.

"No," Slate said. "You should get the kind that attaches to your key chain. It's harder to lose, and you're more likely to have it at hand if something happens. You can buy it at Red's, downtown."

"Thanks." It looked like Jake and Dieter were going to cover for me. "I'll do that. Thanks." Stomach knotting, I sidled out of the winery and race-hobbled to my truck.

I drove down the winding drive. In spite of my run-in with the cops, my trip to Trivia Vineyards had been worth it. I'd learned the truck that had dumped Romeo's body had been his own. He'd been enraged over the loss of half a million dollars' worth of wine. And he'd probably gone after the culprit, or the person he *thought* was the culprit. I really, really hoped it wasn't Leo.

The breeze from the window tossed my hair. I checked the dash clock. I needed to relieve Leo at the museum.

But first, I stopped at Red's. I'd lied my butt off at Trivia Vineyards, and at least I could make my deception half true by picking up pepper spray.

Red's sold pseudo-military supplies and martial arts equipment. The Asian man behind the counter turned out to be the owner, Red. He tried to upsell me on camo pants, but I stuck with the pepper spray.

Clipping the faux-leather case to my key chain, I wore it out the door and drove to the museum, parking in the alley.

I walked down the bamboo-lined hall into the tea room. Women scarfed afternoon tea cakes stacked on modern-looking, tiered white ceramic plates. The Fox and Fennel smelled of pumpkin and cinnamon, and in spite of everything, my mouth watered. Working next door to what amounted to a dine-in bakery could be torture. Delightful, decadent torture. Clenching my jaw, I breezed through the bookcase door and into the Paranormal Museum.

Mrs. Gale whirled on me, her loose black pants and tunic flaring, a carving knife raised shoulder level.

I shrieked, fumbling for my pepper spray. "Don't do it!"

"Oh, goddess!" She dropped the knife and it clattered to the floor.

Leo hurried in from the gallery, a black pumpkin with gold stripes cradled in his arms. "What happened?"

I clutched my chest and leaned against the bookcase, shutting it with my weight. "'Oh, goddess'? Are you Wiccan now?"

Mrs. Gale bent and picked up the knife. "Certainly not! I'm simply exploring the goddess archetypes."

"What are you doing here?" I asked.

"I came to see you, and then Leo explained the problem with the pumpkins."

"Problem?" I asked.

"If we carve them, they go rotten in a day." Leo laid the pumpkin beside the cash register. "But just having plain old pumpkins lying around is lame. We're a paranormal museum."

"So I suggested non-violent alternatives," Mrs. Gale said. "And then it seemed more fun to help than leave him with instructions. It's been ages since I've decorated for Halloween. Now that my kids are gone, it just isn't the same. My son used to build amazing haunted scenes in our front yard. I'm afraid my place is a disappointment now at Halloween."

"I can help you decorate your house," Leo said.

"You would?" she asked.

He shrugged. "There aren't many kids trick-or-treating in my neighborhood. I can shut the house without worrying about getting egged. Besides, you helped me decorate the pumpkins. It's only fair."

I smiled. Maybe Leo had found some parental-type supervision on his own.

Mrs. Gale clapped her hands together, her rings clacking. "That would be marvelous! Why don't you come by this weekend and we can discuss ideas for the yard?"

They agreed on a time, and I tucked my messenger bag beneath the counter. I had to admit it, the pumpkins were eye-catching. A row of miniature ones, painted with a sinister code of gold rectangles, lined the windowsill. Larger white pumpkins decorated with brass upholstery tacks sat in a pyramid. They added a touch of elegance to the museum.

"So if you weren't using the carving knife," I said, "what do you have a carving knife for?"

Leo shrugged one shoulder. "I forgot to return it to the Fox and Fennel the other day."

"And then I knocked it to the floor," Mrs. Gale said. "You startled me just as I was picking it up."

Mystery solved. "You said you came here to see me?" I asked Mrs. Gale.

She floated to the counter, GD sniffing at her heels. "It has come to my attention that certain people are spreading rumors that I had something to do with Romeo's death."

I blinked. "I would never spread rumors!"

"Not you, dear. That gargoyle from Ladies Aid." Her upper lip curled. "Eliza Bigelow."

Leo's dark brows drew together. "Why would anyone think you had something to do with my father's death?"

She shook her head, her crescent moon earrings swinging. "It's utter nonsense. They have it in their heads that I might have used him to sabotage the grape stomp. As if I would lower myself to sabotage!"

"You did sort of, er, threaten it," I said.

She laughed. "Oh, that! I was just blowing off steam, dear. Now, I'm rather embarrassed about my outburst. Your mother, of all people, did not deserve to be the focus of my ire. Even if I don't agree with her tactics, she's only trying to do what's best."

"Tactics?"

"At any rate," Mrs. Gale said, "I just wanted to assure you both that it's untrue." Her chin dipped. "And Eliza will not get away with this."

"You see, those are the sorts of things that some people might misconstrue as a threat," I said.

"Merely a promise, my dear. Merely a promise." She turned to Leo. "So, Sunday evening then?"

He nodded.

"Ta!" Waggling her fingers at us, she fluttered out the front door. The bell jingled behind her.

"How long was she waiting for me?" I asked.

"Long enough for the paint to dry on those pumpkins." He nodded to the window. "I think she's lonely since her kids moved away."

"Yeah. I stopped by your winery today."

Leo's eyebrows squished together. "My winery?"

"I assume Trivia Vineyards is yours now?"

He scratched his cheek. "I guess."

"They said there'd been some sabotage there Friday night. Someone had turned the taps on the wine barrels in the cellar and poured nearly half a million dollars' worth of wine on the floor."

His breath hissed inward, his eyes widening. "What? I worked those harvests! Dammit!" He paced. "The cellar wine is aging from the last few harvests, back when I was still involved. Just manual labor." He stopped and gazed down at a mini pumpkin on the sill.

"I didn't work this year's harvest. It didn't feel right going there anymore."

"But you went by the winery on Friday."

"Romeo called. He said he wanted to talk. I figured I'd listen to what he had to say. Turned out to be just a bunch of BS about tradition and family and hard work. Like he would know anything about being a family."

"Was he worried or upset?"

Leo's laugh was hard, flat. "Only about me. I wasn't holding up the family name. He wanted me back in the vineyard."

"It sounds like he was trying."

"Maybe." Leo knit his lip. "I think Jocelyn was putting pressure on him to bring me back into the fold." He shook his head. "I dunno. It was weird. I hadn't talked to him in months, and then he called out of the blue. I guess that's why I went over there. His call surprised me."

"Did you see anyone or anything that might have led to the sabotage?"

His fists clenched. "If I had, I would have stopped it. Have you ever worked a harvest? It's work. Real work. Not like here—no offense."

"None taken." I knew what he meant. I'd worked harvests when I was a teen. It was hot, backbreaking work. But there was satisfaction in helping produce something tangible, even when you were too young to drink it. "How did it go here?"

"It's Wednesday."

And not exactly a boom day for tourism. "That bad, huh?"

"Oh," he said, "Mason stopped by."

I straightened. "Did he say anything?"

"Said he'd see you tomorrow."

I slumped.

Well, I'd done that to myself by avoiding him earlier. But heck, I'd tackled a vineyard investigation. I could face Mason.

Tomorrow.

SEVENTEEN

"Here's your roast beef." Leo tossed a paper-wrapped sandwich over the cash register.

I caught it one-handed. "Thanks. I'm starving." Above me, the air conditioner rattled and hummed, fighting a losing battle with the noon-time heat. But if the museum wasn't exactly cool, it didn't seem to deter my Thursday visitors. Half a dozen people roamed the three rooms. A couple in T-shirts and shorts perused the exhibits in cases on the far wall, opposite my perch.

"Why's the motorcycle shop closed today?" Leo asked, pulling a wad of napkins from the pocket of his *Paranormal Museum* hoodie.

Throat tightening, I paused in the act of unwrapping my sandwich. Mason's shop had been closed when I arrived that morning. What was going on?

"I don't know," I said. "Mason must have taken another day off."

"I was hoping he'd look at my bike."

"You have a motorcycle?"

Leo colored. "I got it used."

"You mean, you bought it recently?"

GD leapt to the counter and nosed at the sandwich.

His chin jutted forward. "I'm an adult. It's my money."

Had Leo already started spending in expectation of his inheritance? That wasn't a good sign.

"So what's the plan?" he asked.

GD butted against my hand.

"The plan is I eat this sandwich." I glared at the cat. *Mine.* "Then I take the grape press to the haunted house and make sure everything's ready for tonight's opening." Jorge had helped me load the press back into the truck. "You stay here and hold down the fort."

Leo's brow rumpled. "Are you sure you don't want me to go? I know the electronics."

This was true, but in my role as girl detective, it was my duty to sniff around the haunted house. People would be there who had known Jocelyn and Romeo. Also, I suddenly needed to get as far away from the motorcycle shop as possible. "There may be some administrative stuff with Ladies Aid to deal with there. If I get hung up on the electronics, I'll call, and you can walk me through the tech."

Leo nodded. "You know where to find me."

Gathering my sandwich, I rose from behind the counter and motioned to my wooden seat. "The captain's chair is all yours." I grabbed my messenger bag from the shelf beneath the register and headed through the bookcase to the Fox and Fennel. The tables were filled by babbling diners, but Adele was nowhere in sight. Since I'd been banned from the kitchen (don't ask), I went to her office and rapped on the door. It swung open beneath my fist. Adele, neat in her white blouse and apron, looked up from behind a sturdy metal desk.

"Mind if I eat here?" I asked. "Short of huddling inside the spirit cabinet, there's no privacy to be found in the museum."

"Go ahead." She pulled a pencil from her chignon and made a notation on a spreadsheet. "But you'll be dining alone, I'm afraid." She motioned around the cramped room at the neat bookshelves, the printer, the stacked boxes. "I just came in here to check on an order."

"How's your day going?"

"Busy." She brandished a stack of receipts. "Marcelle called in sick, business is booming due to the haunted house opening tonight, and I have to prep for the Death Bistro."

"Mmm. It's been busier than usual at the museum too."

She set down the papers and peered at me. "Are you all right?"

"Yeah. Sure. Why wouldn't I be?"

"How are things with you and Mason?"

"You noticed his shop was closed too?"

"Is it? Why?"

"I don't know."

"Oh. Is something wrong?"

"Not something. Just about everything." I unloaded—the ex-girlfriend, the evasions, his declaration of love.

Adele listened, frowning. "Mason strikes me as an honorable man," she said. "I don't think he'd tell you he loved you if he didn't mean it. Is that why you've been avoiding him?"

"I haven't been avoiding him. Mostly he's been avoiding me, or he's just been unavailable."

"Mostly?" Her left brow rose. "It doesn't sound like you've been trying too hard to get to the bottom of this. What are you afraid of?"

"I'm afraid something's gone wrong."

"And so you're fixing it by avoiding the problem?"

It sounded stupid when she put it that way. "I planned to talk to him today, but his shop is closed."

"Have you tried calling him?"

"Of course. I mean, I left a message. If I call again, I'll seem desperate."

"Oh, we're playing that game, are we? You're better than that, Maddie." She stood and edged from behind the desk. "Call him. I'll give you some privacy." Leaving the room, she closed the door softly behind me.

Adele was right. I was being at worst a coward and at best a fool. Digging my cell phone from my messenger bag, I called Mason.

It went to voicemail, and my breath hitched. I shouldn't have run when I saw him yesterday.

He rumbled through his greeting.

I plastered a smile on my face because I'd read that people can sense over the phone when you're not smiling. "Hi, Mason, it's Maddie. It's been a while since we've spoken, and I know you wanted to talk to me about something. It seemed like you had a lot on your plate, so I thought I'd give you some space, but now I'm feeling like I was wrong. Anyway, please call me when you can. I miss you."

I hung up, making a face. Good thing I was an independent woman in the twenty-first century who was not going to make mountains of molehills. Ha. I ripped the paper off my sandwich and tore into it, wishing I'd asked Leo to buy barbecue chips too. Sue me. I'm an emotional eater.

Picking a slice of jalapeno from the damp paper, I popped it in my mouth, enjoying the vinegary burn. I could limp to the corner market and buy those chips I was craving. They would take my mind off Mason for maybe thirty seconds. Or I could step up and get some actual investigating done.

I scrounged for Detective Slate's business card in my leather wallet. He picked up on the second ring.

"Slate here."

"Hi, this is Maddie Kosloski. I was wondering if you'd found anything on that old murder-suicide?"

"I found the file in the archives—actually, the archivist found it for me—but I haven't had a chance to go through it. Things have been busy around here."

"An understatement, I'm sure. Is there any chance I could come by and take a look at it?"

"Sure. I've checked it out in your name. If I have to go anywhere, I'll leave it with the desk sergeant."

"I'll be there in ten minutes."

Crumpling up the remains of my sandwich, I dropped it in the metal wastebasket beside Adele's desk and left through the alley door.

I unlocked my pickup and glanced up at Mason's apartment windows.

His blinds were shut, and that meant he probably wasn't home. Mason was all about natural lighting. Where *was* he?

I climbed into my truck and drove to the police station.

In the mint-green reception area, I announced myself to the desk sergeant.

He made a call, and Detective Slate strode into the room. He was jacketless, his shirt sleeves rolled up, a manila folder in his hand. Smiling, he jerked his head toward the hallway. "This way."

He led me to a glass-walled conference room and dropped the folder on the long wooden table. "Are you planning another mock retrial?" Back in the spring, I'd cosponsored a mock retrial for the McBride case.

"Do we need one?" I tweaked the pull cord on the dusty mini-blinds, energy fizzing through my veins. This was exactly what I needed—more research, less moping.

"Not if this file is anything to go by. There's not much here."

He opened the folder and spread a series of black-and-white photos on the table. "Crime-scene photography came into its own in the 1920s. This was the only murder that year, so the local photographer went all out. Unfortunately, it still doesn't give us much to work with."

I leaned over the photos. "Alcina's burnt cottage." Even in grainy black-and-white, the photographer had captured the horror. Charred bodies sprawled on the floor, the ruins blackened rubble.

Slate's dark brows rose. "You knew?"

"The bit about the remains being discovered in her burnt cottage was in that old newspaper article I showed you. But what I don't understand is, who burned the cottage? If this was a murder-suicide, and both bodies were found inside, who set the fire?"

"Luigi could have set the fire after killing Alcina, and then shot himself before the flames consumed him. It's not that uncommon. The murderer is ashamed of what he's done, so he tries to blot out the evidence before he kills himself."

I grimaced. And that was the difference between a professional investigator and amateur Maddie. Slate actually knew what he was talking about.

"At any rate," he added, "the police report seems cut and dried." He drew out a yellowed piece of paper and handed it to me.

Our fingertips brushed, and again electricity shivered through my core.

Not daring to look up, I laid the paper on the table and focused on the writing. We'd reached the era of the typewriter, so the report was legible even if some of its letters had faded. "Alcina's father had to be hospitalized from shock and smoke inhalation after trying to put out the fire." The poor man. When had he realized his daughter was inside the burning cottage? I shook my head. I couldn't imagine that sort of loss.

"There wasn't much police and fire department cooperation in those days," Slate said. "It's kind of impressive that the two worked together in this case."

"The good old days, when San Benedetto was cutting edge."

"You should read the police reports on bootlegging. San Benedetto was a hotbed of excitement."

"You're kidding. I thought San Benedetto avoided all that business by selling grapes direct to homes so people could make their own wine?"

"Yeah. Well. Whenever you make something illegal, someone will find a way to make a profit from selling more."

"So much for San Benedetto as sleepy backwater. And as far as the Paganini murders, I don't suppose you've—"

"Maddie, you know I can't discuss those cases, especially not with you."

My hands curled around my middle. "I get it. I'm a suspect."

"You're sticking your nose in. Last time you tried that, you nearly got yourself killed. You're lucky I haven't charged you with impeding an investigation."

"Impeding? How have I impeded?" And how had he managed to keep Laurel from charging me with something?

"That story about dropping your pepper spray in the Trivia parking lot? Do you really think I'm that gullible?"

"No." I picked up the folder. "But a girl can hope. Thanks for turning me on to Red's, by the way." I lifted my key chain from the front pocket of my messenger bag. The pepper spray jangled against my keys.

"Let me see that."

I handed him the key ring, and he removed the spray canister from its leather wrap and squinted at it. "All right, this stuff's okay. It expires in a year, though. You'll have to buy another next October."

"Pepper spray has an expiration date? Really?"

He slid the canister back into the leather. "The date's on the canister."

"Does it really expire, or is that just one of those marketing gimmicks to make you buy more?"

"Expired spray isn't as effective. You might also want to take a class in using it."

"I think I can figure out how to press a button on my own."

He grinned. "Just make sure the wind's blowing in the right direction."

"I should have gotten a Taser."

He laughed, an infectious baritone. "Do you want to take the file with you?"

"Yes, please."

"You've got it for two weeks, then I come after you."

"I'll return it before you have to put out a warrant."

Slate walked me down the hall, past an open cubicle area. Uniform and plainclothes officers milled in the hall, hunched over computers. A female officer hailed him, waving him over.

We stopped in front of a largish empty cubicle with his nameplate on the wall. "Do you mind waiting here?"

I shook my head. "Nope."

"And don't even think about rifling my desk for clues."

"If I thought you had a clue—"

"Don't say it." He hurried to his colleague. She spoke to him in a low tone and motioned toward her computer monitor.

He bent over it, squinting.

Rifling his desk would have been rude, even if I'd had the nerve to do it in front of a dozen cops. So I satisfied myself with a hands-free perusal. Nature calendar pinned to the cubicle wall and surrounded by a random design of pushpins. Computer (off). Stack of multi-colored index cards (blank). Box of lemon bars…

Lemon bars?

I rocked on my heels. Ladies Aid had boasted they "owned" a cop. And they'd used lemon bars to extract donations from one man. Was Ladies Aid using the pastries to literally keep their inside man at the police station sweet?

But Detective Slate? I didn't know what was worse—that he could be corrupted, or that he'd been corrupted and *still* wouldn't tell me the details of the investigation.

Lemon bars! I swayed, grasping the edge of the cubicle divider. There had been lemon bars at Jocelyn's house the night she'd been killed. She'd set them out on the table along with a bottle of sparkling wine. But she and Ladies Aid were on the outs—Jocelyn was part of Mrs. Gale's splinter group. How could she have gotten her hands on the coveted lemon bars? Unless someone from Ladies Aid had brought them to her, perhaps as a peace offering. The killer?

I shook my head. Corrupting a cop was one thing, but murder? Could someone in Ladies Aid possibly ...? And my mother! This put a whole new slant on why she'd gotten me involved in the investigation. I took a deep breath. It wasn't possible. Just another case of my imagination—

"Maddie? Are you okay?"

I shook myself.

Detective Slate loomed over me, his face creased with concern.

"Lemon bars!" I stabbed my finger at them. "How could you?"

He blinked. "Do you want one?"

"No. And I'll find my own way out of the police station, thank you very much."

I turned and headed left.

"The exit's to the right," he called.

Turning, I hobbled in the opposite direction. Were lemon bars the new street drug? Did they lure its victims with their sunshiny innocence, and then hook them with sweet and sour decadence?

Manila folder pressed to my chest, I stumbled from the police station.

I had to face facts.

My mother was dealing.

———

I drove through the vineyards and mulled the lemon bar connection. There was probably an innocent explanation. But there was definitely something weird about those bars.

234

A massive new gate rose at the entry to CW Vineyards. Shiny with fresh paint, it stood open, and I turned down the gravel track.

I bumped past the colonnade of almond trees, slowing to a halt in the packed parking lot of the Gothic haunted house. Women in blue T-shirts buzzed around, their gray caps of hair no doubt concealing devious plots. On the south side of the lawn, the barn's tall doors were shut fast.

I should have asked Leo to come set up the grape press and final electronics. But sending him into this lion's den of matronly mafiosa hardly seemed fair. I was the boss, and I would take the risks.

Slithering out of the truck, I limped to the rear and unlocked the tailgate, sliding out the dolly. I maneuvered the grape press to the edge and hefted it onto the ground. My vision blurred, and I clutched the press's circular handle. Was it my imagination, or had my life gone south ever since the press had entered, stage left? Maybe it *was* cursed.

Oh, what was I thinking? The only person I had to blame for the current chaos in my life was myself. Jamming the dolly beneath the press, I rolled it to the porch steps and bumped it up and inside.

A narrow-faced woman gripped a clipboard and gazed at me over her spectacles. "And you are?"

I flinched. Name, rank, and serial number only. And if I could avoid giving out my name, I would. "Paranormal Museum. Here to finalize the preparation for the Haunted San Benedetto room."

She consulted her clipboard. "Ah, yes. Miss Kosloski."

She knew my name! Ladies Aid was worse than the NSA.

The woman pointed with her pen to one of the openings beside the divider. "Through there."

I scuttled through the entrance to my Haunted San Benedetto room, rolling the dolly before me. The room looked pretty much as I'd left it. Blank-faced mannequins surrounding the table with the ghost-hunting equipment and TV monitor. The fencing for the grape press stood hooked in a square, defending empty space.

I shoved the fence aside, put the grape press where it belonged, and lifted the fence over the press.

Whisking the *Invisible Haunted Grape Press* sign from its hook, I rummaged in my bag. The original *Haunted Grape Press* placard was buried beneath a wad of receipts from the taqueria. I hung it on the fence and hobbled to the electronics table.

Footsteps and women's laughter tumbled down the stairs.

I froze, hoping no one would peek around the hanging divider wall and find me. What had I gotten myself into? More to the point, what had my mother gotten herself into?

"What are those things?" a masculine voice asked.

"Augh!" I jumped, turned, landed on my bad foot, and groaned.

Chuck grinned through his elaborate facial hair. He tucked his tie beneath his tweed vest. "Sorry. Didn't mean to scare you."

"Why would I be scared? Just because San Benedetto is in the grip of a conspiracy, and I'm in a haunted house, and there's a killer on the loose? Is there a basement here? Because if there is, I think I'll go investigate, alone, and twist my ankle on the way down the steps."

He angled his head. "Bad day?"

I began to agree, but my problems paled in comparison to Leo's. And poor Jocelyn. At least no one was trying to kill me, but if that was my low bar for happiness, then my attitude needed adjusting. I changed the subject. "How's the other setup going?"

"I've been assured all will be ready when we open at seven," he said. "I find it hard to believe, but at this point, things are out of my hands."

"You're a risk-taker."

"What do you mean by that?" he asked.

"Putting your tasting room in the hands of Ladies Aid for the haunted house."

He shrugged. "Oh, right. Well, it's Ladies Aid, isn't it? It's not like I'm joining forces with the mob."

"I wouldn't bet on it," I muttered.

"What?"

"Nothing. I'd better get back to the electronics. Do you know who's going to be in charge of the actual event? I'd like to show them how to turn the equipment on and off."

Chuck looked around the room. "I think Betsy Kendle is the lady you're looking for. I saw her upstairs earlier."

My stomach plunged. It would have to be the dragon lady's second in command. "I'll check there. Thanks."

Chuck shambled off.

I approached the ghost-hunter table. The mannequins regarded me, their gazes critical.

Ignoring them, I tackled the monitor setup. After a few misfires with the tangle of cables and remote controls, I set the video to replay the five minute loop.

Satisfied, I surveyed the room. The video screen flickered, and the mannequins watched, diverted. The grape press stood, in all its haunted glory, in the center of the room. At the far side, above the display about the McBride murder, the noose swung morosely from the balcony.

I did a double take. Swung? Why was it swinging? No one should have been up on that balcony—not after I'd nearly gotten flattened by an empty wine barrel. Had Chuck reached up and jiggled the noose on his way out? Uneasy, I hurried to the stairs, keeping a wary eye on the barrels above.

On the second floor, I searched for Betsy and found her in the haunted library. She teetered on a stepladder, stringing spider webs between bookshelves. Cadaverous portraits frowned down at us. Yellow police tape marked the shape of a body on the wooden floor.

Something brushed the top of my head and I darted sideways, sucking in my breath.

Betsy twisted on the stepladder and laughed, her cornflower-blue eyes twinkling. "Gotcha!"

Feeling foolish, I brushed the fake spiderweb away. "And in broad daylight. Nicely done."

She clapped her pudgy hands together, delighted, and I felt silly. There was nothing menacing about Betsy, even if she was part of the Ladies Aid crew. I'd once again let my imagination run wild.

"And the eyes in the portraits glow red," she said. "Did you need something?"

I explained about the electronics. Dutifully, she followed me downstairs and watched me demonstrate.

"It seems simple enough," she said. "I'll make sure they're turned on before start time and off when we pack your room away for the night. I'm glad you kept things simple. If I had to rehang cobwebs every afternoon, I'd go mad."

I lifted the tablecloth. "There are some spare batteries down here."

"Got it." She walked beneath the noose to the McBride display and touched a finger to the photo of the victims. "Who would have thought a small town like San Benedetto would have so much horror in its history?"

My gaze flicked to the loft. "Not to mention its present."

"Oh." Her expression turned serious. "Jocelyn and Romeo. Have you gotten any farther on your investigation?"

"I really can't say," I said, playing it cool.

She winked. "I understand. I'll tell the committee you're closing in."

"There's a murder committee?"

She laughed. "Heavens, no. The external affairs committee."

"Of course," I murmured.

"Your mother has called in a lot of markers for you."

"What do you mean?"

"Not everyone approves of your museum, or your ... activities. Your mother's always been your champion." Her eyes glinted. "It would be a shame to let her down. You know how organizations can be. Some people might take a failure the wrong way."

I gulped. No, that didn't sound like a threat. No, not at all.

EIGHTEEN

Bamboo tea tray in her arms, Adele walked through the open bookcase. She stopped short, brown eyes widening. A coil of black hair slipped from her chignon to her shoulder, twining around the strap of her crisp apron. "You!"

Harper waggled her fingers. "Hi, Adele."

"You're not..." She looked about the museum. Small, circular tables covered in black cloths clustered about the room. In the center of each table stood a flameless candle amidst mini pumpkins and autumn leaves.

Elthia, in a long skirt and black, high-necked Victorian blouse, greeted a couple in black denim at the door.

GD surveyed his kingdom from atop a bronze skull.

Adele swallowed. "Harper, tell me you're not a member of this Bistro of Death."

"No." Harper crossed her legs sheathed in tight designer jeans. Her olive-colored V-neck shirt made her skin look golden. "I'm a member of the Death Bistro."

I edged backward, putting more counter between myself and the coming explosion.

"YOU were the one responsible for those flyers!"

Harper raised her hands in a warding gesture. "That wasn't me, though I did suggest your tea room for our meeting. The Fox and Fennel is fantastic, Adele, and the atmosphere is so much more elegant than that health food store we've been using."

Adele raised her chin. "Of course it is." Laying down the tray, she arranged its contents—small plates of mini scones and cookies—on one of the tables. "But really, Harper, a Death Bistro? People will think you're..." She looked around for eavesdroppers and lowered her voice to a whisper. "Weird."

"We all die," Harper said. "The only choice we have in the matter is how we deal with it."

Adele blew out her breath. "Fine. I'm happy to cater future Death Bistros, as long as they're in the Paranormal Museum. Besides, I'd think you'd prefer to be in here, among all the momento moris."

Elthia turned and walked to us. "Did I hear 'momento mori'? Have you got any from the Victorian era?"

I pointed to a shadowbox on the opposite wall. "A fan made of hair, from Philadelphia, 1853. Believed to be haunted by the hair's owner."

Shuddering, Adele busied herself at the other tables, laying out pastries.

"This entire museum is a momento mori," Harper said. "There are memories of death in every corner."

"We should have thought of moving the Bistro here earlier," Elthia said.

The bell above the door tinkled, and Elthia whipped around. "Chuck!" She bustled over to him.

"How long has this Bistro been going on?" I asked Harper.

"About six months."

"And you just talk about death?"

"You'll see. You're staying, aren't you?"

I might have gone upstairs to hang out with Mason while the party went on. But not tonight. Mason still hadn't returned my calls. His apartment lights were on, but I couldn't bring myself to knock on his door.

I forced a smile. "I wouldn't miss it for the world."

Her gaze softened, looked past me. "You're afraid of what you'll find if you push, aren't you?"

I blinked. Was she talking about Mason or my so-called murder investigation?

She shook her head. "Sorry, I was drifting for a moment. How's your investigation going?"

"A reliable source informed me I'm getting dangerously close to interfering in a police case. It seems that's illegal."

"A reliable source?"

"Detective Slate."

Harper sighed. "He could put me in handcuffs any time."

"Not funny."

"No, I guess it isn't." She straightened off the counter. "For a moment there, back in my office, I thought they might cart me off for interrogation."

"Have they come back to you with more questions?"

"No," she said, her tone repressive.

A woman emerged from the gallery. "Are those Ouija boards for sale?"

"They are! I'll be right there." I hustled toward the gallery, but Chuck touched my arm.

"Hey," he said.

"Hi." I edged toward the potential sale. "What are you doing here? I thought you'd be at the haunted house."

He laughed. "Are you kidding? I couldn't wait to get away from it. At this point, if something goes wrong, I don't want to know."

Ouija-board lady caught my eye.

"Excuse me," I said. "I need to help a customer." Hurrying into the gallery, I got caught in a discussion of the history of Ouija boards and the American spiritualist movement. I knew more about either topic than was healthy. But I'd entered a brave new world of corpses, runaway boyfriends, and Death Bistros.

I returned to the main room to ring up the board, and Detective Laurel Hammer strode through the front door. Pulling a wallet from the pocket of her blue blazer, she flashed her badge at Elthia.

The Death Bistro hostess reared away and clutched her chest, as if Laurel had presented her with a viper.

Laurel grabbed a chair from a table and moved it against a wall. Running her hand through her short blond hair, she sat.

GD strolled in from the Fortune Telling Room and stopped, one paw raised, ears swiveling. Spotting Laurel, he lowered his body closer to the ground.

I scooped him up and set him on the counter beside a plate of tea things, then sat behind the register.

Torn, the cat shifted his gaze between Laurel and the shreds of roast beef dangling from one of the sandwiches.

Elthia went to stand behind an empty chair at one of the tables. She rapped a teaspoon against a teacup. "Everyone? I'd like to start, if it's okay."

Guests made their way to the tables. Chair legs scraped against the linoleum floor.

My eyes widened. Wearing a peach-colored tunic, Mrs. Gale sat at one of the tables. What was the renegade from Ladies Aid doing here?

Elthia rattled through Death Bistro business—collecting fees for the night, their new website. "And next month, Harper Caldarelli will discuss advanced health care directives." She looked down at the table, her fingertips pressing into the black fabric. "And of course, Romeo. We'll need to vote in a new president. It seems strange, so soon after he's gone. It's as if we're erasing his memory."

The group burst into denials.

"He understood better than anyone that we need to make the most of our finite lives," a dark-haired young woman said. "We mourn him, and we move through the loss. We can't pretend it didn't happen."

I cleared my throat. "Especially since Romeo's wasn't an ordinary death. It was murder."

Elthia gestured toward me. "This is Maddie, our hostess for tonight and the owner of the Paranormal Museum. She discovered Romeo's body. I can only imagine how shocking it must have been."

Murmurs of sympathy drifted around the tables.

Elthia resumed her seat. "And she's right. How he died can't help but color our reactions."

The conversation veered into weird-and-terrible-deaths-I-have-known.

I jiggled my leg, trying to think of ways to bring the conversation back to Romeo. But this wasn't my party. If I wanted to learn more about Romeo's death, I'd have to be patient.

GD butted my hand. I offered him a morsel of roast beef from the tiny sandwich. The cat sniffed, considering, then nipped it from my fingers.

"I can't believe someone killed him," the dark-haired woman said.

An opening at last. "You all knew Romeo," I said. "Who might have done this? Did anyone have a grudge against him?"

Laurel drew a notepad from the inside pocket of her blazer.

Elthia's grip on her teacup tightened, her knuckles whitening. "You can't be suggesting one of us—"

"Of course none of you," I said. "But did he say anything? Was he worried or stressed out?"

"Everyone loved Romeo," Elthia said.

Grimacing, a burly thirty-something scratched his beard, the red-gold of a sunset. "That's not entirely true."

Elthia went rigid. "Of course it is!"

"I ran into him in the hardware store a couple weeks back," the redhead said. "He took a phone call. I don't know who he was talking to, but he seemed pretty tense."

Laurel made a note.

"What did he say?" I asked.

He rubbed the back of his thick neck. "I can't remember exactly. Something about money and keeping your grubby hands off my winery."

"Was he talking to a man or a woman?" Peeling a watercress leaf from a shred of roast beef, I handed the meat to the cat.

He shrugged. "I couldn't tell, but it sounded like something was going on with his business."

"He had a successful winery," Elthia said. "I'm sure it was nothing. It's not as if he had money troubles."

"Someone sabotaged Trivia Vineyards," I said. "They dumped nearly half a million dollars' worth of wine on the floor. That might have caused financial problems."

Harper's expression shifted. "When did that happen?"

"The night he died," I said.

"So they went ahead with it." A Marilyn Monroe look-alike crumbled her scone, scattering bits of dried apricot and coconut on her plate. Her sleepy cat-eyes narrowed.

"Went ahead with what?" Harper asked.

"He told me he'd been getting threats," the platinum blonde said.

"What sort of threats?" I asked.

The blonde shook her head. "He wouldn't say. I think he was a little proud of it, and more angry than scared."

Elthia pinked. "That's impossible. He didn't say anything to me. You must be mistaken."

"I don't think so," the blonde said, cool. "I was there when he got the phone call. Romeo swore, told the person where he could shove his threats, and hung up. Afterward, he tried to laugh it off, said he was getting prank calls, but I could see he was furious." She glanced at me. "And no, I couldn't tell you if it was a man or a woman."

Detective Hammer's jaw clenched.

Whoops. Maybe I should have let her ask the questions. I slipped GD the last of the roast beef.

"This doesn't get us any closer to finding Romeo and Jocelyn's killer." Chuck knit his hands together on the table. "They were murdered. It's obvious that someone had it out for them."

Voices rose, a confused babel.

Gaze fixed on the detective, GD tried to slip from the counter. I grabbed him, pulling him onto my lap. Yowling with indignation, he dug his claws into my jeans.

"Back off or no leftovers for you," I hissed.

He subsided, growling, ears twitching.

Elthia rapped on her cup with her teaspoon, silencing the crowd. "I think we're getting off topic."

Harper quirked a brow. "Our Death Bistro president and his wife were murdered. I can't think of anything more on topic."

"We're not crime solvers," Elthia sputtered. "We dishonor Romeo's memory—and Jocelyn's—by focusing on the person who killed him, rather than on his life. Now, on to the next item of business. Elections."

The group voted Elthia in as president of the Death Bistro and made Harper VP. Judging by the look on Harper's face, she wasn't thrilled by the new position.

At least I'd learned something: Romeo had been getting threats. So the murder probably wasn't a spur of the moment thing. Resentment had been simmering—assuming the same person who made the threats killed him.

The Bistro wound down, GD attempting the occasional bolt for freedom. I was kept busy ringing up sales of *Paranormal Museum* mugs and T-shirts, and Halloween art from the gallery, so I had to release the cat.

Laurel mingled with the guests, handing her business card to the two who'd reported hearing the threats. GD cat slunk around people's ankles, his narrowed gaze fixed on Laurel.

Mouth taut, I rang up a Halloween-themed tarot deck. Laurel was a big girl and could handle GD by herself.

Adele and her team whisked away the plates and tables. By the time I came up again for air, the Death Bistro folks had gone, leaving Adele, her cleanup team, and Harper.

Harper smiled crookedly and slung her leather bag over her shoulder. "Well? What did you think?"

"Sales were better than I expected," I said. "You were right about the group."

"I meant about Romeo's murder. Interesting that Laurel was here."

"Yeah. I may be a hot suspect, but at least she's looking at other angles." Unless the only reason she'd come to the Death Bistro was because she knew I'd be there.

"I'd no idea Romeo had been threatened," Harper said.

"Do you know the names of the two who mentioned those threatening phone calls?"

"Sure. Got a piece of paper?"

I slid a yellow pad across the counter, and Harper wrote down two names in her neat script. "I can get you their contact info if you want it." She looked up at me and grinned. "Now that I'm VP of this club, I have access to our membership roster."

"Is that why you agreed to do the job?"

"I agreed because no one else would. But being VP isn't hard. I just run the meeting when the president can't."

"And should something happen to the president, you step into the position."

"A good reason to do everything in my power to keep Elthia healthy," she said.

Adele strode through the open bookcase and stopped in the center of the empty room, hands on her well-clad hips. The tables had been removed and the museum returned to order, or as much order as a paranormal museum could manage. "I think my work here is done," she said. "Harper, can you give me a lift back to my place?"

"What happened to your car?" I asked.

"It's back in the shop, and I've told Mel in no uncertain terms that I'm not paying twice for the same repairs."

Harper rummaged in her bag and drew out a set of keys. "Sure. I'm parked out front. Are you ready to go?"

"Desperately ready," Adele said. "I'll do the washing up tomorrow. Get me out of this madhouse. No offense, Maddie."

"None taken." I was tired too, but at least I'd been well fed. And I'd managed to fulfill my promise to GD, snagging him a leftover roast beef sandwich. I dropped the meat in his food bowl behind the counter.

"Don't stay too late," Adele said.

I locked up after them and cleaned the crumbs from my counter. After a quick sweep of the checkerboard floors, I reviewed the gallery. The Death Bistro members had bought some of my more expensive pieces. I'd need to restock the barren pedestals and empty spaces on the walls.

I checked my watch. It was just after nine o'clock, and I'd rather get the work out of the way now than deal with it in the morning. And it beat going home to face my silent phone.

Walking through the open bookcase, I strode into Adele's office and selected replacement stock. A new Ouija board. A grinning jack-o'-lantern man riding a raven. Primitive paintings of pumpkin patches and spooky houses.

I returned through the darkened tea room to the museum, arranged the new items, and recorded them in my ledger.

GD growled. His bowl was empty. He looked toward the open bookcase door, his tail twitching.

"Sorry, there's no more roast beef." I slid from my chair. There would be hell to pay if GD went questing for food scraps in Adele's tea room.

When I was halfway to the bookcase, something clicked, metallic. The lights went out, plunging the museum into blackness. Hair rose on the back of my neck.

A streetlamp glowed through the window blinds. Using its faint light as a guide, I fumbled my way to the light switch, flicked it up and down.

Nothing.

I swallowed. If the streetlamp was on, it wasn't a general power outage. It was only here, at my haunted museum.

But if ghosts were on the loose, GD would let me know. "Probably just a blown fuse," I told the cat.

Feeling in my purse, my hand fastened on my key ring with its mini flashlight. Head down, I edged through the bookcase door, pausing in the opening to feel my key ring for the light. My fingers brushed something rough and cylindrical. The pepper spray.

The bookcase slammed, bisecting me, squeezing the breath from my lungs. I grunted, too winded to cry out. The door pinned me, the pressure crushing. I struggled to push it open, free myself, but a dark figure held me fast, pinned like a butterfly.

Stars danced before my eyes.

The figure shifted. I raised my arm in a warding gesture, remembered the pepper spray, and squeezed.

My attacker yelped.

The pressure released.

Gasping, I sagged to the floor, my lungs burning. A metallic crash, and the rear door clanged shut.

Coughing, I curled on the cool bamboo floor and gulped air.

GD mewed and sat beside me.

I rose to one elbow and coughed, tears springing to my eyes. My thoughts tangled, hot and angry.

Think. I had to think. Someone had been inside the tea room. The rear door should have automatically locked behind him, but I crawled to my feet and crept down the dark hall to check.

Heart thudding, I gripped my flashlight with one hand, the other clenching the pepper spray. My foot kicked an overturned bucket and I jumped backward. No one leapt at me from the shadows.

I checked the rear door with my flashlight.

Locked.

Retreating into the museum, I shut the bookcase. For good measure, I moved the rocking chair in front of it. It wouldn't stop someone from opening the door, but it would give me advance warning if anyone tried.

Hands trembling, I dumped the contents of my messenger bag on the counter and found my phone. I called Mason.

Voicemail.

I hung up and stared at the phone. And then I cried.

NINETEEN

A SQUAD CAR AND a blue sedan rolled to a halt on the dark street in front of the museum. The pavement glittered, its sheen of mist reflected by the street lamps.

I stood on the brick sidewalk, coughing into the sleeve of my *Paranormal Museum* hoodie. Shivering, I rubbed my arms for warmth.

Slate, rumpled in a navy blue V-neck sweater and jeans, stepped from his sedan. He strode toward me.

I winced. "You were off duty?"

"Given the circumstances," he said, "I'm glad you called. Are you sure you're all right?"

"I'm fine."

Two uniformed officers emerged from the squad car.

"Tell me again what happened," he said.

I ran him through the attack.

"Did you touch the fuse box?" he asked.

"Not tonight."

He nodded. "Good."

Cowardice rather than quick thinking had motivated me. I hadn't wanted to return to the dark tea room. "What about the rear door?" he asked.

"I checked to make sure it was locked. I didn't touch it, but my prints will be all over it anyway. I use that alley door almost every day."

"Okay. Wait here."

He spoke to the uniformed officers, and all three men walked into the museum. Slate stepped outside a few moments later. "How do you open that bookcase?"

"There's a book that says *Open* on the spine. I'll show you." The book could be hard to find if you didn't know what you were looking for.

He held the door for me, and I passed inside. The two uniformed cops skimmed their flashlight beams over the bookcase.

Edging the rocking chair aside, I pressed the book and the case swiveled open. The two uniformed officers darted through.

"This is where he pinned you?" Slate asked.

"Or she."

"A she?"

The lights flooded on, and I winced.

"I'm sorry," I said. "The person seemed big, but it happened fast and was dark. I didn't get a good look at whoever it was." My throat thickened with shame. But it might have been the pepper spray I'd inhaled.

"So he would have had his hand on the bookcase?" Slate said.

I nodded.

"All right. We'll take prints there as well. Tell me more about this Death Bistro."

"In spite of the name, it's a strangely normal group of people who talk about issues around death and dying. Romeo used to be president of the group, and I suspect his interest in death ran deep. Did you know Trivia was the Roman goddess of death?"

"Otherwise known as Hecate, goddess of the underworld and magic." Slate smiled. "I do my research."

My face warmed. Of course he did. "Laur—Detective Hammer was here tonight, taking notes."

As if she'd been summoned by a dark force, the museum door burst open and Laurel strode inside. "What happened?"

"Someone assaulted Miss Kosloski after the Death Bistro ended." Slate explained about the attack.

Laurel swore. "What is it with this place?"

"It's not the museum's fault," I said. And technically, the attack had occurred between the museum and the tea shop.

My stomach quivered. I'd found a body in that exact same place last winter. *Was* there something about the museum? I shook myself.

"Is there anyone who might have it in for you?" Slate asked.

"The mystery is who wouldn't want to kill you," Laurel muttered.

"Now you're just being mean," I said.

Slate shot us repressive looks.

"Sir?" a male voice called, from the other side of the bookcase.

Slate and Laurel walked into the tea room. Since they hadn't told me to stay put, I followed.

A cop squatted beside a square table. He lifted the white tablecloth and pointed to a stainless steel folding knife. "It doesn't look like the other kitchen cutlery."

"That's a pruning knife," I said.

They looked at me.

"Sorry," I said. They hadn't asked my opinion, but that was a farmer's knife. It didn't belong in a tea room.

"She's right," Laurel said. "Bag it." She pointed at me. "And you. Out."

I backed through the open bookcase. Romeo had been stabbed. So had Jocelyn. Was that knife the murder weapon? My legs went wobbly. Had I been the intended next victim?

Laurel shrieked.

GD streaked from the tea room, roast beef and a limp watercress leaf dangling from his mouth.

"Were you in her kitchen?!" I glared at the cat. If Adele found out, she'd call out a hazmat team and stick me with the bill.

The cat dropped the meat into his bowl and sat, smirking.

Laurel stuck her head through the secret door. "And keep that overgrown rat away from me!" She slammed the bookcase shut.

GD and I looked at each other.

"I agree. The rat comment was uncalled for."

Making an O with my mouth, I sucked in my breath. There were cops in Adele's tea room, dusting for prints, and I hadn't bothered to give her a heads-up.

The trend for the evening was not improving.

———

Morning sun slanted through the miniblinds, warming my shoulders through my *Paranormal Museum* T-shirt. I sold a ticket to a retired couple and eased back onto my high chair behind the counter. A spectacular bruise purpled my torso, and I was moving carefully.

New York chic in a black turtleneck and slim skirt, Adele sipped a mug of tea. She leaned one hip against the glass counter, rumpling her *Fox and Fennel* apron. "I told you no good would come out of a Bistro of Death. We shouldn't have let them anywhere near us." She tucked a stray wisp of hair behind her ear, brushing a finger against her pearl earring.

"I went into the storage room to get new stock," I said. "What I can't figure out is why whoever it was didn't attack me at that point. They must have been lurking since after the Death Bistro ended."

"Maybe he wasn't sure if everyone had gone yet." Adele's knuckles whitened on her mug. "Or maybe he was a she."

I coughed. It felt like a fragment of pepper was wedged inside my throat. "At least Leo is off the hook. He wasn't at the Death Bistro."

"Unless he used an accomplice to attack you and give him an alibi."

"A conspiracy in San Benedetto?" I started to laugh but thought of Ladies Aid. Maybe it wasn't so far-fetched. "I don't know. Two killers seems like an awful lot for a small town."

Adele put her mug down with a clatter. "For a small town, we've certainly been racking up the bodies."

Meowing, GD pawed at her pink heels.

She scowled at him. "And you, sir, are not in my good graces! You know perfectly well my tea room is off limits."

His green eyes widened, mournful.

"He's only sucking up to you because you've got that kitchen," I said. GD never looked penitent for me, though he had plenty of offenses to regret.

"Speaking of which," Adele said, "I'd better get back to work before the morning tea crowd arrives." Picking up her mug, she walked to the open bookcase and slipped through, closing it behind her.

I gazed down at GD. "Well? After your performance last night, you'd better find some ghosts for the paying customers."

Whiskers twitching, the cat joined the retirees into the Fortune Telling Room.

I slumped on my seat. Mason's shop was closed again today, and he hadn't returned my messages. What was going on? My stomach rolled.

The wall phone rang. I jerked, startled, then lifted the receiver. "Paranormal Museum, this is Maddie speaking."

"Maddie, this is Harriet Jones from the Historical Association."

"Hi, Harriet. Have you found something about that old murder-suicide?"

"I have, and I think you'll find it intriguing. We have a journal belonging to Alcina's father, Gian. It's mostly financial, but may I bring it to you at the museum today?"

I canted my head, surprised by the special delivery. "Yeah, that would be great. Are you sure it's okay to remove the journal from the Association library?"

She laughed. "For you, of course! I was at the haunted house last night. Your Haunted San Benedetto room was delightful. It provided a real flavor of the town's darker history. And so spooky! Besides, it's been ages since I've been inside the Paranormal Museum. I keep walking past and seeing your Halloween exhibit through the window. It's time I paid a visit."

"Then the entrance ticket's on me. I'll be here all day."

"Excellent! I'll see you soon." She hung up.

I drummed my fingers on the counter. A journal sounded promising. I was making progress on the real story behind the grape press. But I needed to focus on the modern murders. It was time to turn the screws.

Gritting my teeth, I dug a phone number out of my wallet and dialed Mrs. Bigelow.

"Yes?" the Ladies Aid president snapped.

"This is Maddie—"

"I know who it is. Have you something to report?"

"Yes. Someone tried to kill me last night. I'm done with the investigation."

There was a pause. "I see."

"Unless you have some actual information I can use to move the investigation forward, that is. I think you're the kind of woman who knows the people around here well. There aren't a whole lot of local secrets you don't know, are there?"

The pause lengthened. "Romeo and Jocelyn were having marital problems."

"What sort of problems?"

"Jocelyn knew about his affair with that oddly dressed woman—"

"Elthia?"

"Just so. When Romeo was killed, I was certain Jocelyn had something to do with it."

"And now Jocelyn's dead."

"Indeed. Either she had an accomplice who killed her to keep her quiet, or I was wrong."

"Why didn't you tell me this sooner?"

"I do not engage in idle gossip."

"You told me Mrs. Gale was responsible for Romeo's death."

Mrs. Bigelow hesitated. "I'm sorry to say that I wanted her to be guilty. I was angry, and she was on the scene, so to speak. But I hope

I'm honorable enough to admit when I'm wrong. I think you're an honorable person, too, and I'm glad you're investigating. I rather liked Romeo," she said, wistful.

"Did you know him well?"

"No, but he was quite charming, in a European sort of way. Let's just say we had a moment, and leave it at that."

My brows skyrocketed. *A moment?* "What else can you tell me about Romeo?"

The retired couple emerged from the gallery and wandered to the bookcase. The man pressed on one of the book spines, frowned.

"Romeo and I were friendly acquaintances, no more," Mrs. Bigelow said. "Ladies Aid interacts with most of the vintners one way or another. On my part, that interaction was only on a superficial basis. I do not care for alcohol."

"But?"

"But there was something odd going on with him. Unfortunately, I cannot say more as I do not know any more. I suggest you ask your friend Miss Nakamoto about it."

"What does Adele have to do with this?"

"That is an excellent question. Oh, and by the way, you have to remove your grape press from the haunted house. It's too haunted."

I stared at the brass skull, high on a shelf. It needed dusting. "Too haunted? How can a grape press be too haunted?"

"Excuse me?" The retiree pointed at the bookcase. "How does this open?"

I covered the mouthpiece with my hand. "Lower left corner. Press the spine that says *Open.*"

"… quite another thing when adults burst into tears," Mrs. Bigelow finished.

"Sorry, what? Who burst into tears?"

The retirees found the proper book and the case swung open. Looking pleased, they strolled into the tea shop.

"Some ridiculous woman. Said she was a sensitive, whatever that means. But she disturbed the other guests, and I'm afraid word is getting around. We don't want *that* kind of haunted house."

"What kind?"

"The haunted kind. I thought you could replace the exhibit with that silly invisible grape press. You know, that thing you had at the festival?"

"But who was the woman? Do you know her name?" Elthia had said she was a sensitive, but she'd been at the Death Bistro last night, not the haunted house.

"How on earth can I be expected to know the name of every tourist who wanders through our haunted house? I'm not psychic."

Or sensitive, apparently. "All right, I'll change the exhibit."

"The haunted house opens at seven." She hung up.

And tonight the museum closed at six, leaving me just enough time to remove the grape press and swap the signs.

The display had actually made someone cry? GD had reacted to the press, but it couldn't be that horrifying. The blood stains weren't even visible, unless you were a cop.

I banged my hand on the counter. "I'm an idiot!"

GD leapt onto the rocking chair, setting it nodding in agreement.

"It wasn't a murder-suicide at all! It was a double murder."

TWENTY

I DRUMMED MY FINGERS on the counter. The sunlight streaming through the blinds glinted off the glass, highlighting the dust. I grabbed a spray bottle and paper towel from beneath the counter and wiped it down.

Harriet hadn't said what time she'd stop by, and I slid from my chair, pacing. Would Gian Constantino's journal prove my theory? Was the old grape press crime truly a double murder and not a murder-suicide?

GD growled from the rocking chair.

"You're right," I said. "I have to keep focused on the present-day murders." Throwing the paper towel into the wastebasket, I called Mrs. Gale.

She answered, breathless. "Hello?"

"Hi, Cora. This is Maddie Kosloski."

"Oh! Hello, dear. The Death Bistro last night was lovely. Thank you for hosting."

"You're welcome. I wonder if you can help me? After you left last night, someone attacked me in the museum."

"What? Are you all right?"

"I'm fine, but I think someone from the Death Bistro might have snuck into the tea room and lain in wait." Lain? Laid? "Did you notice anyone?"

"No, although I thought Elthia was behaving rather oddly."

Losing your lover can do that to a woman. My heart clenched and I stared out the window, willing Mason to walk past. Had I lost him?

I thrust that thought aside. "I heard that Jocelyn had defected from Ladies Aid to join your Rebelles group. How close were you two?"

Mrs. Gale sighed. "Now I wish we'd been closer. She was clearly a troubled woman. I should have made a greater effort to reach out to her."

"Oh?" Using the flat of my hand, I rolled a pencil along the glass counter.

"As you may have heard, there was trouble in that marriage. I was rather surprised to hear Elthia suggest last night that the Paganinis' vineyard was doing well. Many months, Jocelyn had to dip into her own salary as a professor to help cover the bills."

"So the loss of all that wine last week—"

"Must have been devastating. She loved viticulture, and she was dedicated to wine making. But she was losing patience with Romeo's insistence on quality at all costs. He demanded the very best staff and equipment. But those things all cost money that neither of them had. However, in the weeks leading up to their deaths, something seemed to change. I sensed a cautious, no . . . a conflicted hope in Jocelyn."

"Conflicted?"

"I don't know how to describe it. Although her mood had improved, there seemed to be some cloud of guilt around her. I should have pressed her more. Perhaps then I could have helped."

"Why do you think someone would kill them?"

"That I don't know. I'm sorry I can't be of more help, and I'm sorry you're involved in this."

So was I, but it was too late to back out now. We said our goodbyes and I called my mother.

"Madelyn! How are you?"

"When I found Jocelyn, she had lemon bars on her table."

"What? So?"

"Lemon bars! Stop protecting Ladies Aid. Jocelyn's dead, and she had your lemon bars."

"I think you're being a teensy bit melodramatic. If you had your sister's talent for singing, you could join her on the stage. Did you hear the news about her new contract? She's—"

"Look, Mom, I don't know what's going on, but there were Ladies Aid lemon bars in a murder victim's house. Who might have delivered them?"

"Do you really think someone from Ladies Aid killed Jocelyn?"

"Mommmmm..." I buried my head in my hand. Now I sounded like a whiny teenager. "What's the source of the lemon bars?"

"Mrs. Salvatore. She's a dear, but she's ancient. We've all been trying to get her recipe, but she refuses to share. And a breeze could knock her over. She couldn't have hurt Jocelyn. Are you certain they were her lemon bars?"

"No. I didn't exactly have time to conduct an analysis."

"Sarcasm does not become you," she said. "Were they squares or rectangles?"

"Excuse me?"

"Squares or rectangles?"

I thought back. "Squares."

"Then they weren't our bars. Mrs. Salvatore cuts hers into rectangles."

"And Detective Slate?"

She hesitated. "It isn't what you think."

"So those *were* Ladies Aid lemon bars on his desk!"

"They were Mrs. Salvatore's lemon bars."

The bell over the door jingled. A portly twenty-something in a comic book hero T-shirt slouched into the museum.

I sold him a ticket and he meandered to the far wall, staring at the haunted photos.

"Why did he have Mrs. Salvatore's lemon bars?"

"It's got nothing to do with your investigation."

"Whatever it is, I'll keep it to myself."

My mother blew out her breath. "One of the neighbors complained about the state of Mrs. Salvatore's lawn. As I said, she's rather fragile, so I'm afraid she's let it run to seed. It's embarrassing, but Detective Slate mowed it for her."

"Why is that embarrassing?"

"Because I should have taken care of it myself. She's a member of Ladies Aid, after all, and if we can't rally around to help one of our own members, then what good are we? Ever since Cora ... Well, that's neither here nor there. At any rate, as a thank you, Mrs. Salvatore asked me to deliver a box to Detective Slate, which I was happy to do. He, also, wished his good deed to remain private. Please don't say anything."

"Then who's the cop that Eliza Bigelow has in her pocket?"

Comic Book Guy glanced over his shoulder at me.

I swiveled in my seat, avoiding his gaze.

"Really, Madeline. I could hardly tell you that."

"Why not?"

"It would be unethical."

"Bribing the police is unethical," I hissed.

Comic Book Guy sidled into the Fortune Telling Room, and I relaxed.

"They're just lemon bars, darling. You know, that bakery on San Benedetto Avenue sells square lemon bars. They're not as good as Mrs. Salvatore's, but they're a close second. Perhaps Jocelyn bought them there?"

Great. Was I supposed to go to the bakery with a photo of Jocelyn to confirm it? My stomach rumbled. Why was I griping? I love bakeries! "I'll check it out," I said.

I hung up and searched for Jocelyn Paganini online. The community college website had a brief biography and a photo. I printed out her photo and read the bio. The latter consisted mainly of a list of professional accreditations. I whistled. She'd been a Master of Wine? There were only about three hundred of those in the world.

A few customers trickled in, and I sold them tickets. One bought an American primitive Ouija board—they really were popular. Could I convince the artist to let us continue selling her boards after the exhibit ended? Oooh! Or even design a special edition Paranormal Museum Ouija board?

The bell above the door tinkled and Harriet walked inside. Her lightweight, floral-patterned blouse stuck damply to her ample curves. She smoothed the front of her khaki skirt, shifting the manila envelope beneath her arm. She paused and adjusted her spectacles, ruffling her white hair.

I slid from my chair and walked around the counter. "Harriet, thanks for coming by."

She waved her hand, dismissive. "As much as I enjoy the Historical Association house, it's nice to get out and about." She leaned forward, and I smelled peppermint schnapps. "Sometimes I wonder if that old house we're in is haunted."

"Really?" I asked.

"Haunted by the past, my dear." She handed me the packet. "Such a sad story. I'd read, of course, that poor Mr. Constantino was a broken man after his daughter's death. Everyone knows that's why his vineyard fell apart. After he sold it, he ended up in a sanatorium. But after reading his journal, I wonder if perhaps the death left him a bit unhinged?" She tapped her head with a gnarled finger. "You do bring me the most interesting research projects. I'm ashamed to say that when I cataloged the journal all those years ago, I merely skimmed it. You forced me to read it more closely." She shook her head. "What a tragedy. I can't imagine what it would be like to lose a child. The poor man was wracked with guilt for being unable to save his daughter."

I opened the envelope and tipped its contents onto the glass counter. Old black-and-white photographs. Sheets of typing paper. A battered notebook with a thick green cardboard cover.

"May I browse your museum?" she asked.

"Please, be my guest."

She wandered to the haunted rocking chair, stooping to pet GD. "Delightful animal." She clucked and moved into the Fortune Telling Room.

GD shot me a satisfied look and yawned.

"That's just one opinion." I examined a photo: a group of workers in rough, old-timey clothing grinning around the grape press. So my grape press had indeed belonged to the Constantinos.

I flipped over the photo of the workers. The only notation on the back was a date: 1919. Was Gian, Alcina's father, or Luigi Rotta, her supposed killer, in the photo?

I rifled past a shot of an old barn to a formal portrait of Alcina Constantino. She'd been a doe-eyed beauty, her dark hair finger-waved back from her delicate profile.

Laying the police photos on the counter, I scrutinized the burnt cottage. My heart beat faster. "Of course it isn't here," I muttered. "It couldn't be."

GD dropped from the rocking chair and strolled across the linoleum floor. He stopped beside my chair and gazed up, unblinking.

I opened the antique notebook, dated 1921. It was more a ledger than a journal—lists of expenses and sales. As farmers went, Gian had been prosperous. The first two years of Prohibition had been good to him, and he'd shipped zinfandel grapes to home brewers across the country at exorbitant prices. I flipped through the pages. Amounts owed and paid, the payday rolls... Luigi was one of the lower-paid farm workers. An expansion of the vineyard... Interesting for a student of historical viticulture, but why had Harriet found this so fascinating?

Three-fourths of the way through, the handwriting changed, grew shakier. I checked the dates and drew in a breath. There'd been a two-week gap between the prior entry and the beginning of the shaky writing.

Alcina had died during that gap.

I turned the page. Someone had covered it in scrawls of black ink, as if trying to blot out the writing beneath. The next three pages were the same—a mass of black scribbling. And then two pages filled with shaky writing: *My fault my fault my fault my fault.*

Flesh pebbling, I thumbed through the rest of the book. The pages were blank.

I read Harriet's cover sheet. The Constantino Vineyards began operations in 1895, when young Gian and his wife emigrated to California. They built a wine production facility in 1899. Gian's wife died giving birth to Alcina in 1901. The vineyard prospered until 1922. After the tragic murder of Alcina by her would-be suitor, Luigi Rotta, the winery fell into disuse. Gian sold the land to a local farmer in 1926 and died one year later.

According to Harriet's report, local legend about the relationship between Alcina and Luigi varied. One version had it that Alcina had spurned Luigi. In the other, her father had refused to allow his daughter to associate with a lowly farm worker.

I smoothed a photocopied newspaper clipping from Harriet dated October 10, 1922. It included a photo of an old barn, which I presumed belonged to the Constantinos, but otherwise provided no new information.

"Well?"

My hand jerked, scattering papers and photos to the floor.

Harriet bent to pick them up. "I'm sorry. I didn't mean to startle you. History can be riveting, can't it? Your museum has certainly piqued my interest in the nineteenth-century spiritualist movement."

I hustled around the counter and knelt beside her. "I'll get those."

"Nonsense. I'm not helpless, you know. Not yet, at least."

I swept up the photos. "That local legend about the romance—"

"Ah, yes. I'm sorry I had to resort to historical gossip, but the whole affair is shrouded in mystery." She winked, straightening. "That suggests a scandal hushed up, does it not?"

I rose. "You think Alcina didn't rebuff Luigi's advances?"

"You didn't get a chance to go through all the documents, I see."

"No."

"I did find one other newspaper article, which I think you will find intriguing. If I may?" She held out her hand.

I gave her the stack of materials, and she shuffled through the papers and photos.

"Read this." She handed me a photocopied newspaper article.

AN ENGAGEMENT ANNOUNCEMENT.

Mr. Gian Constantino, of San Benedetto, announces the engagement of his daughter, Miss Alcina Constantino, to Paul Harris Wesson, of Lodi, California. Miss Constantino is well known as a soloist at Our Lady of Mercy Catholic Church. Mr. Wesson is a graduate of the University of Redlands, California. He is taking graduate work at Harvard in business. Upon the completion of his studies, Mr. Wesson plans to join the Constantino vineyards.

I leaned against the counter, nonplussed. "She was engaged to someone else?"

"Indeed." Harriet's eyes twinkled.

"Why would someone who went to Harvard want to return to San Benedetto to work on a glorified farm?"

She peered at me over her glasses, and my cheeks warmed. I'd come back to San Benedetto to work in a paranormal museum. But I didn't have an Ivy League degree.

"Would you like me to do some research on Mr. Wesson?" she asked.

I was going to have a whopping credit card bill this month, but I'd been doing well on those Ouija boards. "Here's the thing," I said.

"The police found decades-old bloodstains from a man and a woman on the grape press." I pointed to the photo of the workers surrounding the press. "We know that it did indeed belong to the Constantinos, because here it is in the picture." I slid the photo across the counter to her. "But there's no grape press in the crime scene photos. There couldn't be, because the press wasn't damaged in the fire. It's sitting, unburnt, at the haunted house right now. So if that's Alcina and Luigi's blood on the press, their bodies were *moved*—away from the grape press, into the cottage. Someone else set that fire."

"There are bloodstains on the grape press?"

"Not that you'd notice, but the police found some."

"And are you certain the blood belonged to Luigi and Alcina?"

"No," I said. "Detective Slate said it was too old to learn much from. I think I'm lucky I got as much information as I did."

Harriet cocked her head, tapping her powdered cheek. "Still, there's a haunted legend attached to that grape press for a reason."

"I think so too," I said. "At some point, someone connected the grape press to the deaths of Luigi and Alcina. It never made any sense to me—why would a ghost attach itself to a grape press? It was just some equipment Luigi had used while working."

"But if they were murdered beside it—"

"Exactly!"

"Little wonder Luigi can't rest in peace if he was unjustly accused of killing the woman he loved. We need to find the truth."

"Yes!"

She stared at me.

One beat. Two.

I exhaled. "Put it on my card."

———

270

Leo, a dark cloud, wandered into the museum and slumped over the counter.

"It's your day off," I said, edging the tip jar aside.

"I'm bored."

"I'm hungry." It was well past lunch. I could have ordered in, but I'd been too engrossed in my Internet research and ticket sales. "If you're looking for something to do, want to take over for an hour?"

"Deal."

I let him have my seat and slipped through the bookcase into the tea room.

Harper was leaning over the sleek, almond-colored counter, chatting with Adele.

I tapped her shoulder. "Hey, guys."

Harper turned and flicked a speck of dust off the lapel of her pin-striped suit. "I was just going to go bug you. Want to grab a bite?"

"Here?" I asked.

Adele thrust her hands onto her aproned hips. "What's wrong with the Fox and Fennel?"

"Nothing," I said, except I'd been eating her food a lot lately. "I love your roast turkey sandwich with pesto and arugula."

"I'll get you a table."

We followed Adele to a corner table, warmed on two sides by sunny windows.

Harper dropped one of the shades, obscuring our view of the building next door. "Adele told me what happened last night. Are you okay?"

"Bruised but not beaten."

Adele pulled up a chair and sat beside us. "The killer must think you're close."

"Then the killer is sadly mistaken," I said in a low voice. "I'm going around in circles. Romeo was having an affair with Elthia, and she was at the Death Bistro last night. She could have stayed behind to crush me in the door. Maybe things went wrong between Elthia and Romeo and she killed him, a crime of passion?"

"And then she killed Jocelyn?" Harper braced her elbows on the white tablecloth. "Why?"

"Because Jocelyn knew they were having an affair and suspected Elthia of Romeo's murder?" I shrugged. "And then there's Chuck."

"What about Chuck?" Harper asked.

"Well," I said, "he might have been having an affair with Jocelyn. He was hanging around her enough in the days before she died."

"So another crime of passion?" Adele fiddled with a butter knife. "He killed Romeo to have Jocelyn, and then Jocelyn found out, rejected him, and he killed her too?"

"It's a theory," I said. But I wasn't happy with it. "Chuck was at the Death Bistro. And I saw him around the haunted house before that empty wine barrel nearly fell on me."

"Wasn't Leo helping you with the display setup when the barrel fell?" Adele asked.

"He'd left by then." But had he gone far? I shook myself. I just didn't believe Leo was guilty. "Leo wasn't at the Death Bistro." But my stomach knotted.

"Maybe not," Adele said, "but I saw him through the window when we were cleaning up. He was standing on the sidewalk talking to Cora. I remember because he was wearing one of those black *Paranormal Museum* hoodies. You said you couldn't see your attacker. Was he wearing black?"

"I don't know," I said, staring at my hands. "It was dark."

A waiter paused beside our table and took our orders.

When he'd bustled off, and Harper turned in her seat toward me. "Which one was Cora?" she asked.

"You remember Mrs. Gale," I said. "She used to be president of Ladies Aid, but she left and started her own group. Wait—you mean she's not a regular member of the Death Bistro?"

Harper shook her head. "The older woman? No, tonight was the first time I'd seen her. How do Leo and Cora know each other?"

"She came by the museum to see me and stayed to help him decorate pumpkins."

"That's an odd pairing," Harper said.

"She's an empty nester," I said. "Leo's lost his parents. Maybe they'll be good for each other."

Harper chewed on her lower lip. "I shouldn't tell you this."

"If you know something," Adele said, "yes, you should. Maddie was nearly killed last night."

Harper looked around and leaned over the table. "Look, this is confidential."

"I can keep my mouth shut," I said.

"I know you can." Harper's smile wavered, her brows drawing in. She hesitated.

"Harper, it's Maddie!" Adele gestured, impatient.

"All right." Harper's voice lowered to a whisper. "Romeo was dropping his life insurance policy. Leo was the beneficiary."

I sat back in my chair, my heart slithering south. Now Leo had an even stronger financial motive.

"So that's why you and Romeo were parting ways," I said. "You won't work with someone unless they've got life insurance to cover their kids. Leo isn't twenty-one yet, the cut-off age." I should have guessed.

Harper nodded.

"Do you think Leo knew?" Adele asked.

She shook her head. "I don't know."

"But why drop the policy?" I asked.

"Romeo was looking for ways to cut costs. He saw the policy as a drain."

"So there were financial issues at the winery," I said.

"I wouldn't know about that," Harper said. "I only dealt with his personal finances. And that's all I can say."

"Will the police have this information?"

Harper nodded. "His request to drop the policy is in our files, though we hadn't gotten started on the paperwork. Romeo had already paid up for the year and had three months to go before the next premium was due. Maddie, I know you see yourself in Leo—"

"I do not."

"—but you need to be careful around that kid."

I shook my head. There was no way my assistant was a killer, and no reason for anyone to believe his innocence.

TWENTY-ONE

I FLIPPED THE SIGN on the door to *Closed*.

GD curled on the haunted rocking chair, eyes shut, exhausted from a long day of doing... Well, as far as I could see, his day consisted of eating, napping, and ignoring me. When I die, I want to come back as a museum cat.

Sighing, I did a quick cleanup. A spider had snuck its web into a corner, attaching to the shiny, black crown molding. I knocked the web down with a broom, turned off the lights, and slipped through the bookcase.

From the tea room closet, I borrowed the dolly and wheeled it to my pickup. I was getting kind of tired of hauling the grape press around.

The sun hadn't quite set, and the alley lay deep in shadow. I craned my neck.

Mason's apartment lights were on.

Enough was enough. Taking a deep breath, I left the dolly by my tailgate and trudged up the narrow concrete staircase. I stopped in front of the metal security door. My stomach flipped, tight and empty.

I smoothed my hair and the front of my *Paranormal Museum* T-shirt, and I knocked—*shave and a haircut*. The door clanged beneath my knuckles. He'd know it was me because I always stopped before the *two bits* part.

A bolt slid back, a chain rattled. The door opened, and there stood my worst nightmare—the young woman I'd seen in the motorcycle shop, taller than me, thinner than me, prettier than me. Long auburn hair fell in gentle waves past her shoulders. There were faint lines on her forehead and at the corners of her eyes, and I sensed they weren't from a lifetime of laughter.

"Hello," she said, smiling. "Can I help you?"

"Hi, I'm Maddie Kosloski. Is Mason here?"

"He's in the shower, but he should be out any minute."

The shower. A cold dagger plunged into my heart. *Stay calm. Stay calm.* "Do you mind if I wait?"

She edged aside, and I stepped past her.

A blond-haired boy slumped on Mason's black leather couch. He stared between his shoes, propped on the glass coffee table, at a video game on Mason's big screen TV.

Takeout boxes piled high on the counter dividing the kitchen from the living room.

I glanced toward the glass bricks that formed a barricade between the bedroom and living area. Something shifted behind them, a door opening. Mason emerged, neck bent, head buried in a towel. He wore a fresh pair of black jeans and a T-shirt.

Mason had done more than just get in touch with his ex. It looked like she'd moved in.

"Did I hear someone at the door?" He straightened, whipping off the towel. Slowly, his arm lowered. "Maddie."

"Hi, Mason. Your shop's been closed for the last two days. I was getting worried." *Tell me there's an innocent explanation.*

"Yeah, sorry. I should have called you." He rubbed the back of his neck. "This is Anabelle. I mentioned her to you."

She shook her head. "I'm sorry, where are my manners? I should have introduced myself. Mason's told me so much about you, Maddie."

"And you must be his old girlfriend." That sounded catty. "I don't mean old. You're not old. Just, um, Mason, could you help me get a dolly into the back of my truck?"

He smiled. "Sure."

In silence, the two of us walked down the stairs and into the alley. I unlatched the tailgate, and Mason easily lifted the dolly inside.

"She seems nice—"

"I'm sorry, I should have called," he said at the same time.

I sat against the open tailgate and studied him. His glacier-blue eyes were downcast, his expression uncertain.

My throat squeezed. Oh, God. We were breaking up. He'd fallen in love with her again.

He looked away. "He's my son."

I gripped the edges of the tailgate. "What?"

"I didn't know. I didn't know she was pregnant when I returned to the military. Neither did she. And then when I didn't come back to her, she found someone else, got married, and never told me about Jordan."

"Your son?" The words came, broken monosyllables I struggled to push past my lips.

"I'm sorry I've been avoiding you. I didn't know how to tell you, because I'm still wrapping my brain around the situation." He clawed his hands through his mane of golden hair.

I shook my head, rallying. Mason hadn't known. Of course it was a shock. "Why did she decide to tell you now?"

"Her husband passed away last year and things fell apart. She lost their house." His voice dropped, and he glanced up at the lit apartment windows. "They've been living out of a van for the last three months."

So she'd told him about his son when she'd needed him. My jaw clenched. The thought was unfair. He deserved the truth from her, no matter the motivation. "How awful for them both."

We stared at each other, silent.

"A son," I finally said. "That's a lot for anyone to process. How are you handling this?"

He laughed, bitter. "I pushed you aside and stopped working. That's how I handled it. Badly."

"Mason—"

"He's my son. I can't let them live in a van."

The door to the Fox and Fennel clanged open. Adele, in her black turtleneck and apron, staggered outside carrying a garbage bag. She glanced at us and tossed the bag into the dumpster, then returned to the tea room. The door banged shut.

"What are you going to do?" I asked.

"I don't know. Right now, they're living with me until she can get a job, get back on her feet."

Living in his studio apartment? A chasm opened in my chest. My mouth opened, but no words formed.

He watched me.

I couldn't read his face. Hope? Expectancy?

Mason would do the right thing. He'd always do the right thing, and that was why I loved him. Of course he'd take care of his son. I swallowed. "You can't let them live in a van. In your shoes, I'd do the same."

"It's only temporary." He grasped my shoulders. "I meant what I said, Maddie. I love you. This doesn't change my feelings."

I nodded, wooden. He loved me, and he was living with the mother of his child. Temporarily. But what else was he supposed to do?

I wanted to ask if he was sure Jordan was his, if he could trust her. But I didn't. Those were all questions Mason had no doubt asked himself and didn't need me to echo.

A roar of sound flooded from the upstairs windows—the video game. There was a shout, and someone turned down the volume.

A smile flit across his face, not reaching his eyes. "I should get back up there. You'd be amazed at the destructive capacity of a ten-year-old boy."

I nodded and he released me, stepping back. "I'll call you tomorrow."

"Sure. Tomorrow." Watching him jog up the steps to his apartment, I slid off the tailgate.

I couldn't blame him for something that happened ten years ago, something he hadn't even known about. And I couldn't blame him for doing whatever it took to keep Jordan and his mother off the streets. So why were my lungs tight, my stomach twisting with nausea?

Turning, I slammed the tailgate shut. Tears pricked the backs of my eyes, and I blinked them back. I was better than this. I hadn't lost Mason. This was the twenty-first century and lots of families were blended. What was I worried about?

And why did I have to find out about this the hard way?

He'd had to take some time. Mason needed to sort his feelings before talking to me. That was all. It wasn't unreasonable. By taking Anabelle and Jordan in, he was choosing the right, the responsible path. That was what I loved about him.

I needed to go. The haunted house was opening soon.

But my legs, leaden, didn't want to move.

My keys pressed into the flesh of my palm. I unlocked the alley door and returned to my sanctuary, the museum.

GD looked up from his spot on the rocking chair, his emerald eyes unblinking.

"No ghosts tonight?" I tried to sound cheerful, but my voice cracked. I tried to keep my hands steady as I flipped on the computer, but they trembled. I tried to tell myself I was overreacting, that I wasn't losing Mason, but I didn't believe it. My imagination was a curse.

Or was it? I'd sensed something was off early into Mason's self-imposed disappearance. My imagination had been right; our relationship had been wrong.

The bookcase eased open and Adele walked in. "Maddie? Are you all right?"

"I'm fine."

She approached the counter. "I saw you and Mason talking. You didn't look all right then, and you don't look all right now. If you don't want to talk about it, I won't bother you. But are you sure you don't want to talk?"

I opened my mouth, shut it. But Adele was sensible where it counted. She'd put my imagination in its place. I unburdened myself, telling her everything.

She listened, her expression grave. "What are you going to do?" she asked.

"Do?" She expected me to do something? "It's not Mason's fault this happened."

"No, it isn't his fault, but it *has* happened."

"And I don't know what else he can do. He can't let Anabelle and his son live on the street."

"I'm assuming he doesn't have the money to put them up in an apartment of their own?"

"I don't know. We haven't talked about money." And it didn't feel like it was my business to question his decision. "Mason's still in shock. I'm in shock. And I feel like I'm overreacting. He didn't cheat on me. This happened years before we met. And the only thing it says about the man he is today is that he's responsible and trying to set things right."

She nodded, her eyes dark with sympathy.

"I'm not overreacting, am I?"

She patted my hand. "You did the right thing," she said. "You found out what was going on, and you didn't react in anger. Of course the situation has thrown both you and Mason."

The wall phone rang, startling me. I picked it up. "Hello?"

"Maddie, it's Harriet. I was so intrigued by your little mystery that I began researching the mysterious Mr. Paul Wesson right away. It wasn't hard—I really don't think I should charge you for this. He's all over the Internet."

"Of course, I'll pay," I said faintly.

"A wedding announcement in Cambridge, Mass. I've just emailed it to you. October 15, 1922. He married someone else. Later, he went on to become a rather successful chemical manufacturer on the east coast. The wedding took place only a week after Alcina was killed."

"Huh."

"I wonder if he even knew she'd died?"

I wondered if he even knew that he and Alcina were engaged. "Thanks. That's helpful." We murmured goodbyes, and I hung up.

"What was that about?" Adele asked.

"It doesn't matter. Just the grape press mystery."

She angled her head to one side. "Let's get out of here. I'll call Harper. You can drive me home, and we'll uncork a bottle of reserve wine."

"I'm not up for a pity party."

"There will be zero pity, I promise. Why should there be? You're not a wronged woman. There's nothing pathetic about the situation. It simply requires large quantities of friendship and wine."

Her family's reserve wines were awfully good. And I really didn't want to deal with the grape press. "All right. Let's go."

We locked up. Adele called Harper, and I drove. We stopped at the local doggy daycare to pick up Adele's pug, Pug. She clasped him to her chest. He wriggled, shedding tawny fur across her black turtleneck.

"Did you miss me?" she cooed, scratching the dog's fawn-colored head.

We drove out of town, into the vineyards. The temperature had dropped and I rolled up my window. The setting sun blinded me, turning the sky to fire.

Wincing, I lowered the truck's visor. "Adele, there's something I've been meaning to ask you."

"Oh?" She arched her neck, evading Pug's pink tongue.

"Mrs. Bigelow from Ladies Aid said there was something odd going on among the local vintners. She thought you might know something about it."

"Odd?"

"I'm sorry. I don't want to pry, but I overheard an argument between your parents. Is something happening at the winery?"

She blew out her breath. "I'm not supposed to say."

"Okay." I didn't have the heart to push.

"Someone made Daddy an offer," she burst out.

"An offer?"

"To buy the winery. And he's actually considering selling! Can you believe it?"

"Is it a good offer?"

"Of course it's a good offer. That's why he's considering it. Daddy has always been a businessman first, a vintner second. He's in it because he likes being his own boss, and my mother's in it because she loves making wine. They're a perfect team. I guess I didn't understand that to him, it's not the family business, it's just business. But I grew up on Plot 42, and he and my mother spent so much time building their Haunted Vine label. I'm trying to be objective, but selling out feels like a betrayal."

"Who's the buyer? Not the vampire?"

"The vampire? What are you talking about?"

"Tall, pale, good-looking in a you-can-never-be-too-rich-or-too-thin sort of way?"

She snorted. "Oh, him. Yes, he's the one. He represents one of those big international wine conglomerates."

I frowned. Others had told me outsiders wanted to invest in San Benedetto's wine industry, not buy it up. Was it the same investor? Or had I misunderstood?

I slowed, turning down a long dirt driveway and parking beneath an oak tree.

Adele stepped out, setting Pug on the ground. On stubby legs, he bounded up the porch steps of her wedding-cake Victorian. He raced back in forth in front of the screened front door, his tongue hanging from his mouth.

I followed, my feet hollow on the steps as she unlocked the door. The setting sun made long prison-bar shadows of the rows of grapevines. An oak trembled in the uneven breeze, drizzling dried leaves atop my truck. I zipped my hoodie higher. It felt like autumn, the last traces of summer warmth vanished with the darkening sky.

Pug raced inside, through the all-white living room and into the kitchen. Crunching and snuffling sounds drifted through the house.

"Don't they feed him at that daycare?" I asked.

Adele laughed. "You know Pug. There's never a bad time to eat." She headed for the kitchen.

I sank onto the snow-white couch and stared into the unlit, white-brick fireplace. A branch scraped against the window.

"Mind if I start a fire?" I asked.

"Go right ahead. There's wood in the basket beside the fireplace." I set up the fire. By the time I had it crackling, Harper had arrived. She'd changed out of her pinstripes and into jeans and a caramel-colored knit top.

Harper took two glasses of blood-colored wine from Adele and passed one to me.

I rose in front of the fireplace, and we clinked glasses.

"To good friends," Harper said.

Adele and I echoed the toast. I sipped the wine, savoring the flavors of dark berries and black pepper and licorice. "Reserve" meant "expensive," and one didn't gulp reserve wine like cheap beer. Not that I have anything against cheap beer.

"What's going on, Maddie?" Harper asked.

We sat on the snowy couch and I told her about Mason. Adele puttered in the kitchen, heating hors d'oeuvres. "Mini quiches?" she called out.

"Yes, please," Harper shouted back. Scratching her jaw, she turned to me and sipped her wine. "So what are you going to do?"

"I don't see a whole lot of options. Either I go along with the program, or …" Or what? Break up? My mouth went dry and I took another sip. Was breaking up really a possibility? I wasn't a fan of the first option, but the second sickened my stomach. I couldn't make a decision tonight. I'd sent myself halfway to Crazy Town because of Mason's silence, and I wasn't sure I was thinking clearly now.

Someone knocked on the front door.

"Can one of you get that?" Adele called from the kitchen.

I lurched off the couch, setting my goblet beside a stack of wine and travel magazines on the coffee table. Trotting to the door, I opened it.

Mr. Nakamoto stood on the porch. The chill breeze ruffled his thinning gray hair. A *Haunted Vine* windbreaker flapped around him, too large on his narrow frame. "Maddie. Hi. I was looking for my daughter."

I stepped away from the door. The Nakamotos often popped in and out of each other's homes. "She's in the kitchen," I said.

He strode past me and into the kitchen. I returned to my warm spot on Adele's couch and reached for my glass.

A shriek from the kitchen split my ears, and my hand jerked. The goblet tilted. Fumbling, I caught it before zinfandel could spill onto the white shag rug.

Harper winced. "Did I miss something?"

Adele ran into the living room, her father following more slowly behind her. "We're not selling! Plot 42 and Haunted Vine are still ours!" She clapped her hands together, doing a little dance. Pug hopped around her heels and barked.

Mr. Nakamoto grimaced. "So you girls heard."

"I didn't," Harper said. "You were thinking of selling the vineyard?"

He nodded.

"I heard there were investors in town," I said. "And a big investor?"

"I don't know about the others, but the group I spoke with is certainly big. They're trying to buy up a collection of vineyards." Mr. Nakamoto frowned. "The other vintners won't be happy."

"Why not?" I asked.

"It's an all-or-nothing deal. If one winery doesn't sell out, no one can. For this to work, Pryce needs a large block of land—not little pieces of vineyard here and there."

"Which other vineyards are involved in the deal?" I asked. Chuck hadn't said anything about selling, but the vampire had been hanging around his place as well. And he'd been talking to Jocelyn.

Mr. Nakamoto shook his head. "The company rep played things close to the vest. They made us sign a confidentiality agreement. He wouldn't tell me which other wineries were involved, and no one else is talking."

"This is the guy who looks like a Regency-era vampire? He was at your house a few nights ago when I came by to pick up Adele?"

Mr. Nakamoto's dark eyes twinkled. "Pryce, a vampire? No wonder you agreed to take on the Paranormal Museum. What an imagination."

"I thought Pryce looked like a consumptive Victorian dandy," Adele said.

Laughing, he kissed her on the top of the head. He said goodbye to us and left, the door snicking shut behind him.

"This calls for a celebration," Adele said. "It's time to break out the reserve wine."

"I thought this was reserve wine." Harper eyed her glass askance. She faltered, biting her lip. "Oh. Right!"

"Adele..." I began.

She crossed her arms over her chest, her cheeks pinking. "Well, the reserve is expensive, and I'm a small business owner on a budget."

I reached for my phone, wanting to talk this over with... the thought stumbled in its tracks. Mason. I couldn't call him. Not now.

My vision blurred. What had happened to us?

TWENTY-TWO

Mason didn't call.

Not that night.

Not all the next day.

Sunday arrived, and the setting sun slanted through the blinds, illuminating everything that was wrong with my museum. The floor in the main room looked shabby next to the new linoleum in the gallery. The photo frames lining the walls were cheap, battered. The brass skull needed polishing. But I'd known this would never be a high-class establishment. That was part of its paranormal charm.

And no customer likes a mournful museum curator. So I sat in my long-legged chair and smiled at the milling customers.

The wall phone rang, and I pounced on it. "Paranormal Museum, this is Mad—"

"You promised to pick up that grape press on Friday!" Mrs. Bigelow shouted.

I winced, holding the phone away from my ear. The museum was busy, tourists clotting the rooms thanks to the haunted house.

"Sorry," I said. "Something came up."

"I did not accept excuses from my children, and I assume your mother does not accept them from you."

"Mrs.—"

She hung up.

I checked my watch, flipped the sign to *Closed*. It was past five o'clock. Time to shoo out the crowd and leave.

They trickled from the museum, their arms loaded with goodies. I sold three coffee mugs, a painting of a pumpkin patch, and a Ouija board. Normally, the sales would make me cackle with capitalist glee. Today I just shoved the money in the register and slammed it shut. Thank God the day was over.

I locked up after the last of the customers and checked the cat's food bowl. A quick search assured me GD hadn't escaped into the tea room (he was sleeping on top of the spirit cabinet). I whisked a broom around the linoleum floor and escaped.

I pulled out of the alley and braked to a stop, sinking my head onto the steering wheel. That damned grape press. I needed to get it from the haunted house.

But I didn't like being shouted at by Mrs. Bigelow. Mason hadn't called. And I was exhausted.

"Screw it." Bigelow could wait one more day.

I drove home, settling in with a delivery pizza and a bottle of wine.

Past midnight, I stumbled into bed, trying not to think of Mason. Each time my thoughts wandered in his direction, the muscles in my neck and shoulders bunched. So I pondered the murders instead.

Did the police know about the vineyard deal? From what little I'd heard about Romeo, he didn't seem the type to sell. But the sabotage at his vineyard had cost him dearly, which would have increased the pressure on him to take the deal. Had that been the motivation for the sabotage, or was it more personal?

Assuming Romeo had been asked to be part of the deal, there were plenty of suspects who'd have wanted him to sell. Other vintners. Jocelyn, perhaps, but she was dead and out of the running as a murder suspect. Leo? With his father and Jocelyn dead, he could sell out, do whatever he wanted with the money.

I wasn't sure if Elthia had a dog in this particular hunt. But her family owned a small vineyard. What if they wanted to sell out, and she, being Romeo's mistress, knew he was scotching the deal?

I rolled over, and the bed creaked beneath me. Moonlight streamed through the window and made eerie silhouettes of the oak branches outside.

And speaking of vineyard owners, what about Chuck and the vampire, Pryce? I'd seen them with Jocelyn in the wine tent—sealing the deal once Romeo was dead? If Jocelyn had been ready to sell, how would her death have affected the deal?

Frustrated, I fisted my hands in the warm sheets. There were too many suspects with too many motives. *Please, please, let the killer not be Leo.*

My thoughts tumbled to the grape press mystery. If Romeo's murder had been a crime of finance, Alcina and Luigi's murders appeared to be crimes of passion.

Or were they? Back in 1922, air travel was in its infancy. Poor roads made cross-country travel by car a long and bumpy proposition. Alcina's fiancé couldn't have committed the crime and made it back to Harvard a week later for his wedding. But someone had moved and set fire to those bodies.

I had a dark suspicion who the killer was, but I feared it would take a séance to prove it.

I rolled over, knocking a pillow to the floor.

And what if I was wrong about Romeo's murder being a crime motivated by money? He'd been having an affair with Elthia, and love made a depressing motive for murder. Just ask poor, long-dead Alcina.

Past and present crimes jumbled together. I fell into an uneasy sleep and dreamed of grape vats and vineyards and vampires.

———

Eyes gritty, I dragged myself from bed late on Monday. The night had brought me clarity, and I knew now what I had to do.

I showered and dressed in beige drawstring slacks and an army-green tank top. Then I called Mason.

"Maddie, it's good to hear from you."

His voice was a warm rumble, and I squeezed my eyes shut. "Hi, Mason. How are things going?"

"Yesterday I took Jordan and Anabelle to Old Town Sacramento. We stuffed ourselves on fudge."

In spite of myself, I smiled. It was hard to imagine Mason of the rippling muscles as a chocoholic. "Are you free for coffee this afternoon?" My mouth went dry. It felt like I was asking for a first date.

"When and where?"

I considered the Fox and Fennel, but we needed privacy. "Three o'clock? The Wok and Bowl?" A 1950s-themed bowling alley and

Chinese restaurant, the Wok and Bowl brewed rocking java. Plus, it was noisy, so no one would overhear our conversation.

"I'll be there." He paused. "It felt strange going out without you yesterday."

My throat constricted. "You need time with your family. I'll see you this afternoon."

We hung up, and I blew out my breath. Next up: present-day murder investigation. I called Dieter.

"Yeah?" On his end of the line, a circular saw screamed, winding to silence.

"It's Maddie, I needed to—"

"I'm at your mom's house."

Even better. "I'll be right over."

I drove to my mother's ranch-style home and parked beside Dieter's truck. A bead of sweat trickled down my neck and I lifted my hair, knotting it into a bun. The circular saw shrieked, cutting the cloudless sky.

I crunched across fallen leaves, following the noise to the back yard. Waiting a respectful distance away, I watched Dieter cut through a redwood plank. Sawdust swirled in the balmy air. It filmed his goggles, drifted to rest in his spiky brown hair. One end of the board thunked to the concrete patio.

Turning off the saw, he stepped back, rubbing his palms on the front of his overalls. He raised his goggles to the top of his head. "What's up, Mad?"

I stepped out from behind a camellia bush. "What are you doing?"

The sliding glass door scraped back. My mother, neat in a silky blouse and pressed jeans, stepped onto the patio. "He's helping with my new low-water garden. What brings you here this morning?"

"Dieter, you mentioned you repaired the gate at Chuck's vineyard. What happened to the old one?"

"Chuck told me one of his workers hit it. He must have hit it pretty damned hard, because the thing was off its hinges and busted into eight pieces. Why?"

"Just curious." I turned on my mother. "Mom, what's really going on with Ladies Aid?"

She raised a brow. "Really going on? I don't know what you mean."

"You're up to something," I said.

"Madelyn, I explained to you about the lemon bars—"

"Lemon bars?" Dieter asked.

"Then why did you insist I investigate Romeo's murder?"

She toyed with the silver squash-blossom necklace at her throat. "I was worried about Cora. I knew Eliza would blame her for Romeo's death and thought it would ease her mind if she knew you were in her corner. Oh! Did I tell you? Your brother Shane got a promotion!"

"Huh." Bringing up my brother was a cheap attempt to divert me. There was more to this story.

"He wasn't clear on what the promotion was, exactly," she said, "but I'm sure we'll know soon."

"No doubt." I folded my arms over my chest.

Dieter slung a two-by-four over his shoulder. "What's with the lemon bars?"

"They're addictive," I said.

"I have some in the kitchen," my mother said. "Would you like some?"

"I wouldn't start if I were you," I said. "*Highly* addictive."

His gaze ping-ponged between the two of us. He shifted his weight. "Um, maybe later, Mrs. Kosloski. So how's the investigation going, Mad?" he asked, trying to look disinterested.

"You'll have to wait and see, just like all the other bettors." I lowered my head and stared at my mother.

"I don't actually bet," Dieter said. "I simply facilitate—"

"Whatever." I flapped my hand at him. "I'm off to crime-solve."

I stomped to my truck. Maybe I shouldn't have tackled my mother in front of Dieter.

Meh, she wouldn't have come clean even if we'd talked in private.

Levering myself into the cab of my truck, I slammed the door. A light breeze wafted through the open window, rustling the oak branches above me. I leaned my head against the rest. I was getting closer, but I still had zero proof to back up my suspicions.

There was one stop I hadn't made, and even though my stomach fluttered with nerves, I was looking forward to it. I drove into town and glided along San Benedetto Avenue. Parking on the street, I hopped out and fed the meter.

Green-and-white-striped awnings fluttered above the pastry-filled windows of Sugar Hall Bakery. I walked inside, my skin shivering in the air conditioning. The scents of baking flour, sugar, and butter tangled in the cool air. Heaven.

Like my museum, the bakery had a checkerboard floor. Unlike my museum, their glass cases were filled with a dizzying array of pastries.

I stepped up to the gleaming counter. An aproned man with salt-and-pepper hair dealt change to a plump elderly woman. She lifted a white box from the counter and tottered off.

He adjusted his paper hat. "Can I help you?" he asked in a Slavic-sounding accent.

"I hear you've got fantastic lemon bars."

He grinned, showing off a gold tooth. "The best in San Benedetto. How many would you like?"

"A dozen?" I could hardly grease the wheels by ordering just one bar.

I followed him along the counter to the lemon bars, gold and sugar-dusted and perfectly square. Those looked like Jocelyn's all right. "My friend, Jocelyn, raved about them," I said, throwing a note of what I hoped was sadness into my voice.

"Mrs. Paganini was one of our best clients." He shook his head, loading lemon bars into the white bakery box. "Tragedy. A real tragedy."

"Had you seen her recently?"

His eyes narrowed. "Why do you want to know?"

"I was at her house the night she died, and she had some lemon squares on the coffee table. I thought—"

"YOU!" He snapped the lid of the box in place and glared at me across the counter.

"Me?"

"You are the woman who is trying to solve the crime. I tell you nothing!"

"But why?"

"I make bet with Dieter. No help! Take your lemon bars and go!" He stomped to the register and rang me up, punching the buttons.

Dieter and his stupid bet! I gripped my wallet, clutching it to my chest and feeling like I'd been caught with my hand in the cookie jar. (That happened a lot when I was growing up.)

Gulping, I paid and scuttled back to my truck with the lemon bars. The baker hadn't confirmed Jocelyn had bought the bars the day of her death. But she had been a customer, and these looked like the same bars. Ladies Aid was off the hook.

Sitting in the truck, I found Elthia's phone number in my wallet, dialed.

"Hello?" she asked, her tone cautious.

"Elthia, this is Maddie Kosloski."

"Oh! What … What do you want?"

"I'd like to meet."

"I'm super busy right now."

"We can do it later, if it's more convenient."

"No, I don't think so."

Well, it had been worth a shot. "You told me Leo had once threatened Romeo."

"I don't remember saying anything of the sort."

"Well, you did. Now, what exactly did Leo threaten Romeo with? And please think carefully before answering. It's important."

She hesitated. "I may have only *thought* Leo threatened Romeo. You know they had a tense relationship."

"Leo is a teenager whose father left his mother and married another woman. Of course he had issues. But that's a long way from a real threat."

"I don't know why you're defending him. He's an angry young man who happens to benefit from the deaths of both his father and Jocelyn. If he looks guilty, don't blame me." She hung up.

Elthia was lying. I thought I knew why.

TWENTY-THREE

A FAMILY KNOCKED DOWN pins at the Wok and Bowl. I watched from the far side of the bowling alley, turning the cooling coffee mug in my hands. The AC was up higher than I liked, and I shivered in my tank top. Sitting in the red faux-leather booth, I pulled my museum hoodie from my messenger bag.

I glanced at my watch for the third time, comparing it to the '50s-style diner clock above the alleys. My watch wasn't wrong. Mason was late. Only by fifteen minutes, but it wasn't like him. When it came to punctuality, the military had left an impression on Mason.

He strode into the bowling alley five minutes later and looked around. He wore his usual jeans and tight T-shirt stretched across his broad chest. Catching my eye, he waved and jogged down the steps to my booth, smiling.

He kissed me on the cheek, slid into the seat across from me, and raked his hand through his blond mane. "Sorry, Maddie. I was at the school with Jordan and his mother. We're trying to enroll him, but the soonest they can take him is after the December break."

And suddenly I felt I was cheating with a married man. That wasn't me. It never would be. I would never be the other woman, the one who broke up a family. "What's Jordan going to do in the meantime?" I asked, stalling.

"Anabelle's going to homeschool him as best she can to make sure he's caught up when he starts."

A waitress, poodle skirt swirling, appeared at our table.

"I'd like a cup of coffee, please," he said.

She left, and he eased back in his seat. "You're a sight for sore eyes." He smiled, his blue eyes crinkling.

"You've been busy," I hedged, pushing my hair out of my face. I'd never expected this conversation, and felt like I was tiptoeing barefoot through broken glass.

"So have you." Reaching across the table, he took my hand. "How's the haunted house going?"

"I have to take back the grape press. They say it's too haunted." *Just say it, Maddie. Just say it!*

He grinned. "Too haunted? What does that mean?"

"I'm not sure. Mason, I think we should take a break."

He withdrew his hand, his expression stilling. "A break?"

"You're dealing with a lot right now, and your ex-girlfriend is living with you." My throat tightened. This was the right decision. But I was having a hard time breathing.

"She's not staying with me forever," he said. "Just until she can get back on her feet."

"Anabelle wasn't able to find a job after her husband died and ended up on the street. I imagine it will take a little time for her to find one here."

"Sure, maybe a few months. It's been hard for her. She was a stay-at-home mom."

A few months! I took a slow, steadying breath. "I can't even imagine how hard it's been for her. She's lucky to have you."

"If this is about the last week—"

"It is, and it isn't. You've left me in limbo."

He began to speak, and I held up my hand.

"I get it," I said. "And it's not all your fault. I could have tried harder to track you down. And the situation would have thrown anyone for a loop. I know you're doing your best to make things right. But I haven't handled the ambiguity well, and I don't think I'm going to start handling it well any time soon. For both our sakes, I need to step away. That will give you and Anabelle time to figure things out, and I won't be trapped in relationship purgatory."

His eyes darkened. "Is that how you feel? Trapped?"

"No," I said quickly. "I didn't mean it like that. But do you really feel like things are the same between us?"

The waitress brought his coffee and winked. "Here you go, sir." She swished away.

Mason looked after her, a pulse beating in his jaw. "You're right." He cleared his throat. "This situation isn't fair to you."

"It's not about fair, it's about what's right for everyone." I swallowed. "If you need anything, I'll always be there. I wasn't lying when I said—"

"I know. I meant it too. I still do." He rose and laid some bills on the table, then bent to kiss my forehead. "I'll see you around, Maddie."

Heart breaking, I gripped my coffee mug and drew ragged breaths. It had been the right thing to do.

Hadn't it?

On shaky legs, I walked to my truck in the Wok and Bowl parking lot. The afternoon sun radiated off the macadam. Sweat prickled my back and I peeled off the hoodie. I opened the door, letting the heat escape. Leaning against its hot metal side, I blinked back tears.

I had done the right thing.

Mason might be fine with living with his ex, juggling sudden fatherhood, and dating me. I wasn't.

I didn't know if that made me a bad or a weak person, but I hadn't liked myself much last week—the neediness, the panic, the insecurity. Months or more of some sort of half-relationship with Mason would send me around the bend. I needed to find my footing again. And Mason needed to deal with his family without another woman in the mix.

Once my breathing evened out, I stepped into the truck and drove into downtown. The shops were busy, pedestrians hurrying down the brick sidewalks. A young man in black slouched toward me. Leo.

I pulled into a free spot on the side of the street and tapped the horn. Leo looked up and jogged to my truck.

I leaned out the window. "What's up?" My voice was strained, and I forced a smile.

He didn't seem to notice, lifting one shoulder, letting it drop. His black hair was lank, his face pale. "Just walking. Where're you off to?"

"The haunted house. I need to pick up that grape press and turn the exhibit back into the invisible haunted grape press."

He shook his head. "When are they going to make up their minds?"

"Never, is my guess."

"Need some help?"

"Sure." I leaned across the seat and unlocked the passenger door. He slid inside and buckled up. "You got the dolly?"

"In the back."

"Cool." His lower jaw went sideways, twisting his mouth.

I drove on, focusing on the road. A pink Cadillac cut in front of me and braked, drifting into the gas station.

"I've been taking a web design class at the JC," Leo said.

"Oh?"

"We need to do a shopping cart project for the class. You know, online sales? I was thinking maybe I could work on the museum website?"

It was an answer to my frugal capitalist prayers. "Why not?"

We drove through town, beneath the welcome arch, past the Wine and Visitors Bureau, and into the vineyards.

Leo rolled down his window. "Ever think of getting air conditioning?"

"In this old truck? It would ruin the charm."

A truck full of oranges bounced past us.

"Do you attend the junior college Jocelyn worked at?" I asked.

"Yeah."

"Did you see her around much?"

"I'm not in the viticulture program."

It wasn't really an answer, but I let it lie and turned at the massive gates to CW Vineyards. We bumped down the shaded gravel drive and pulled in front of the tasting room/haunted house. A few cars parked there. A sandwich-board proclaimed, *Yes, we're open for tasting!*

I frowned. "Chuck planned to keep the tasting room running when the haunted house wasn't operating. I don't know where they've moved our exhibit. Let me go inside and see where everything's at before we drag the dolly out."

I trotted up the porch steps and into the tasting room. The hanging divider had vanished along with the Haunted San Benedetto exhibit. Couples stood at the tall round tables, drinking wine and sampling cheese. Others lined up at the cash register.

Elthia worked behind the tasting bar, filling a box with bottles of wine.

I waved to her, and her eyes narrowed.

"Hi," I said. "I just came to pick up the grape press."

"Sure you are." Her mouth twisted in disbelief.

"Hey, I didn't know you worked here."

"Part-time." She handed a customer the box. "And I don't know anything about the press. You'll have to ask Chuck."

"Where is he?"

"Barn."

Nodding, I strode out of the tasting room and across the yard. The barn doors were open, but I hesitated outside.

"Can I help you?" Chuck asked from behind me.

I jumped a little and turned.

He stroked his beard, grinning. "Sorry, did I startle you?"

He seemed to make it a habit.

"Ladies Aid wanted me to remove the grape press and replace it with my invisible grape press exhibit," I said.

He chuckled. "Right. I heard there was a commotion the other night."

"What sort of commotion?"

"Some type of mass hysteria. One woman started sobbing when she got near the press on the first night, said she was a psychic or something. People heard about it, and now everyone's imagining stuff. Someone actually fainted last night."

"Fainted? Were they hurt?"

"No, the woman's fine. I think she got a rise out of the attention. Anyway, all of your things are in the storage room. You'll find it unlocked, behind the tables in the tasting area, beneath the loft."

And beneath all those wine barrels. Great.

"Will you be able to manage on your own?" he asked.

"Leo's with me, and we've got a dolly." I walked back to the truck and collected both.

Leo carried the dolly into the tasting area and wheeled it to the storage room door.

I opened it and followed him inside. The room was cool and dim and I fumbled for a light, switched it on. Its bulb flickered, clicking. The grape press stood beside stacks of *CW Vineyards* boxes.

Leo's lip curled. "That stuff is no better than table wine."

I raised a brow. Leo hadn't hit drinking age yet.

"That's just what I heard," he said hastily.

"Sure it was. And don't be a snob. Table wine has its place." I switched the haunted grape press sign for the invisible haunted grape press sign.

The air in the closet congealed, cold and cloying. Gooseflesh prickled my skin.

I grasped the grape press, my grip damp, and heaved. The press shifted an inch. Had it always been this heavy? A shadow crawled across it. I blinked and it vanished. I stared hard at the press. It was too easy to imagine splatters of blood on its decaying wood.

Leo put his back into it, but the grape press resisted, squeaking, crawling, edging across the floor. I panted. The air seemed thick, oppressive, and I gulped.

My now ex-boyfriend wouldn't have had any problem lifting the press, and cold silence slithered inside my heart. What had I done? I'd never find someone like Mason again. I knew girls who picked up new boyfriends within weeks of discarding the old ones. I wasn't one of those girls.

A puff of mist appeared before Leo's mouth. "This place is a freezer," he grunted.

"I know. They must be keeping it cool for the wine."

"Wine's supposed to be cellar temperature. Not refrigerated."

I nodded. I'd lost Mason. For good. My chest ached. My movements were clumsy, useless.

We tipped the press at an angle, shuffling it into place.

Leo grasped the dolly handles and his shoulders slumped. He blinked rapidly, as if trying to repress some emotion.

Sadness.

I'd felt it every time I'd gotten near the grape press. Could the vintage press be somehow triggering it?

I shook my head. No, my first instinct had been right. I was attributing powers to the object because others claimed they'd experienced something dark.

Chuck stuck his head in the storage room. "You two doing okay in there?"

"Got it." Leo grunted.

"Careful with that curse now," Chuck said.

"It's not cursed." I shook my head to clear it. The fluorescent light flickered in the ceiling. "It's the key to a murder mystery."

"Oh?" Chuck leaned against the door frame, blocking our exit.

Scalp prickling, I shifted. I wasn't scared of Chuck, not with Leo beside me and a tasting room full of wine drinkers outside the door. So why was my skin crawling? "Two burned bodies were found in a cottage in 1922—Alcina, daughter of a vintner, and Luigi, one of the workers. Everyone thought Luigi killed Alcina because she'd turned him down. Male and female blood was found on this grape press—"

"Male and female?" Chuck asked.

"But the grape press wasn't burnt." The storage room was airless and I struggled for breath. "It wasn't inside the cottage when the building was set on fire. Photos from the crime scene prove this. So if a man and woman were shot beside the grape press, how did their bodies end up inside a burned-out cottage?"

"I don't know," Chuck said. "How?"

Leo angled the dolly back and tested the press's stability. He lowered it to the ground and wiped his brow, his pale forehead beaded with sweat.

"The killer gave himself away during the cover-up." I raised my voice enough to carry into the tasting room. "And I think it might have been Alcina's father. I think her father wanted her to marry someone else, a Harvard man, not a lowly worker in his vineyards. But you can't force something that's not meant to be, and the Harvard guy wasn't with the program. He married someone else a week after Alcina's murder. Maybe Alcina had been jilted and found comfort with Luigi. Or maybe she had no intention of marrying the man from Harvard either. After her death, her father was wracked with guilt, so much so that he ended up in a sanatorium."

"He went crazy?" Leo asked, his voice thin.

"And in his journal, after the murders, he wrote that it was his fault. Everyone assumed he felt guilty because he hadn't been able to protect his daughter. But what if it really *was* his fault? What if he killed them both? He might not have meant to kill Alcina. Maybe she just got in the way. By all accounts he was devastated by her death."

A tightness I hadn't known I'd been carrying released. I wobbled, light.

"It's a good story," Chuck said. "Good luck proving it."

Leo straightened, shoulders back.

I smiled, a thin line. "It's probably not possible after all these years." But I did know a certain detective with a fondness for cold case files.

Together, Leo and I got the press into the back of my pickup, and we drove to the museum. We hauled it inside beneath the watchful gaze of GD and set it in the center of the main room.

GD sneezed and curled up on the rocking chair, closing his eyes. No hissing, no growling, no bristling fur. Had figuring out the crime been enough to banish whatever was hanging on to the press?

"Do you really think your story about the murder is true?" Leo asked.

"Murders, plural. I may not have all the details, but I think I'm pretty close."

"That Chuck guy is right. It will be tough to prove."

"Maybe."

Leo left. Through the window blinds, I watched him slouch down the street. I drew my cell phone from my bag, made a call.

"Hello?"

I took a deep breath. "I think someone's going to try and kill me again. Tonight."

TWENTY-FOUR

I PACED THE DISTRESSED wood floors of my garage apartment. In the windows, I saw only my own reflection, hazy in the glass, black against the night. The butterflies in my stomach had escaped, cannoning inside my skin, the blood in my veins throbbing.

Catching my foot on the blue rag rug for the fourth time, I sat on the overstuffed couch and picked up my e-reader. A minute later, I set it down on the coffee table. I couldn't read, not when I knew what was coming.

I was certain about the how's and who's and why's of last week's murders. But as with those deaths in the far-off past, I had no real evidence, only a story that made sense. The police had the resources to uncover more, and I didn't doubt they would, eventually. But the killer had already made one attempt on my life, in the museum. My actions today might have been crazy—I'd practically told the killer that I knew—but I was tired of waiting.

A branch scraped against a blackened window, and I winced.

Picking up the e-reader, I read about how to drop ten pounds simply by changing my habits. Ha. As if habits were easy to change. I'd already eaten my way through half a box of lemon bars, but if there ever was a time for emotional eating, this was it. I'd broken up with my boyfriend and taunted a killer. All in the same freaking day. I felt sick, from lemon bars and fear.

Footsteps creaked on the outside stairs.

I froze, rooted to the couch. My heart thumped, frantic, against my rib cage. I angled my head, listening.

Two sets of feet padded up the steps.

I'd miscalculated. The killer had an accomplice. *What had I done what had I done what had I done?*

Gripping the e-reader, I rose from the couch on shaky legs. I'd committed to this course. My only choice was to see it through.

Someone pounded on the door. Even though I'd been expecting it, my muscles contracted with dread.

I trudged to the door, steps dragging as if slogging through molasses. "Who is it?" I called, my voice hoarse.

"We have pizza," Adele and Harper sang out.

I blinked, fumbled the lock, yanked open the door. "What are you two doing here?"

Adele fluttered past me, her pale blue Parisian-style jacket and tulip skirt swishing.

Harper, holding two pizza boxes, followed.

Hastily, I shut the door behind them.

Adele laid two bottles of zinfandel on the coffee table and hugged me. "We heard about you and Mason."

I pried myself free of her embrace. "What? How?" I hadn't told anyone, and I was certain Mason hadn't said anything.

Harper grimaced, tugging at the collar of her caramel-colored turtleneck. Her nearly black hair hung in casual waves about her shoulders. "The waitress at the Wok and Bowl has a crush on Mason."

"Poodle skirt? But how did she hear us in all that racket?"

"She has one of those super-hearing devices," Harper said. "You know, the kind you see on TV for picking up conversations in crowded rooms."

"She spied on us?"

"No," Harper said, "she uses it to listen in on if customers want more coffee. Can I put the pizzas in the kitchen?"

"I'll get plates," Adele said.

"Wait, no," I said. My friends were going to ruin everything. "I really appreciate this, guys. But I just don't think—"

Adele and Harper exchanged knowing glances and walked into the kitchen.

I trotted after them. "Look, I already ate half a dozen lemon bars. I just want to be alone tonight to digest."

Adele opened the sky-blue cupboard and pulled out three dishes. "We know you, Maddie. You're just going to sit here and eat and feel sorry for yourself. You're thinking you'll never find another man like Mason again. You're worried you'll grow old and alone except for your dozen cats. That when you die, no one will find you for days and your cats will feed on your rotting corpse. But you're wrong."

My ears grew hot with embarrassment.

"I'm pretty sure GD's cured her of any desire for a dozen cats," Harper said.

So had the visual of being eaten. I had to get rid of my friends, and I *really* wanted to stop talking about my relationship status.

"I think the lemon bar binge snapped me out of it. I'm okay." The scent of pepperoni and melted cheese coiled around the kitchen. My treasonous mouth watered.

"You've been a wreck all week worrying about Mason." Adele scrounged in a drawer for silverware. "And now the worst has happened. But you'll get through this."

I covered my face with my hands. The hurt of having broken up with Mason was a solid, steady ache. But it was something I knew would come to an end, and that beat the insecurity and confusion of the week before. I had made the right decision. Maybe I'd broken up with him because I was flawed and weak, but I knew my flaws and understood how this situation would affect me.

"It's okay to cry," Adele said. "I know how much you cared about him."

"I'm not crying," I said, dropping my hands. "I'm okay. Breaking up with him hurt. It still hurts. But it was the right call. You don't have to stay."

"But we want to stay," Adele said.

"I'm sure you have better things to do." I ground my teeth in frustration.

"Sadly," Harper said, "we don't."

"You're both great friends," I said, "and I appreciate what you're trying to do. But I need to be alone tonight."

"We're not leaving you," Adele said, "and that's that."

"You really should leave," I said.

"Yes, Adele." Chuck aimed a gun at us through the open kitchen door. "You really should have left." His moustache curled like a cartoon villain's, but there was nothing funny about the gun he aimed.

Adele squeaked, her dark eyes widening.

Harper stilled, hand poised in the act of lifting a pizza box lid.

"Chuck!" I sputtered, scared and furious. "Why couldn't you wait until they'd left? How can you be so damn impatient?"

"I considered waiting. But then I thought, with Adele dead, the 'precious heritage' her parents ruined my deal over wouldn't matter."

"What's he talking about?" Adele whispered, face pale.

"The wineries," I said, inwardly cursing myself. I should have told my friends to get the hell out and not worried if I'd upset them. But no, I had to be selfish and put our friendship before their safety. Stupid!

"He's desperate to sell CW Vineyards," I continued, watching Chuck, "but he can't sell unless all the wineries involved agree. Romeo wouldn't sell, so he tried to pressure him by sabotaging him. But it wasn't hard for Romeo to guess who the guilty culprit was, was it, Chuck? He took off in his truck and drove right through the CW Vineyard gates to get to you."

"He had that hot Italian temper," Chuck said.

"So you killed him, and used his truck and his keys to dump his body at the festival."

"It wasn't my fault," Chuck said. "It was self-defense."

"Maybe," I said, "but Jocelyn's death wasn't. You thought she'd sell the winery. But she had second thoughts about selling Leo's inheritance."

"What does that have to do with me?" Adele wailed.

Chuck snarled through his beard. "I came here for Maddie, not you. I had to stop her before she went to the police. She'd obviously figured it out." He looked back at me. "I knew it that first time I saw you at the haunted house, when you were dropping those hints about the Mafia and conspiracies."

"That's why you dropped the wine barrel on me?"

"Too bad it missed," he said. "But you kept pushing it, twisting the knife. You never should have made that crack about the cover-up giving it away."

"And the Buick?"

"What Buick?"

"The one in the parking lot outside the festival grounds."

"What?" he asked.

"Oh. You mean that really was an accident?" So it was true. Not everything is about me.

"But what does that have to do with me?" Adele asked again.

"Chuck thinks your father is holding on to the winery because of you," I said.

"Am I wrong?" he asked.

Adele didn't respond.

"I thought not," he said. "With you gone, he'll sell." Gun steady, Chuck edged into the kitchen.

Dammit, this wasn't the plan. I wasn't action hero material. There were too many variables now. I might succeed in dragging one of my friends out of the line of fire, but the odds of saving them both were low.

"Get out while you can, Chuck," I said. "You've left too many bodies, too much evidence. If I figured it out, the police must be close as well, and unlike me, they have crime labs. You don't need to add more murders to the list. Just go. Run."

"Shut up."

Harper hurled the pizza box. It arced through the air like a throwing star.

Chuck raised his arm, deflecting it. A gunshot blasted, and plaster rained from the ceiling.

I flinched, involuntarily shutting my eyes, my ears ringing.

Adele shrieked.

"DROP IT," Detective Slate roared.

I looked.

Slate stood in the kitchen doorway, gripping a gun between two hands, his eyes hard as agates.

Laurel skidded into view in the pass-through window to the living room. She aimed her weapon through it.

Chuck gripped Harper by the hair, his gun wedged beneath her chin. Cheese and pepperoni dripped off the front of his khakis and puddled on the floor.

Harper whimpered, an ugly sound.

I had to think. It was my fault Harper was in this. Aside from Harper, I was the person nearest to Chuck. My fault, my responsibility. I edged closer.

"It's over, Chuck," Slate said. "The house is surrounded. You're not getting out of here. You may as well drop the gun."

"Back off," he snarled. "I have a hostage."

Harper grabbed his wrist and pushed, jerking her head away.

I lunged, clutching Chuck's gun arm. My feet slipped in pizza. Wrapping both my arms around his, I pulled his wrist to my chest. We both went down, Chuck landing on top of me. I gasped, the air knocked from my lungs.

The gun fired, Chuck's arm jerking against my chest. Wood and dishes exploded.

Adele screamed.

Chuck went limp atop me. Our arms and legs tangled. After what seemed an age, he was rolled off me and I could breathe again.

Against the sink, Harper sat, panting, one leg extended along the linoleum floor. Adele brandished a wine bottle like a baseball bat, her nostrils flaring.

Detective Slate crouched beside Chuck, who was unconscious on the linoleum. The detective pressed two fingers against Chuck's neck. "He's not dead, but he needs medical attention. Nice swing, Miss Nakamoto."

She nodded, her chest heaving, and lowered the bottle.

Unclipping a radio from his belt, Slate called for an ambulance.

In seconds, the kitchen swarmed with cops. They'd heard everything. I thought of Adele's lecture on my miserable love life and flushed. Yeah, everything. Laurel lined Harper, Adele, and me up on the couch: Hear No Evil, See No Evil, Speak No Evil.

Adele's head rotated toward me. "The next time you tell us to leave," she said, "we'll leave."

Dazed, I looked at Harper. "I can't believe you attacked a gunman with a pizza. Pizza really is the ultimate food. You can put all four food groups on it, and it can be weaponized."

"Someone had to do something." Harper slumped. "Even if my follow-through was a failure."

"Excuse me," Adele said. "I did knock him out cold with a wine bottle. Maybe wine's the ultimate beverage."

"No talking," Laurel snapped.

"I'm really sorry about this," I whispered.

Harper waved her hand. "Not your fault."

Except it sort of was my fault. I stared at my sneakers.

There was a scuffle at the door. Dieter burst past two uniformed officers. His tie was flung over one shoulder of his navy business suit, his face pale. "Adele!"

"Dieter!" She sprang from the couch and raced into his arms. They covered each other in kisses.

Harper and I gaped, open-mouthed. I wasn't sure what stunned me more, the embrace or Dieter's suit.

"Huh," Harper said. "What were the odds of that?"

TWENTY-FIVE

My MOTHER ROSE FROM her seat at the Fox and Fennel. The peak of her witch's hat brushed a light fixture, and she straightened the brim. A dozen women in witchy attire sat around the wide round table littered with teacups and scone crumbs. Bats on near-invisible wires danced around a centerpiece of miniature pumpkins.

I leaned against the granite counter, thumbing through a newspaper. I was an invited guest at the Witches' Tea, but one of Adele's waiters had unexpectedly gotten sick, so I'd pitched in as a server. Now I was perusing the Historical Association article I'd coauthored: *Who Killed Alcina Constantino?* It was still speculation, but the evidence of her father's guilt was compelling.

And the spectral evidence? Harper had checked out the grape press and proclaimed it haunt-free. GD concurred.

My mother cleared her throat, raising her hands in benediction. "To paraphrase Shakespeare: By the pricking of my thumbs, something wonderful this way comes. Thank you all for your hard work on this year's haunted house." She smiled wickedly. "This lets you hard workers off the hook for the upcoming Christmas Cow event. However, I'll be there, and we need volunteers, and it's a fun and, frankly, easier event than the haunted house. So please see me if you're interested. Happy Halloween!"

The ladies cheered.

Mrs. Gale rose from her chair, applauding. "And let's hear it for our new president!"

The other ladies rose as well.

Adele braced her elbows beside mine on the cream-colored counter. "How on earth did your mother wrest control from that old battle axe, Bigelow?" she whispered.

"No idea." But Cora Gale and her splinter group had returned to the Ladies Aid fold once my mother was in charge.

"What a harvest." Adele arched, pressing her hands into the small of her back. She smoothed her apron over her black silk top. "Thank God the worst is over."

"I hope so." Life did seem to be getting back to normal. I gazed through the front windows. The gauzy curtains blocked the setting sun.

I saw Mason and Anabelle walk past on the sidewalk. He smiled at her and ruffled Jordan's hair.

A ribbon around my heart snapped, came undone. I drew a deep breath. It had been the right decision.

Straightening off the counter, I turned to my friend. There was one more thing I had to set right. For some reason I wasn't clear on, for the past few weeks we'd all been tiptoeing around what had happened. It was guilt that choked my throat, caused me to avoid the gazes of my best friends and skip our regular girls' nights out in favor of working the haunted house.

"About that night—" I began.

Adele waved a hand. "The only person responsible for that night was Chuck. I still can't believe … Do you think my father might have been in danger?"

I hoped not, but killing had seemed to get easier for Chuck the more he'd practiced. Good thing his third attempt had not been the charm. "Nah," I said.

"I still don't understand why he wanted to kill *you*," she murmured.

"Like he said, he realized I'd figured it out. That woman from Ladies Aid—Betsy—told him I had a 'hot clue,' and when I started asking him pointed questions, he assumed I was looking in his direction. And after that, the more questions I asked, the more it looked like I knew something. He got paranoid, and everything I said seemed suspicious. Telling him that the cover-up had been the undoing of the grape press murders was sort of the last straw. The more he tried to cover up his crimes—moving Romeo's body, attacking me, killing Jocelyn—the more evidence he left behind."

"How much do you think Vampire Pryce knew?" Adele asked.

Pryce had left town after Chuck's arrest. A wall of corporate lawyers had met the cops when they'd tried questioning him. But Pryce must have known how badly Chuck wanted to sell—Chuck had practically been acting as his liaison. "I doubt we'll ever know," I said. "But after this, I don't think his company will be doing business in San Benedetto."

Adele shuddered. "Definitely not. Even some of the vineyard owners who were interested have told me they're glad now they didn't sell."

Enough. I couldn't put it off any longer. "When you and Harper showed up at my door, I suspected that Chuck was on his way. Or that he might already have snuck into my house."

She blinked. "I knew."

"You knew?"

"Dieter warned me about what was up. Why do you think Harper and I refused to leave?"

"You..." Tears pricked the backs of my eyes. "You came over when you knew a killer was going to be there?"

"Both of us knew. That's why we came. We couldn't let you do it alone."

"But... the pizza! How did you have time?"

"Oh, we were coming over with the pizza anyway. Dieter called and told us when we were on the way."

"But how did Dieter know?" I was still trying to wrap my head around their new relationship. I wasn't surprised Dieter was in love with my friend, but I'd had no idea she was interested in him too. They seemed such opposites. Maybe together they came to a sort of balance.

Adele looked around, making sure no one was listening. "Dieter was listening to his police radio," she whispered. "He heard the cop chatter about your house and called me. He thought I might already be there."

"He has a police radio?" I filed that nugget away for future use. "Aren't those illegal?"

"He thought it would help him keep track of your investigation for his, er, side business." The color rose in her cheeks.

I chewed it over. Knowing what they were walking into, Adele and Harper had come anyway, to protect and support me.

They were nuts.

I couldn't imagine better friends.

Leo emerged through the bookcase door. Nodding to Mrs. Gale, he slumped onto a chair in a corner far from the Witches' Tea. Leo

319

and Mrs. Gale—now there was another unlikely pairing, though not a romantic one. She'd confessed to me that she missed having her children around, and Leo reminded her of her son.

"Hey, wait a minute." I turned back to Adele. "You *knew* the cops were listening, yet you blathered on about my depressing love life? Thanks to you, the entire police department—"

"Knows you're single? You're welcome."

The Witches' Tea broke up, the ladies filtering out of the Fox and Fennel. Leo rose and stretched. Slinging Mrs. Gale's purse over his shoulder, he followed her out the door.

Whipping off her witch's hat, my mother strode to the counter. "Thank you, Adele. The tea was impeccable as usual. Do you have the bill for me?"

"Just a moment." Adele hurried into the small hallway and vanished around the corner.

My mom flapped the hat, using it as a fan. "Another harvest season done. Let's hope the next one's not as eventful."

"Mom, what happened to Mrs. Bigelow?"

She colored. "Eliza was a strong president, and we are all sorry to see her go."

"Out with it."

"If you must know, she was taking things too far. Ladies Aid was always efficient, but it was fun, too, until she took over."

"And?"

"And I knew with a little push, Ladies Aid would rebel. There was already dissention in the ranks."

"And my investigation was the push?"

"Of course not!" She squeezed her eyes shut. "Well, the danger to you was the final straw, but I hadn't planned that. I had no idea you'd nearly get killed over her silly investigation."

"Her investigation? But *you* dragged me into it!"

She blinked. "You know that, and I know that, but Eliza didn't know that." She raised her hands, let them drop. "I knew you were going to investigate no matter what I said. You were always like that, even as a child, picking off scabs to see what was beneath."

"To get rid of them more quickly."

"There was no way you were going to let it go, not with the grape press throwing suspicion on you, and the Death Bistro throwing suspicion on Adele. Since you were going to investigate anyway, I simply dropped a few hints to Eliza."

"Hints?"

"I reminded her of your prior success solving a murder, and she took the bait. You have no idea how sorry I am. I accused Eliza of going too far, but I'm just as guilty." She pinned her arms against her stomach. "I became obsessed with becoming president, and now that I've got the job—"

"You realize what a pain it is?"

"Are you joking? I love it! But I realized I was trying to fill the gap left by your father."

"Oh, Mom." My eyes grew damp. "I miss him too."

"I know you do, dear." She hugged me. "I hope you forgive me."

"Mmph. I would have poked around anyway. I've got a process."

"It's so good to have you home."

Adele bustled into the room and laid an invoice on the counter. "Here you go."

My mother extracted reading glasses from the purse over her arm and examined the bill. "That seems in order." Taking out a checkbook, she paid.

Detective Laurel Hammer strode through the door of the tea room. She'd dressed in an official-looking blue blazer, white blouse, and blue slacks. Working in a museum didn't include the glamour of carrying a gun, but at least I could wear the clothes I wanted. Today was hot out, a reminder of summer. I felt bad for her.

"Oh, I'm sorry," Adele called. "We're closed."

Laurel's face darkened. Her gaze landed on me and she crooked a finger. "You. Outside."

Again? Laurel had been coming after me for weeks, asking questions and generally making me feel criminal. I'd learned just to nod and take it. Eventually she'd get bored and leave me alone.

"Sure, no problem," I said. Meek, I followed the detective onto the sidewalk. My mother watched us, eyes narrowed.

A plum tree dropped leaves onto the hood of a blue Camaro parallel parked behind my mom's Lincoln. "How can I help you?" I asked.

Laurel jabbed a finger at me. "You can keep your nose out of police investigations."

"Okay."

"If I had my way, you'd be charged with obstruction of justice, but Slate has some weird soft spot for you.

"But I didn't obstruct. I went straight to the police when I figured Chuck was going to make his move." Besides, obstruction was only for people who lied or covered up during an investigation—I'd checked online. But I decided not to argue the point.

"And do you have any idea what it was like, having to listen to your friend vomit the story of your pathetic love life?"

I swallowed. "Oh. You heard that?" I really should have forced Adele and Harper from my apartment sooner.

"I was in the van, listening. It turned my stomach."

"Mine too." At last we were in agreement on something.

"You think this is funny?" She stepped closer.

I shook my head. "No."

My mother popped out of the tea room. "Is everything all right out here?"

A pulse beat in Laurel's jaw. "Fine," she ground out. She strode around the muscle car, opening the driver's door. Her phone rang. Unclipping it from her belt, she walked forward, leaving the door ajar. "Yes?"

"Madclyn," my mother said in a low voice, "*is* everything all right?"

"Laurel's just upset she couldn't get a scone."

"I'll get her a scone. We've got several left over. Do you think she'd like pumpkin or lemon poppy seed?"

"Ah…"

"I'll get one of each. Wait here." She darted inside the Fox and Fennel and the door drifted slowly shut behind her. This left me stuck on the sidewalk, waiting for my mom, rather than running as far from Laurel as possible.

Edging away, I gazed into the windows of the Paranormal Museum. Tomorrow we'd have to take down the black Halloween streamers, but the pumpkins could stay in the window through Thanksgiving.

I smiled. This had been a good month for the museum, but I still had a lot of work to do. Leo had gotten started on the shopping cart for our website. Now I needed to write the copy and photograph our products. I wanted our online sales up and running by December 1st to take advantage of the holiday shopping.

I glanced back at Laurel.

She glided sideways.

I blinked. And then my brain caught up to reality. Laurel wasn't moving, her car was.

"Laurel! Look—"

She howled, dropping the phone.

"Laurel!" I ran to her.

She jerked backward, staggering into the street.

A black cat streaked from the driver's side door of the Challenger. The car tapped my mother's bumper, halting.

I stared after the cat, which was bounding down the street. "GD?"

My mother emerged from the tea room brandishing a white paper bag. "Scones!"

Laurel hopped on one foot, her face crimson. "Your cat! Your cat drove the car over my foot!"

"I'll take you to the emergency room," I said.

"Don't change the subject." Laurel snarled, leaning against the hood and gripping her injured foot. "Your cat tried to kill me."

"You probably didn't set the parking brake," I said.

She growled low in her throat. "Don't tell me I didn't set the brake. I always set the brake. And your cat—"

"That wasn't my cat," I said. After all, one black cat looks like another. And you don't really own cats. They sort of just decide if they're going to stick around.

I shifted my weight. The cat *had* looked like GD. And lately he had been kind of stalking Laurel. But it wasn't as if he knew how to operate a car. And how could GD have even gotten outside?

I remembered Leo entering the tea room through the bookcase, the slowly closing secret door.

Nah.

"If I catch that mangy sack of fur," Laurel said, "I'll—"

"You'll what?" my mother asked.

Laurel swallowed. Her jaw clenched. "Nothing."

"You're in pain," my mother said, "and you're not thinking clearly. I'll drive you to the emergency room, since my car is closest." She frowned. "Did you dent my bumper?"

We helped Laurel into the passenger side of my mother's car. When we'd closed the door on her, my mother turned to me. "Really, Madelyn, must you taunt her?" she whispered.

"I had nothing to do with—"

"It *is* your cat."

"We don't know that."

"I'll meet you at the emergency room." She got into the car and drove off.

Did I want to know? I looked skyward. A puffy cloud floated past. A scattering of burgundy leaves skipped down the street.

Hanging my head, I walked into the tea room. The clash of metal bins floated down the long hall—Adele taking out the trash.

The bookcase stood open. I walked through it into the museum.

GD perched atop the grape press, his tail coiled around his feet. He glanced at me and got busy cleaning one of his paws.

"I guess you're off the hook. It must have been a different cat."

But the alleyway door had been propped open while Adele dumped the garbage. And the bookcase had been open as well. GD would have had time to race to the alley and return to the museum...

I shook my head.

"Nah."

THE END

325

ABOUT THE AUTHOR

Kirsten Weiss writes paranormal mysteries, blending her experiences and imagination to create a vivid world of magic and mayhem. She is also the author of the Riga Hayworth series. Follow her on her website at kirstenweiss.com.

———

Enjoy the book? Then keep the magic and mystery going!
The Paranormal Museum is offering a *free*
5-Day Fortune Telling Challenge.
Sign up at www.kirstenweiss.com/fortune-telling-challenge